DUANE SWIERCZYNSKI

SEVERANCE PACKAGE

ILLUSTRATIONS BY **DENNIS CALERO**

 ST. MARTIN'S MINOTAUR ⊷ NEW YORK

SEVERANCE PACKAGE. Copyright © 2008 by Duane Swierczynski. All rights reserved. Printed in the United States of America. No part of this book may be used or reproduced in any manner whatsoever without written permission except in the case of brief quotations embodied in critical articles or reviews. For information, address St. Martin's Press, 175 Fifth Avenue, New York, N.Y. 10010.

www.minotaurbooks.com

Library of Congress Cataloging-in-Publication Data

Swierczynski, Duane.
    Severance package / Duane Swierczynski.—1st St. Martin's Minotaur ed.
        p.   cm.
    ISBN-13: 978-0-312-34380-4
    ISBN-10: 0-312-34380-9
    I. Title.
PS3619.W53S48   2007
813'.6—dc22

2007026527

First Edition: June 2008

10 9 8 7 6 5 4 3 2 1

TO **JAMES ROACH,**
WHO TAUGHT THE MOST DANGEROUS GAME

Contents

WAKE-UP CALL 1

ARRIVALS 8

MEETING 27

AFTER THE MEETING 45

THE MORNING GRIND 63

ONE-ON-ONE 101

MIDMORNING BREAK
(WITH PEPPERIDGE FARM COOKIES) 126

BACK TO WORK 148

EARLY LUNCH 176

CLEANUP 206

CLOSING TIME 234

OUT OF THE OFFICE 258

ACKNOWLEDGMENTS 267

SEVERANCE PACKAGE

WAKE-UP CALL

Pleasure doing business with you. —*ANONYMOUS*

His name was Paul Lewis . . .

. . . and he didn't know he had seven minutes to live.

When he opened his eyes, his wife was already in the shower. Their bedroom shared a wall with their bathroom. He could hear the water pelt the tile full-blast. Paul thought about her in there. Naked. Soapy. Suds gliding over her nipples. Maybe he should step into the shower, surprise her. He hadn't brushed his teeth, but that was fine. They wouldn't have to kiss.

Then he remembered Molly's morning meeting. He glanced at the clock. 7:15. She had to be in early. So much for a reckless Saturday morning.

Paul sat up and ran his tongue around his mouth. Dry and pasty. He needed a Diet Coke, stat.

The central air had been running all night, so the living room was dark and cool. On top of the entertainment center sat the two DVDs they'd rented last night: two ultraviolent Bruce Willis thrillers. Surprisingly, they had been Molly's idea. She usually didn't like action movies. "But I have a crush on Bruce Willis," she'd said sweetly. "Oh you do, do you?" Paul replied, smiling. "What's he got that I don't?" His wife ran her fingernails down his chest and said, "A broken nose." That was the end of the DVD viewing for the evening, with about thirty minutes left to go on the first movie.

There were two boxes on the dining room table. One, Paul knew, was for Molly's boss. What, the man couldn't pick up his own mail? The second box was white cardboard and tied with string. Probably full of vanilla muffins or chocolate-filled cannoli, picked up from Reading Terminal Market on her way home last night. Molly was way too kind to those stuck-up jerks at the office, but Paul would never tell her different. That's just who Molly was.

Paul turned the corner and walked into the kitchen. For a second, he was worried that he'd left the Chinese food containers on the counter, and their leftover fried rice and lo mein and Seven Stars Around the Moon had spoiled. But Molly had taken care of it. The white-and-red containers were neatly stacked on the fridge shelves, right below the row of Diet Cokes—he'd been on regular Coke until Molly had pointed out how much sugar he was drinking every morning—and above a white Tupperware container with a blue lid and yellow note taped to it: FOR LUNCH ONLY!!! LOVE, MOLLY.

Oh, baby.

Paul lifted the edge of the lid, and the sweet aroma hit him in an instant. Molly's potato salad. His favorite.

She's made him potato salad, just for today.

God, he loved his wife.

Paul had grown up in a large Polish family—before it was Lewis, it was Lewinski, and boy was Paul glad they changed that name fifty years ago—so he ate the requisite Polish foods. His grandmother Stell was famous for a decidedly non-Polish dish:

potato salad, which had accompanied every holiday meal since Paul was a baby. But Grandma Stell died when Paul was thirteen, and since then, nobody could replicate the potato salad. Not Paul's mother, or her sisters, or any second or third cousins. A few months after they started dating, Paul confided in Molly how much he missed Grandma Stell's potato salad. She said little, just smiled at him and listened, which is what she usually did. But inside, she had been thinking. And in the weeks that followed, Molly Finnerty—later to become Molly Lewis—did some research.

The following Easter, Molly presented her fiancé with a Tupperware container. Inside was a potato salad that defied imagination. It tasted just like Grandma Stell's, down to the sweetness of the mayonnaise and the sideways cut of the celery. This potato salad was a surprise hit among the Lewis family. Molly was cemented into their hearts, now and forever more.

Today she'd made it for him, apropos of nothing.

Paul reread the admonishment, FOR LUNCH ONLY!!! and smiled. Molly was grossed out whenever she woke up Christmas or Easter morning and caught her husband with a tablespoon inside the Tupperware container hours before company was due to arrive.

Ah, but today isn't a holiday, Paul thought. No company coming.

He fished a tablespoon out of the drawer behind him, then helped himself to a mouthful of the most delicious food known to man. The moment the special mayonnaise blend touched his taste buds, a narcotic-like rush flooded his bloodstream. It was a taste that reminded him how lucky he had it, being married to a woman like Molly.

A moment later, Paul started choking.

It felt like an impossibly large chunk of potato had lodged in his throat. Paul thought he could just cough once and everything would be okay, but it was weird—he was unable to draw any air. Panic replaced that warm-and-fuzzy potato salad feeling. He couldn't breathe or talk or yell. Paul's mouth flopped open, and half-chewed potato chunks tumbled out. What was going on? He hadn't even swallowed the first bite.

His knees slammed against the linoleum.

His hands flew to his throat.

Upstairs, Molly Lewis was finishing up in the shower. The warm water felt good on her back. Just one more strip of flesh to shave on her leg, then a rinse, and the shower would be over. She wondered if Paul was still sleeping.

Paul's legs kicked out wildly, as if he were running on an invisible treadmill knocked on its side. His trembling fingers scratched at the floor. No. This can't be it. Not this incredibly stupid way to die. Not Molly's potato salad.

Molly.

Molly could save him.

Up.

Must stand up.

Reach the top of the stove, grab the silver teakettle, and start banging. Something to get her attention.

Up.

Gray spots spun wildly in Paul's vision. His palm adhered to the linoleum, and it was enough to pull him forward a few inches. Then his other palm, already damp with sweat. It slipped. Paul's nose slammed into the floor. Pain exploded across his face. He would have screamed if he could.

He had only one thought now:

Kettle.

Reach the kettle.

He'd given the kettle to Molly for Christmas two years ago. She loved tea and hot cocoa. He'd found it at a Kitchen Kapers downtown. It was her favorite store.

Up.

Molly turned off the hot water first, then the cold about two seconds later, relishing the blast of icy water at the end. Nothing felt better in August. She then turned the knob that would drain the water from the shower pipes into the tub. The excess splashed her feet.

She opened the curtain and reached around the wall for her towel. As her hand grasped the terry cloth, she thought she heard something.

Something . . . clanging?

Paul slammed the teakettle on top of the stove one more time . . . but that was it. He had been deprived of oxygen far too long. His muscles were starving. They required immediate and constant gratification—oxygen all the time. Greedy bastards.

After he fell, and rolled toward the sink, Paul tried pounding his fist into his upper chest, but it was a futile gesture. He didn't have the strength left.

A potato.

A little wedge of potato had caused his world to crash down around him.

Oh, Molly, he thought. Forgive me. Your life, changed forever because I was stupid enough to spoon some potato salad into my mouth on a Saturday morning. Your sweet potato salad, a mayonnaise-soaked symbol of all the kind things you've done for me over the years.

My sweet, sweet Molly.

The kitchen faded away.

The kitchen they'd redone a year ago, ripping out the old metal cabinets and replacing them with fresh-smelling sandal-wood maple.

She'd picked them out. She liked the color.

Oh, Molly . . .

Molly?

Was that Molly in the doorway now, her beautiful red hair dripping wet, a white terry cloth towel wrapped around her body?

God, she was no hallucination. She was really standing there. Looking down at him, strapping jewelry to her wrists. Thick silver bracelets. Paul couldn't remember buying them for her. Where did they come from?

Wait.

Why wasn't she trying to save him?

Couldn't she see him, choking, trembling, jolting, scratching, pleading, *fading*?

But Molly simply stared, with the strangest look on her face. That look would be the last thing Paul Lewis would ever see, and if there were an afterlife, it would be an image that would haunt him, even if his memories of earthly life were to be erased. Molly's face would still be there. Perplexing him. Who was this woman? Why did she make his soul ache?

So it was probably merciful that Paul didn't hear what his wife said as she looked down upon his writhing, dying body, "Well, this is ahead of schedule."

ARRIVALS

Executives owe it to the organization and to their fellow workers
not to tolerate nonperforming individuals in important jobs.
—**PETER DRUCKER**

His name was Jamie DeBroux . . .

. . . and he had been up most of the night, tag-teaming with Andrea, marching back and forth into the tiny bedroom at the back
of their apartment.

What hurt the most, after being awake so many hours, were
his eyes. Jamie wore daily-wear contacts, but lately he hadn't
bothered to take them out at night. Without them he was practically blind, and he was too new a father to risk changing a diaper
or preparing a bottle of Similac with impaired vision. Bad
enough they had to work in the dark, so Chase could learn the
difference between night and day.

Sunlight.

Darkness.

Sunlight this morning, which was turning out to be a blaz-
ingly hot Saturday in August. Their window air-conditioning
unit was no match for it, and Jamie had to get dressed and head
into the office. His eyes swam with tears.

Life with the baby was now:

Day

Night

Day

Night

Melting into each other.

Nobody told you that parenthood was like doing hallucinogenics. That you watched the life you knew melt away into a gray fuzz. Or if they did, you didn't believe them.

Jamie knew he shouldn't complain. Not after having a month off for paternity leave.

Still, it was strange to be going back on a Saturday morning, to a managers' meeting led by his boss, David Murphy. Last time he'd seen his boss was late June, at Jamie's awkward baby shower in the office. Nobody had brought gifts. Just money—ones and fives—stuffed into a card. David had provided an array of cold cuts and Pepperidge Farm cookies, which were the boss's favorite. Stuart ran to the soda machines for Cokes and Diet Cokes. Jamie gave him a few singles from the card to pay for them.

Being away from that place had been nice.

Very nice.

And now this "managers' meeting." Jamie had no idea what it could be about. He'd been gone for a month.

Never mind that Jamie wasn't a manager.

There was nothing to do about it now, though. What could he do? Change jobs and risk losing medical insurance for three months? Andrea had left her job in May, and with it went the other benefits package.

Besides, David wasn't so bad to work for. It was everybody else who drove him up the wall.

The problem wasn't hard to figure out. Jamie's job was "media relations director," which meant he had to explain to the rest of the world—or more specifically, certain trade publications—what

Murphy, Knox & Associates did. Thing was, not even Jamie was entirely clear on what their company did. Not without it making his head hurt.

Everyone else, who did the real work of the company, formed a closed little society. They put up walls that were difficult, if not impossible, to breach. They were the driving force of the company. They were the Clique.

He was the staff word nerd.

Murphy, Knox & Associates was listed with Dun & Bradstreet as a "financial services office" that claimed annual sales of $516.6 million. The press releases Jamie wrote often dealt with new financial packages. The information would come straight from Amy Felton—sometimes Nichole Wise. Rarely did it come from David, though every press release had to pass through his office. Jamie would drop a hard copy into the black plastic bin on Molly's desk. A few hours later, the hard copy would be slid under Jamie's door. Sometimes, David didn't change a thing. Other times, David would rework Jamie's prose into an ungrammatical, stilted mess.

Jamie tried to talk him out of it—taking the liberty of rewriting David's rewrite, and presenting it to him with a memo explaining why he'd made certain changes.

He did that exactly once.

"Repeat after me," David had said.

Jamie smiled.

"I'm not joking. Repeat after me."

"Oh," Jamie said. "Um, repeat after you."

"I *will* not."

"I *will* not." God, this was humiliating.

"Rewrite David Murphy's work."

"Rewrite your work."

"David Murphy's work."

"Oh. *David Murphy's work.*"

So yeah—David could be a tool every once in a while. But that was nothing compared with how the other Murphy, Knox employees treated him on a daily basis. It wasn't a *lack* of respect; that would imply there had been respect to begin with. To the Clique, Jamie was just the word nerd.

To be dismissed completely, unless you needed a press release.

Worst of all: Jamie could understand. At his former job, a reporting gig at a small daily in New Mexico, the editors and reporters were tight. They pretty much ignored the newspaper's controller—the bean-counting cyborg. What, invite him out for a beer after work? That would be like inviting Bin Laden home for turkey and cranberry sauce.

And now *Jamie* was the cyborg. The press release–writing Bin Laden. No wonder he wasn't exactly rushing back to the office this morning.

Somehow he pulled it together. The memory of Chase, sleeping, reminded him of why.

The air-conditioning quickly cooled the interior of Jamie's Subaru Forester. The vehicle was newly equipped with a Graco baby seat in the back. The hospital wouldn't let them leave without one; both of them had forgotten about it. He'd had to run to a Toys "R" Us in Port Richmond, then spent the better part of a humid July night trying to figure out how to strap the thing in.

He looked at Chase's seat in the rearview. Wondered if he was up yet.

Jamie reached into the front pocket of his leather bag. Grabbed his cell, flipped it open. Held down the 2 key. Their home number popped up.

Beep.

No service.

What?

Jamie tried it again, then looked for the bars. Nothing. In its place, the image of a telephone receiver with a red hash mark across it.

No service.

No service here—a few minutes from the heart of downtown Philadelphia?

Maybe David had canceled the free office cell phone perk since he'd left. But no, that couldn't be right. Jamie had used the phone yesterday, calling Andrea from CVS, asking if he had the right package of diapers for Chase.

Jamie pressed the button again. Still nothing. He'd have to call Andrea from work.

His name was Stuart McCrane . . .

. . . and his Ford Focus was halfway up the white concrete ramp before he saw the sign. He hit the brakes and squinted his eyes to make sure he was seeing right. The Focus idled. It didn't like to idle, especially on such a steep incline. Stuart had to rev it to keep it in place.

Weekend rate: $26.50.

Unbelievable.

The Saturday-morning sun blazed off 1919 Market, a thirty-seven-story box of a building. You couldn't call it a skyscraper, not with Liberty One and Two just two blocks down the street. This was where Stuart reported for work, Monday through Fridays. He had no reason to know the garage rates. He almost never drove. The regional rails carried him from his rented house in Bala Cynwyd to Suburban Station, no problem, all for just a few bucks. But this was a Saturday. Trains ran much slower. And without much traffic downtown, it was faster to drive. Apparently, it was more expensive, too.

You'd think a cushy government job would come with free parking.

Then again, you'd think that a cushy government job wouldn't haul you in on a Saturday.

Hah.

But really, he had no idea why he was being dragged in on a weekend morning. Stuff he did—erasing bank accounts, leaving your average wannabe jihadist with a useless ATM card in one hand, his dick in the other—could be done anywhere, really. He could do it at friggin' Starbucks. There was nothing more simple and yet nothing more satisfying. Maybe some guys got off on the idea of picking off towel-heads with a sniper rifle. Stuart loved doing it by tapping ENTER.

Guess he'd find out what this was about soon enough.

Stuart threw the Focus in reverse, gently lifted his foot off the brake. The car rolled back down the ramp. Another vehicle turned the corner sharply, ready to shoot up the ramp and, judging from its speed, *over* the Focus, if need be.

Brakes screamed. The Focus jolted to a stop, pressing Stuart back into his seat.

"Man," he said.

He slapped the steering wheel, then looked into the rearview.

It was a Subaru Tribeca. With a woman behind the wheel.

Stuart crouched down into his seat, checked the rearview again. Squinted.

Oh.

Molly Lewis.

Stuart allowed the Focus to roll backwards. The Tribeca got the hint and reversed back down the foot of the ramp and backed onto Twentieth Street. Stuart steered the Focus until it was parallel with the Tribeca. Traffic was light this morning. It was only 8:45. Stuart rolled down his window. The Tribeca did the same, on the passenger side.

"Change your mind about work?"

"Hey, Molly. Yeah, I wish. I'm just not paying twenty-six fifty to park. I'll find something on the street."

"Then you've got to feed the meter."

"Then I'll feed the meter. I'm not paying twenty-six fifty."

"David told me we'd be here until at least two o'clock."

"What? I thought noon."

"He e-mailed me this morning."

"Man. What is this about anyway? I've got my laptop at home. I can do whatever he wants from my living room."

"Don't shoot the messenger."

Stuart watched the Tribeca—fancy wheels for an assistant, he thought—shoot up the ramp. He continued up Twentieth, turned left on Arch, then Twenty-first, then Market down to Nineteenth. He drove past the green light at Chestnut, then hung a right on Sansom. There were no available spots on the 1900 block, or the next. Didn't look like much farther down, either.

He flipped open the ashtray. One quarter, a few nickels, many pennies.

"Man."

But then, movement. The red taillights of a Lexus. Pulling back. McCrane pressed his brakes. Slowed to a stop. Watched the Lexus maneuver out of the space.

Even better, it was a Monday-through-Friday loading space. Weekends, it was fair game.

"*Yes,*" Stuart said.

Her name was Molly Lewis . . .

. . . and she eased the Tribeca into a spot on an empty level in the 1919 Market Street Building's garage. The nearest car was at least ten spots away. She turned off the engine, then opened the suitcase on the passenger seat. Inside, on top of a yellow legal pad, was David's package.

Molly's cell phone played the guitar riff from "Boys Don't Cry." She put in the earpiece and pressed ANSWER. A voice spoke to her.

She said: "Yes, I remembered."

And a few seconds later: "I know. I followed the protocols."

The packages had arrived last night. Paul had asked what she'd ordered *now*—smiling as he said it—and Molly truthfully replied that it was something for David. She had carried them to the glassed-in patio and sat down on a white metal garden chair. Then she carefully clipped away the masking tape with a pair of blue-handled scissors and then opened the flaps of the first box.

She had put the contents—David's delivery—into her own briefcase, then gone back to order dinner from the gourmet Chinese place a few blocks away. Paul hated calling it in, and always complained until Molly did it.

Then she went back out to the patio to open the second box. She was staring at the contents now:

A Beretta .22 Neo.

Ammo—a box of fifty, target practice, 29 gr.

"I am," she said now. "See you soon."

Molly opened a white cardboard box, dumped most of the doughnuts and cannoli out onto the concrete floor of the parking garage. Let the pigeons enjoy them. She quickly assembled and loaded the pistol, then nestled it between the two remaining doughnuts. Sugar jelly.

Paul used to love sugar jelly.

Her name was Roxanne Kurtwood . . .

. . . and they were driving toward downtown Philadelphia.

"We're closing," Roxanne said.

She'd been waiting all morning to say that.

"We're not closing," Nichole said. "Our kind of business doesn't close. Not in this market."

"Then why a Saturday meeting?"

"Whatever, but we're *not* closing."

Nichole and Roxanne had become fast friends three months ago, ever since Roxanne was promoted from her internship. Before that Nichole hadn't said much to Roxanne, other than to chastise her for forgetting to return the shared key to the ladies' room. The day the promotion memo made the rounds, though, Nichole sidled up to Roxanne's cubicle, asked her to go to Marathon for lunch. Since then they'd had lunch together every day.

Roxanne appreciated the friendship, but it was also frustrating. Nichole was like most Philadelphians: cold and standoffish, right up until the moment they're not.

Even after their friendship suddenly and miraculously bloomed, the office was *so* secretive. How many times had she walked into Nichole's office, only to find her quickly hit a key sequence that blanked her screen and brought up a fake spreadsheet? Like Roxanne wasn't supposed to notice?

"We're not closing," Nichole repeated, "but I saw the reports."

"And?" Rox asked.

"Top line revenue is just awful. Even considering we budgeted *under*. It's bad."

"*That* bad?"

"Bad."

"How bad?"

"Rox, you know I can't tell you."

"Nondisclosure."

This was Nichole's excuse for everything. I signed a nondisclosure. Sorry, Rox, it's not you, it's the nondisclosure. I'd tell you who I went home with last night after the Khyber, but you know . . . *nondisclosure.* And it wasn't just Nichole. It was the whole office. The whole city, for that matter.

Roxanne kept her focus on the road. Tried to keep her left wheels the exact same distance from the median marker. Tried not to lose it.

"But I can tell you," Nichole said. "Without getting into numbers."

"And?"

"We're at least 850,000 below projections."

Roxanne's Chevy HHR glided down the Schuylkill Expressway. Couldn't do that any other day of the week, save Sunday. She looked out on the hills of Manayunk, and it looked like the neighborhood was roasting alive in its own haze.

Frustrated as she was, Roxanne was glad to be in one air-conditioned environment and headed to another. Her apartment in Bryn Mawr didn't have air. After a night of drinking with Amy, Nichole, and Ethan, she gladly took Nichole up on the offer of her couch. She showered and changed at Nichole's, and was thankful for the AC. Roxanne had grown up in Vermont, where the humidity wasn't often a factor.

How did Philadelphians live like this all summer long? Maybe that was their problem.

Her name was Nichole Wise . . .

. . . and she hated lying to Roxanne, feeding her that crap about "top line revenue." If Roxanne had paid closer attention to things around the office, she might have seen through it.

But Nichole couldn't let that bother her. If this morning went as expected, she could be looking at a promotion.

Something big was going down.

Murphy wouldn't have called this Saturday-morning meeting otherwise.

She wondered if she'd have the chance to deliver a verbal coup de grâce and relish the expression on his stupid face.

You? he'd say, all shocked.

Yeah, she'd say. *Me.*

Maybe—just maybe—her long nightmare assignment would be over.

And if that were to happen, she'd bring Roxanne back with her.

The United States of America needed bright young women like Roxanne Kurtwood.

Her name was Amy Felton . . .

. . . and she wished she didn't need this job so bad.

But she did, and would continue to do so, especially if she kept making stupid moves like last night—grabbing the check at the Continental, saying it was no problem, she had it covered. Nice one, Felton. Another $119 on the AmEx that didn't need to be there. Wasn't even as if she drank very much. Two Cosmos, nursed over a four-hour stretch.

But Nichole and Roxanne and Ethan . . . oh God, Ethan. He'd knocked back enough booze to curl a human liver.

Damn it, why did she pick up the check? Was she *that* eager to please people she didn't particularly like?

Ethan not included.

Thing was, Amy knew she was screwed, because this was part of her job.

David had once told her: "You've got to be my public face. It's not good for the boss to be palling around with his employees. But *you* can. You're their upper management confidante. The one who has access to me, yet remains their friend. So keep them happy. Take them out for drinks."

Sure, take them out for drinks. Pick up the check while you're at it.

She wanted to ask: Why doesn't *the government* pick up the check every now and again?

And this stuff about Amy being the "upper management confidante" was just an easy out for David. He didn't like socializing with anyone below his rank. Amy was his second in command, and *she* hardly had any face time with him. It didn't help that he'd been gone for sixteen days straight and didn't tell her where. Covert government stuff. *Blah, blah, blah.* What David didn't realize was that his impromptu vacations dealt serious blows to office morale. He'd returned this week, but the wisecracks and bitterness hadn't gone away. Nobody liked the boss being away that long.

Especially in an office like this. Considering what they did.

And now this morning's "managers' meeting." People were going to freak. Especially the people who hadn't been invited.

David wouldn't even tell her what it was about, other than it was a "new operation."

As if what they did on a daily basis wasn't important enough?

Just get through it, Felton.

On weekends—on scorching summer weekends, it seemed—the Market–Frankford El only ran every fifteen minutes. She made it to the platform to watch the air-conditioned cars of the 8:21 train pull away from the station. The sun was like a photographer's flashbulb set on "stun." No breeze to cool her down. Not even up here. Philadelphia was in the clutches of still another heat wave—seven straight days of hundred-plus temperatures.

Such temperature spikes used to be unusual in the mid-Atlantic, but for the past four years, they'd become the norm.

At least she wasn't hungover, which would have been intolerable in this heat.

She'd been afraid to drink too much.

Run the tab up too high.

His name was Ethan Goins . . .

. . . and his hangover wasn't just a condition; it was a living creature, nestled within the meat of his brain, gnawing at the fat gray noodles, savoring them, and, as a cocktail, absorbing all available moisture from the rest of his body. The skin on his hands was so dry, you could fling him against a concrete wall, and—if Ethan's palms happened to be facing out—he'd stick. His eyes needed to be plucked out of his sockets, dropped into a glass pitcher of ice water. Might hurt some, but he'd enjoy the soothing *hissssss* of hot versus cold.

Oh, Ethan knew better. Knew he had to report to David Murphy's Big Bad Saturday-Morning Managers' Meeting.

It was why he'd stayed up way too late last night, drinking those orange martinis with Amy.

Rebel Ethan Goins.

Stickin' it to the Man, one French martini at a time.

They'd tasted like Tang. That was the problem. Sweet as a child's breakfast drink. Now, as Ethan stuffed his throbbing, desiccated, burning, aching body inside an aluminum coffin manufactured by Honda, he knew he had only one chance.

McDonald's drive-through.

Large Coke, plenty of ice, red-and-yellow pin-striped straw plunged down into the cup.

Egg.McMuffin. With a slice of Canadian bacon wedged between the soft marble slab of egg and flour-flecked sides of a gently warmed English muffin.

Hash browns.

Three of them. In the little greasy paper bags. Spread across the passenger seat.

Where Amy Felton sat whenever they met to talk, unwind, stare at each other awkwardly . . . before he drove her home. Which was like returning a nun to her convent.

Sister Amy had been the architect of his misery this morning—Ms. "Oooh, let's go out drinking after work." Ethan never even heard of French martinis until Amy had pointed it out on the menu.

Yeah, she could deal with a greasy butt next time she sat in the car.

Come to think of it, maybe he'd buy four hash browns. Have one on hand, just in case. It was probably going to be a four–hash brown morning, all told.

The infusion of meat and caffeine and carbohydrates and protein was the only prayer he had of making it through this morning alive.

He just prayed that the morning meeting would be a brief one—a new assignment, a new bit of training. Whatever. His role at the office wasn't central to their mission. He was just the protector. The dude who could be counted on to snap a neck if somebody tried to mess with the numbers geeks. So they could jabber on about whatever they wanted to this morning.

Just so long as he could make his way back home as soon as possible, crank up the central air, pull down the shades, crawl under a blanket, and suffer through the rest of his death in peace.

Ethan paid for his breakfast with a debit card, grabbed the bag, placed the Coke in the drink holder, fumbled with the paper around the straw, and drove away. By the next red light, the Egg McMuffin was unwrapped and headed to his mouth.

The third hash brown was history even before he reached the on-ramp to the Schuylkill Expressway.

By the time he reached the off-ramp to Vine Street, there was a rumbling in Ethan's belly.

By the time he hit Market Street, there was more than rumbling. There was an escape plan forming.

By Twentieth Street, a full-on revolt was in the works.

Ethan, of course, should have known better: The McDonald's breakfast hangover cure is a fleeting one. A salve to the brain and stomach for only a short while. It is a remedy on loan. The havoc it wreaks on your intestinal tract can be nearly as painful as the hangover itself. It is like pressing your palms to the beaches of heaven shortly before catching the jitney to hell.

Ethan needed a bathroom. *Immediately.*

The office. It was his only chance.

His name was David Murphy . . .

. . . and he was the boss.

David had been in the office since the night before. Drove in under the cover of darkness, parked on a different garage level. Not that anyone would notice. David had rented a different car a few days ago, switched out the plates twice.

Use misdirection, illusion, and deception.

As usual, he was taking things straight out of the Moscow Rules. Like:

Pick the time and the place for action.

He was going to miss the Moscow Rules. Where some men

had a moral compass, David had this loose set of guidelines, developed by CIA operatives at the Moscow station inside the U.S. Embassy during the Cold War. They were good for tradecraft. They were also good for life, in general:

Never go against your gut.

Establish a distinctive and dynamic profile and pattern.

David wished he'd hired one last escort before he holed up here for the night. He could really use a blow job. It would help mellow him out.

But his final assignment beckoned.

Walking toward the parking garage elevator, David had carried two plastic bags, lined with sturdy brown paper bags, along with his black briefcase. That was all he needed.

He should also have hit some drive-through. He was *ravenous,* and it was going to be a busy night.

Maybe he could sneak out for something later.

Maybe even a warm mouth. Some tasty little piece of Fishtown skank.

As the Moscow Rules said:

Keep your options open.

Upstairs in his office, which was not quite as air-conditioned as he would have liked—the building cut back on the AC at night—David knelt in front of the mini-fridge. He unloaded the contents of his bags: three sixty-four-ounce containers of Tropicana Pure Premium Homestyle orange juice, four bottles of Veuve Clicquot. You always wanted more champagne to orange juice; nobody overloaded a mimosa with OJ.

The cookies were already here. He'd purchased them at CVS the day before. He had the urge to open a bag and take a few, but he resisted. He needed them for tomorrow.

Inside his oversized Kevlar-reinforced briefcase were the elevator codes and schematics to the phone system.

The customer service line at Verizon.

The twin packages, the assemblies, the triggers.

All set.

Wait.

Except for one thing: the fax transmission he had to destroy.

It was redundant, actually; David knew who was on that list. As if he could forget. Or miss a name.

Those names would be burned on his brain forever. However long "forever" would be.

Not long.

"Nothing fancy; just kill them."

The last set of instructions he'd ever hear or obey.

David scanned the list one more time:

Jamie DeBroux

Amy Felton

Ethan Goins

Roxanne Kurtwood

Molly Lewis

Stuart McCrane

Nichole Wise

He had to kill them all.

MEETING

To succeed in life in today's world, you must have the will and tenacity to finish the job.

—CHIN-NING CHU

The conference room table was loaded with cookies. Pepperidge Farm, every conceivable make and model: Milano, Chessmen, Bordeaux, Geneva, and Verona. David had encouraged everyone to go ahead, open the bags, help themselves. Also on the table were two towers of clear plastic cups, three cartons of Tropicana, and four bottles of champagne.

Jamie couldn't read the labels on the bottles, but they looked French and expensive. The tops on two of the bottles had been popped and removed, but nobody had poured a glass yet. The cookies also remained untouched.

That is, until David reached forward and grabbed a Milano, then everybody decided having a cookie was a great idea.

Jamie had his eyes on the Chessmen, but held back. He wasn't about to fight the Clique for a cookie. Let them pick over the bags. Chessmen were the least popular. He'd be able to grab a few when the feeding frenzy was over.

"Looks like everybody's here . . . ," David said, scanning faces, then frowning. "Except Ethan. Anybody seen Ethan?"

"His bag's at his desk, and his computer's on," said Molly, who'd taken her usual position: the right hand of the devil.

"Did he make it home last night?"

"He did," Amy Felton said, and then winced, as if regretting having opened her mouth.

"Should I look for him?" Molly said.

David shook his head. There were droplets of moisture on his brow. "No, no. We can start without him."

"Are you . . ."

"I am."

Some boss/assistant drama going on there, Jamie decided.

He hated how David treated Molly.

She had been here only six months, and already working for David had utterly demoralized her. Jamie assumed that was be-cause she was a genuine human being—not one of the Clique.

Out of all his coworkers, Molly was the only one he spent any significant time with. Jamie had once read a story in some mag-azine about "office spouses"—surrogate partners in the work-place with whom you shared your life. It wasn't about infidelity. Jamie read that piece and decided that the closest thing he had to an office spouse was Molly. What made it easy was that Molly, like Jamie, was married. And they were united in their thinking that David Murphy was a serious tool.

"Tool?" Molly had asked, trying to fight a goofy smile that threatened to wash over her entire face.

"Yeah, tool," Jamie had said. "Never heard that expression before?"

She giggled. "Not in Illinois I didn't."

"Stick with me, country girl," Jamie said. "I'll teach you all about the big bad city."

Molly, come to think of it, was the one who'd organized the shower for Jamie. She was the only one who saw him as more than just the media relations guy.

The cookie grab ended. Jamie took the opportunity to snag three Chessmen. He stacked them on a square white paper napkin. The cookie on top: a pawn.

"First of all," David said, "I want to thank everyone for coming up here on a Saturday morning. A *hot* Saturday morning in the middle of August. The time of year when nobody in their right mind stays in Philadelphia."

Stuart chuckled. No one else did. Stuart was a brownnosing ass.

But David was right. Outside, the haze blanketed downtown Philadelphia, making it difficult to see any detail outside of a two-block radius.

David paused to snap a Milano in half with his teeth. He chewed slowly. Brushed crumbs from his place at the table. The man enjoyed taking his time almost as much as he enjoyed Pepperidge Farm cookies.

"I know this kind of meeting runs counter to protocol. But we've come up against a new challenge. I've been tasked with accepting that challenge, and this is why I've brought you all in this morning."

Already, David was being his good ol' obscure self. Protocol? Challenge? Did anyone really talk like that? Did anyone understand what the guy was talking about half the time?

Jamie eyed the Tropicana. He was thirsty. The Chessmen wouldn't help that, and they'd probably only jack him up for a sugar crash this afternoon. He had promised Andrea he'd be home as early as possible and take over Chase duty.

"As of right now," David said, "we're on official lockdown."

"What?"

"Oh, man."

"I came in for this?"

"What's going on, David?"

"Damn it."

Jamie looked around the room. Lockdown? What the hell was "lockdown"?

"Beyond that," David continued, "I've taken some additional measures. The elevators have been given a bypass code and will skip this floor for the next eight hours. No exceptions. Calling down to the front desk won't work, either."

Jamie didn't hear the part about the front desk. He was fixated on the "next eight hours" bit. Eight hours? Trapped in here, with the Clique? He thought he'd be out of here by noon. Andrea was going to kill him.

"The phones," David said, "have been disconnected—and not just in the computer room. You can't plug anything back in, and have the phones back up or anything. The lines for this floor have been severed in the subbasement, right where it connects to the Verizon router. Which you can't get to, because of the elevators."

Stuart laughed. "So much for a smoke break."

"No offense, David," said Nichole, "but if I need a smoke, I'm marching down thirty-six flights of fire stairs, lockdown or no lockdown."

"No you aren't."

Nichole raised an eyebrow. "You going to come between a woman and her Marlboros?"

David tented his fingers under his bony chin. He was smiling. "The fire towers won't be any good to you."

"Why?" Jamie heard himself ask. Not that he smoked.

"Because the doors have been rigged with sarin bombs."

Six wadfuls of toilet paper and a vigorous hand-washing later, and a solemn vow to never *ever* so much as glance at a French martini—or an Egg McMuffin—ever again, Ethan left the bathroom on the thirty-seventh floor and headed for the north fire tower.

Checked his plastic-and-metal Nike sports watch. He was late. What else, right?

Better to be late than to squirm uncomfortably in that over-chilled corner office and have to rush out in the middle of a David Murphy brainstorm.™

Sorry, boss. Got to do the hot squat. Ask Felton for details. She'll tell you all about the effects of the French martini on the lower digestive tract.

In all the time Ethan had used the men's room on the thirty-seventh floor, he'd never stopped to wonder about the companies up here. There was more than one, certainly—there was a directory at the end of the hall.

He didn't stop to wonder now, either.

The air in the fire tower was mercifully warm. Ethan was tempted to take a seat on the cool concrete and savor the varying climes. Breath warm; sweat out the French martini. Meanwhile, let the soothing cool work its way up from the steps, into his buttocks, and beyond, healing the O-ring damage he'd sustained up on thirty-seven.

But the later his appearance on the thirty-sixth floor, the worse off he'd be.

Up, Ethan, up.

Go, Ethan, go.

Down the stairs. Hand on the doorknob. Get it over with.

The cardboard he'd used to prop open the door was still in place.

There were smiles at first, then confused frowns. Was this supposed to be an icebreaker? Jamie thought. Or was this David's strange way of saying there was going to be a Saturday-morning fire drill?

"Stop it, David," Amy said. "This isn't funny."

"*Sarin,* David?" Nichole asked. "Isn't that a little harsh?"

Stuart tried to jump on the bandwagon. "Seriously. Couldn't you have made do with a little burst of anthrax or something? Let the trespasser know you mean business, but live to tell the tale?"

"Biological agents like anthrax take too long," David said. "And it's not as easy to weaponize as you think."

"Right," Stuart said. "I always have trouble with that."

"Plus, you could take a full blast, right in the face, and still figure you were okay for a while. Then you could make your way down the stairs and out to Market Street. I figured the immediate impact of sarin—burning eyes, nausea, constricted breathing, muscle weakness, the whole nine—would be the only thing that could keep you guys on this floor. I didn't use an extravagant amount, but certainly enough to prevent you from reaching the bottom floor. Your throat would close before you made it down three or four flights."

Amy's nose wrinkled. "David."

"Am I being offensive?"

"*Hostile work environment,*" Stuart said in a mock falsetto.

"Okay, we get it, it's lockdown, we're not going anywhere, ha ha ha," Amy said. "So what's the operational plan?"

"Whoa," Nichole said. "Before we start talking about plans . . . David, you do know who's here, right?" She motioned at Jamie.

Me? Jamie thought. Oh, you've got to love the Clique. God forbid I sit in on a meeting with any substance. Freaky as it was.

David tented his index fingers under his nose again. Raised his eyebrows slightly, then opened his mouth . . .

And there was a scream.

Not from David. From somewhere else. Beyond the walls of the conference room. Elsewhere on the floor.

Molly said, "God, Ethan . . ."

Ethan had glanced up at the weird thing above the door just before it happened. Thing was bone-white, cushy, the size of a fanny pack, and had a keypad and bright green digital display with the word READY. He turned around to look at the wall behind him—maybe there were more? His hand was still on the doorknob. As he turned, the door opened another inch.

He heard a clicking sound. A blast of mist hit him square in the face. His eyes burned immediately. It freaked him out.

So Ethan didn't care how it might sound. He screamed.

He screamed like hell.

David and Molly exchanged glances, and David said, "We're going to have to check that out."

"Wait," Amy said. "Was that *Ethan*?"

Jamie stood up. He looked outside, in the haze of the summer morning, scanning for planes. He couldn't help it. He'd worked in a building in Lower Manhattan on 9/11, right at Broadway and Bleecker. His office window had faced the Twin Towers; he'd been taking a leak when the first plane hit. Jamie had walked back to his office and saw, with a start, that the upper floors of the North Tower were on fire. Someone screamed.

The scream, the blaze: forever entwined in his memory.

He'd tried calling Andrea, who worked uptown. No luck. Circuits were jammed. Jamie called his old college roommate in Virginia, who was able to get through to Andrea. While he was waiting to hear back, the second plane hit. He could hear the roar even blocks away.

The scream reminded him of that morning.

"Sit down, Jamie," David said.

"I don't think we're safe up here," Jamie said. Only later, as he thought back over the events of the morning, would he understand that he was momentarily gifted with some kind of precognitive blast. A small part of his brain knew what the other parts would slowly come to experience: *We're not safe up here.*

"Sit down *now*," David commanded.

Amazingly, Jamie found himself sitting back down. What had he planned on doing, anyway? Check the windows for burning skyscrapers?

David cleared his throat, staring at a bag of Geneva cookies that was closest to him.

"I'd hoped to have more time to explain, to set your souls at ease a bit, but I guess that's not to be."

He ran his fingers through his hair. Jamie could swear David's hand was shaking.

"Truth is, I've failed you."

Nobody said a word.

Nobody even reached for a cookie.

This is bad, Jamie thought. He wondered if his most recent résumé was stored on his computer at work, or at home. He just hoped there was some kind of severance package to see them through a few months of job hunting.

"Most of you know the truth about our company," David said, "but for the two of you who don't, I apologize for the shock you're about to receive."

Someone gasped. Jamie didn't see who.

"We're a front company for CI-6, which is a government intelligence agency," David said. "We are being shut down."

Jamie found himself locking eyes with Stuart. We are *what*?

Stuart didn't look a bit surprised.

"You should be doing to me what I'm about to do to you," David continued.

"Oh, no." Roxanne gulped. "You're going to fire us."

David gave her a tight-lipped smile, then a shake of his head. "No, Roxanne, I'm not going to fire you. I'm going to *kill* you. You, and everyone else in this room. Then I'm going to kill myself."

"David," Amy said.

"Molly? The box, please."

It was there in front of Molly—all of a sudden, it seemed. Jamie hadn't noticed it before. He'd had his eyes on the cookies. Like everyone else.

Molly opened the box, which was a plain white cardboard mailing box. She parted some Bubble Wrap, and lifted out a gun. With something bulky around the barrel.

David put his hand out.

Molly was shaking. Hesitating a moment before she handed over the weapon to her boss.

But she did, like a good employee. Then she bowed her head slightly.

David pointed the gun in the general direction of his employees. With a minor flick of the wrist, the barrel could be pointed directly at any of them. Jamie felt his forehead break out into a sweat. He wasn't sure he was actually seeing any of this, but of course, he was seeing it. Because it was real.

Unfolding in front of his eyes.

"What I want you to do," David said, "is mix a little champagne and orange juice together. Each contain a chemical that, when combined, is an extremely effective poison. It is also completely painless. You will lose consciousness within seconds, and that will be it."

"David, stop this," Amy said. "This isn't funny at all."

"I tried it myself a few nights ago. A very *micro* dose. It's totally relaxing. I've never had a better night's sleep."

Stuart was still trying to play the good soldier. "You want us to have a drink with you, boss? We'll drink with you."

David ignored him. "If you choose not to have a drink, then I'll be forced to shoot you in the head. I cannot guarantee that this second method will be pain-free. You may require a second bullet. It may be worse if you all decide to do something foolish like rush me. Make no mistake. If you do, all of you will be shot. My marksmanship is excellent. Any of you familiar with my operational background will know this to be true."

Part of Jamie wanted to believe this was a charade, or a movie, or a bad dream, but all his senses relayed the truth: *This was real.* He also had the feeling that he was really the only one taking David seriously. Everyone else at the table looked like they were still waiting for the punch line, the moral. But Jamie realized: His boss wasn't telling a joke or a parable. He was offering them a choice.

Drink poison champagne and die.

Or get shot in the head.

Jamie believed it as much as he believed he was sitting in that conference room chair. As much as he believed that outside the sweeping conference room windows, Philadelphia stewed in the humid air of early morning.

"You're insane," Jamie said.

David looked at him with pity. "I didn't want to invite you in this morning, Jamie. Swear to God I didn't. You're our press guy. I even said to them, Why the press guy? You're too good a press guy. You approached your job with zeal. But alas, you looked at some things you shouldn't have seen."

"What are you talking about? What things?"

"Your wife and newborn son will believe you died in an office fire," David said. "They will be taken care of."

"David, *please,*" Amy said. "What are you doing? Does anybody else know you're doing this?"

"Yeah this is *so* not funny."

"I'm going to find Ethan."

The shuffling of chairs.

The nervous exhalation of air.

"I'm going with you."

"SIT."

David, commanding.

It worked.

Everyone froze.

"I've given you all a dignified way out," he said. "I suggest you take it."

No one said anything until Stuart, looking around with a goofy smile on his face, stood up.

"You got it, boss."

Stuart knew what this was.

At a previous job—a few years before he was recruited to work here—the HR department decided it was worth the money to send some of the sales associates on an Outward Bound trip. Three days in the woods, learning to tie knots and trust each other.

The penultimate activity: backwards free fall. Go ahead, let yourself tilt back. Free yourself from doubt and worry. Your coworkers will catch you.

Stuart did it, but as he was falling, all he could think about were the times at the Applebee's, when he would try to make conversational inroads, but everyone would look at him like he had a gushing head wound and they didn't want to get blood on their suits. But he allowed himself to drop backwards anyway, allowed himself to trust.

As the Outward Bound leader—a gruff guy who looked like Oliver Stone—had promised, his coworkers had indeed caught him. When he looked up, Stuart saw that nobody was looking down at him, the human being in their hands. Still, no matter; they had caught him. Stuart received a certificate and a small pin, and he noted the achievement on his résumé.

So that's what this was. David's weird version of a trust game. The gun was a prop—probably a flare gun. Maybe even one of those lighters you find at Spencer's. The talk about elevators and windows was meant to simulate something . . . like a hostile environment, just like they'd encountered in Outward Bound. There's no way out. You have nothing but trust. Trust in your coworkers. Trust in your boss.

This was a front company for the government, but it was still a company, and the more Stuart thought about it, the more he knew it was a test of trust. To see who was executive material and who wasn't.

Stuart took the bottle of champagne and poured three fingers' full into a clear plastic wineglass.

"Stu," Jamie said. "Wait."

Stuart waved his hand, as if he were batting away a fly. Jamie was just jealous he hadn't taken the initiative.

"Very wise move, Stuart," David said.

Stuart splashed in some of the Tropicana, and he couldn't help himself. He was beaming. Passing the trust test. There was nothing to stir the champagne and orange juice—were you even supposed to stir mimosas? Whatever. Didn't matter. Not for the purposes of the trust test.

"Cheers," Stuart said, raising the cup in a mock toast.

"Thank you for your service," David said, which gave Stuart the slightest bit of pause. What did that mean?

Jamie stood up now. "Stu, *no*. Don't do it."

Bite it, DeBroux.

Stuart sipped his mimosa, then looked at David.

But David didn't say anything. Just stared at him. So did everyone else. Even Jamie, who sat back down.

And the weirdest thing was, Stuart felt like he was having an Outward Bound flashback. He had the overwhelming urge to drift backwards, in the hands of his coworkers. But this time, they'd all be looking at him admiringly. Because he'd won the Trust Game. None of them could say that. Could they?

Was he still holding the plastic wineglass? Stuart didn't know.

He couldn't feel his fingers.

Or his legs, as they gave out from under him.

Jamie DeBroux

Amy Felton

Ethan Goins

Roxanne Kurtwood

Molly Lewis

~~Stuart McCrane~~

Nichole Wise

Everyone watched Stuart collapse. The hand holding his plastic cup of mimosa hit the side of the conference table. The drink splashed everywhere. Roxanne, who had been sitting next to Stuart, hopped her chair to the side reflexively.

"Oh God."

"*Stuart,*" Amy said. "C'mon, Stuart. This isn't funny!"

"One recommendation," David said, holding up a bony finger. "Try to remain seated when you drink this stuff. You might even want to position yourself on the floor, leaning against a wall, so that you can fall asleep without hurting yourself."

"Stuart?"

"Not that I think Stuart felt anything. The first thing the poison shuts down is your brain."

Amy ran around the side of the table and knelt next to Stuart, whose eyes were still open. She pressed a finger to his carotid artery. Looked up at Roxanne.

"Double-check me. Feel his neck."

"No. No way."

Searching around Stuart's neck, madly, looking for something that resembled a pulse. You can't fake that. You can't just stop your heartbeat voluntarily.

"*Stuart!*"

David shook his head. "He's gone, Amy."

Amy looked up over the table at her boss.

"Stuart chose the smart way out. I hope that the rest of you follow suit. We can drink together, if you like."

Jamie said, "Oh, you're going to kill yourself, too?"

"Yes, Jamie. They want us all gone." David turned to his assistant. "Molly, will you do the honors?"

Molly, who had been silent for the duration of the meeting—including Stuart's suicide toast—raised her head.

Then she reached into a white cardboard box and pulled out another gun. It looked smaller.

"Hey," said David. "I meant mixing the drinks. Like we discussed?"

She aimed the gun at David.

He squinted. "Is that a Neo?" he asked.

Molly screamed—a howling geyser of rage that seemed like it had been building up under a mountain of composure.

"Hey, wait a second . . . *Molly!*"

Then she squeezed the trigger.

BLAM!

Part of David's scalp flipped up from his head, like a piece of toupee caught in a breeze.

David saw an explosion in front of his eyes, then a cold, *cold* sensation on the right side of his head.

As he was thrown backwards, someone pressed PAUSE.

He could see the faces of his employees, frozen in perfect detail. Many of them were slack-jawed in surprise. The others seemed not to be processing it yet.

Then again, neither was he.

Molly.

They'd gone over this. A *lot.* Offer the mimosas. The easy way out. Not that he thought many people would go for it, but hey, you never know. Then if things got ugly, leave the shooting to David. Bow your head and pray for God's blessings. Molly was religious. In every e-mail, she put "God bless" or "God willing" or "Faith in Jesus" before her name. Hearty Midwestern stock— made her perfect for this kind of work. Perfect for following instructions.

Except for this one little time.

My God.

Molly had just shot him in the head.

Molly!

David knew she wasn't supposed to live through this. But *she* didn't know that. He'd promised her a way out. New identity. New life. How had she found out the truth?

Granted, he didn't have the nicest things in the world planned for her. First a shot to the leg that would drop her to the ground. Then, press the gun to her head, tell her to take off her shirt and bra if she wants to live. Check out her tits, kill her anyway.

How had she found out the truth?

David's body hit the conference room floor.

AFTER THE MEETING

The best way to get started is to stop talking and begin doing.
—WALT DISNEY

Everyone stood up.

"H-H-He was going to kill us all," Molly said, her voice trembling.

Her hand, weighed down with the gun, dropped to the surface of the table with a hard thud. The barrel pointed at the space where David had been sitting. Smoke curled around it. Then, quieter now:

"He was going to kill us all."

"I know, Molly. Give me the gun, sweetie."

This was Amy Felton. Face compassionate yet determined.

In.

Control.

"The gun, Molly."

Molly nodded but didn't move.

"I had no choice. He told me he was going to kill Paul if I didn't do what he wanted."

Paul Lewis. Her husband.

"Sweetie," Amy said, her expression softening. "I understand. I'm going to take the gun, okay?"

Amy was able to take the gun. Molly folded her arms on top of the table, then buried her face in them.

"Did somebody check David? Is he dead?"

"Oh, Molly, what did you do?"

"Shut up. Here, take this."

Jamie looked down. Amy was handing him the murder weapon.

"I don't want that."

"I need to check David. Hold this."

It all felt like another 9/11. The shock of it. Molly, shooting David. Amy, trying to hand him the gun she used. David, on the floor, bleeding out of a hole in his head.

The sense that nothing would be the same again. He wouldn't be reporting to work on Monday. None of them would. Instantly, he thought of Chase.

"Jamie."

Jamie took the gun—still warm—and watched Amy trot over to David. The blue-gray carpet around his head was soaked deep purple with blood. David's lips were trembling.

"I think he's still alive," Amy said. "God, I don't know."

"Somebody call nine-one-one."

Nichole made a beeline for the phone in the conference room. Grabbed the receiver. Put it to her ear. There was a confused look on her face. Her index finger stabbed at the hook switch.

"There's no dial tone."

"He wasn't kidding about lockdown, was he?"

"What?"

"My cell's in my bag," Nichole said.

Roxanne said, "Mine's here." She was already dialing. "Wait . . ." She looked at the display more carefully. "No service?"

"David had it suspended as of eight thirty this morning," Molly said, her face still buried in her hands.

"You've got to be kidding."

"It's lockdown, remember?"

Which is why my cell wouldn't work this morning, Jamie thought.

Every one of David Murphy's employees was issued company cell phones, free of charge, to use as they wished. David's only rule: Keep the phone on from 7:00 A.M. until midnight, just in case he needed to reach you. Agree to that, and you could enjoy unlimited minutes, long distance, you name it. Every one of David's direct reports—Jamie, Amy, Ethan, Roxanne, Stuart, Molly, Nichole—immediately canceled their private cells and used their company phones exclusively. David had even sprung for models with built-in cameras and texting capability.

But none of that mattered with the service canceled.

"Why did he cancel it?"

"I should have known . . . ," Molly said, near-wailing. "I saw the signs. . . ."

"What signs?"

Amy, on the floor with David, said, "Forget it. I've still got a pulse, but he needs an ambulance *now.*"

"Was he kidding about the elevators, too?"

Molly wearily said, *"No."*

"I'm going to check anyway."

"We should check our offices. Not all of the phones may be turned off."

"The stairs."

"David said the stairs were rigged with . . ."

"What? Sarin?" Nichole said. "Do you really believe that?"

"He wasn't joking. He showed me a packet. Told me exactly what it was. I think he was showing off."

"He showed you?" Nichole asked. "When? How long have you known about this."

Amy said, "We've got to find Ethan."

Ethan didn't feel so good.

Okay, yeah, maybe he *had* screamed a bit prematurely. But that puff of whatever that'd nailed him . . . c'mon, you'd be frightened, too. In his imagination, it was a burst of ultra-hot steam from a chipped pipe. The kind of steam so lethally hot, it scalded the flesh from his face before his nerves had a chance to relay the pain. From here on out, he'd be stuck hiding behind masks, or at the very least, ridiculous amounts of theatrical makeup.

All of that passed through his mind in about two seconds. His fingers explored his face.

Flesh still there. His eyes, too.

His burning eyes.

Burning, but not about to shrivel up and drop out of their sockets.

Still, they burned. Worse by the second.

He needed water.

He must have been blasted with wet air that had been circulating throughout 1919 Market Street since the place was built—around the time KC and the Sunshine Band were first huge. That air was carrying every germ and virus that had plagued this building's inhabitants in years since. Ethan had a feeling he'd be sick the rest of the summer.

Ethan needed the men's room. Wash out his eyes. His face. His badly burning eyes. Compose himself enough so that when he popped into David's office, he would be able to say, *Screaming? I didn't hear any screaming,* and have it sound believable.

He pulled on the doorknob. The door wouldn't open. He tried it again. Nothing. Locked.

Wait.

Damn it.

He could see it, even through his blurry, stinging vision.

The cardboard had slipped out.

Ethan tugged at it, cursed, then kicked the door. His skin around his eyes was really starting to sting now, too.

"Hey!"

Kicked it again.

"Hey! Anybody!"

He was about to kick again—in fact, his foot was already cocked, ready to deliver the blow, when he heard something

POP!

A car backfiring.

Up here? On the thirty-sixth floor?

"Hey!"

This was ridiculous. Everyone was probably already gathered in the conference room. Probably closed the door, too, for the big secret operational announcement. Which he was missing. Locked on the other side of this door. Eyes burning, face itching. More intense than ever. His throat, suddenly raw.

Nobody was going to hear him yell.

Especially with his throat closing, all of a sudden.

Jamie mumbled something about being right back and walked to his office.

Roxanne gaped at him on the way out, as in: You're leaving now?

With our boss, shot in the head, lying on the floor?

Jamie was trying to think a few steps ahead. Maybe his

monthlong paternity leave had given him a different perspective, but right now, his worry wasn't David Murphy. He was worried about what David had *said.* Elevators, blocked. Phone lines, cut. The cell phone thing, if Molly was to be believed, was troubling in itself.

Jamie's office was the farthest away from David's, but closest to the conference room. This usually bugged him. Not today. He needed to make it to his office as soon as possible.

He needed a few seconds to think.

Jamie had never been a fan of group decisions. Whatever was happening in the conference room, he wasn't an important part of it. He was the company's press guy—the guy who wrote the press release in the event of a new hire or the launch of a new financial product. He wasn't the guy doing the hiring, and he had nothing to do with the financial products. He wasn't a member of the Clique. He took whatever the managers said and translated it into something the trade press could understand. There weren't many trade publications that covered his particular industry; Jamie had been shocked at how small the list was when he started a year ago.

But what had David been saying, right before Molly shot him in the head?

Front company?

Intelligence agency?

I mean . . . *what?*

Jamie sat behind his desk and saw the greeting card tacked to his corkboard. He'd almost forgotten about that.

Andrea had given it to him the day Chase was born, a month ago. It was a card from Baby Chase to his new daddy. On the front was a cartoon duck—a little boy duck, wearing little boy pants. Fireworks burst behind him. HAPPY FOURTH OF JULY, DADDY the card said on the back. "You're just lucky he wasn't born on Arbor Day," Andrea had joked. But Jamie loved that card to an absurd degree. It was the little duck, in the little boy pants. *His* little boy. For the first time, it all clicked. He'd brought it to work with him a few days later as he packed up his Rolodex and notes for his paternity leave. Unpaid, but what the hell. How often are firstborn sons born?

The card was meant to be tacked up temporarily, to put a smile on Jamie's face as he went through the drudgery of answering last e-mails, setting his voice mail vacation message, gathering up manila folders full of junk he knew he wouldn't actually touch for at least a month. But in the hurry to leave, the card was forgotten. Jamie wanted to kick himself, but it wasn't worth showing his face in the office just to recover the card. He'd be sucked back into the vortex too quickly—one more press release, c'mon, just one more . . .

Jamie put his fingers to the greeting card. Smoothed the imaginary feathers on the head of the little boy duck. Then he tucked it in his back pocket.

He desperately needed to call Andrea, tell her what was going on, and somehow convince her that she didn't need to worry.

But his office phone, like the one in the conference room, was dead. Jamie looked out his office window, which faced east. If he craned his neck, he could almost see the corner of his block, off in the distance beyond Spring Garden Street. Just two houses down from the corner were Andrea and his baby boy.

Whatever had happened this morning, Jamie knew it would be many, many hours before he would see his wife and son again. The police interrogations alone would probably keep him here—or down at the Roundhouse—until late tonight.

He just wished the police could be called, so they could arrive, so that they could get it all over with already.

Look at me, he thought. The new daddy. Gone for barely an hour, and already nervous as hell.

Nervous daddy.

Wait a minute.

Jamie saw his soft leather briefcase on the desk. Was it still in there?

It would make all the difference.

The remaining employees split up. If they had any chance of calling an ambulance—for Stuart or David or both, even though Stuart's chances of making it through this without brain damage were next to nil—they were going to have to find their way to another floor. That much was clear.

Nichole announced that they'd be checking the elevators, and it took Roxanne a second to realize that *they* meant her, too. Jamie had already slipped out of the conference room to find a phone or sit behind his desk and cry or something. Ethan was still AWOL. Molly left a second later, most likely to the bathroom to puke. Amy couldn't blame her. She had only *watched* her boss take a bullet to the head, and she felt queasy.

Of course, that left Amy to lock the doors to the conference room, leaving the guns where they were. Let the police sort it out.

It also left her to check the fire escape doors. You know, the ones allegedly rigged with a chemical nerve agent.

Sometimes, Amy felt like the only adult in this company.

There were only two fire escapes in the building; both were accessible only from outside the office. The thirty-sixth floor was a square carved up into two separate offices; their company dominated the floor in a U shape. The remaining sliver was occupied by a local magazine called *Philadelphia Living*—shopping, restaurants, parties, and all of that good stuff. Amy was a subscriber, even though she didn't know anybody who could afford the getaways, clothes, and jewelry highlighted in the magazine every month. It was lifestyle porn: You'll never have it as good as this. Masturbate to the pages, if it makes you feel better.

She walked halfway down the hall that connected the conference room with David's office, then turned left. A security door opened up directly onto a short corridor. Make a left again, and you'd be staring at the north fire escape door.

Which Amy was doing now.

Staring at it.

Should she chance it?

David had told them some wild things this morning. There was not much she could prove right now, except for one thing: that the orange juice and champagne contained some kind of poison, which had killed poor Stuart. Why would David lie about something like putting sarin in the fire towers?

Because it was silly, that's why. Poison's one thing; rigging a chemical bomb is another. This building has security up the wazoo. Like somebody wouldn't notice a bomb rigged to a fire escape door? Somebody leaves a brown-bag lunch on a step in the fire tower and hazmat-suited Homeland Security folks would probably be descending on the scene within twenty minutes.

So if the very idea was ridiculous, why was she nervous about opening the door?

Go ahead, Amy.

Go ahead and do it.

She put her hand on the cool steel, as if she could sense by touch. *Oh yeah, clearly there's a sarin bomb behind this door.*

The problem was, Ethan recognized the sensation.

His throat had closed up once before, halfway around the world.

Before coming to work for David's company, he'd been in the military. Special Forces. Most recently Afghanistan, November

2001, as part of Operation We Think Bin Laden's Here So We're Going to Bomb You Back to the Stone Age, and he and his crew had been duking it out with some obscure Afghan warlord in the desert south of Kandahar. A warlord who just so happened to have a few canisters of ricin lying around. A skirmish went wrong; Ethan and his fellow gunmen found themselves tumbling into a medieval-era sandpit, and the warlord—some screwhead named Muhammad Gur—danced around the edge of the pit, throwing in his precious canisters of ricin, cackling.

Ricin, Ethan later read, was manufactured from the waste of castor beans. In weaponized mist form, ricin asks your body to stop making certain important proteins.

Okay, it's not really *asking*. Ricin pretty much demands it. As a result, cells die. If not treated, the victim follows suit.

All Ethan knew was that his throat was closing up.

He'd been hit the worst out of anybody. He could have sworn that Muhammad Gur jerk had been aiming for him personally. Luckily, Ethan's colleagues blasted their way out of the pit and dragged Ethan across the desert, looking for help. But when somebody looked down and saw Ethan frantically pointing at his throat, it quickly became clear that he might not make it to the medical supply tent.

A tracheotomy is a quick but complex procedure. In an emergency situation, you find the Adam's apple, slide down a bit until you feel the next bump—the cricoid cartilage—then find the little valley between the two. Congrats, you've found the cricothyroid membrane. That is where you cut: half inch horizontally, half inch deep. Pinch the sides so that the incision opens like a fish mouth, then insert the tube. Don't have a tube? Use a straw. Or the plastic tube of a ballpoint pen (with the ink stem removed, of course).

Out in the desert south of Kanadhar, Ethan's savior had a Swiss Army pocketknife and a plastic straw. Saved his life.

But here, inside the fire tower at 1919 Market Street . . .

Ethan was pretty much screwed.

Suffering from a serious Muhammad Gur flashback, Ethan stumbled backwards and imagined, if only for a few seconds, that he was trying to cling to the side of that medieval sand pit. Actually, it was a set of concrete stairs, leading down to the half landing between the thirty-sixth and the thirty-fifth floor.

Ethan tumbled down them. Backwards.

Every step hurt.

But not as bad as the agony in his throat.

This felt worse than ricin.

Castor beans his ass.

This was something else.

Amy stepped back from the door. She thought she heard something on the other side. The pounding of feet? People? Maybe security guards? Cops? A black bag crew? Someone dispatched to clean up their presumed-dead bodies?

Never mind. It could be help.

"Hello?"

She caught herself before pounding on the door. Just on the off *off* chance that the door was indeed rigged; she didn't want to set off any kind of bomb accidentally.

"Hello! Can you hear me?!"

Ethan recognized Amy's voice immediately. Her sweet voice. He wished he could answer her.

Still, he was strangely pleased that she'd come looking for him. So much so, Ethan was even willing to forgive her the French martini thing.

Hello! Can you hear me?!

Yes, honey, I can.

I wish I could tell you to come on in. But for one, my throat is sealed up tight, and for another, I'm thinking you'd receive a face-blast of the same chemical agent if you walked through that door.

Instead, Ethan found himself scrambling through his bag, searching for a pen.

Amy wanted to open the door, but worry gripped her hard. Even an off *off* chance was still a chance. She didn't want her life to end just because she ignored a warning. The warning of a man who—until just a few minutes ago—she considered the smartest guy she'd ever worked for.

But what if help were on the other side?

Help would have answered. Wouldn't it?

The inner office door behind Amy opened.

Molly stood there, tears streaking down her face. Looks like she didn't go to the bathroom after all, Amy thought. She must have been wandering around the office in a daze. It was under-standable. How often did you shoot your boss in the head?

Amy felt bad for Molly, even if she had been part of David's plan from the beginning. She'd said it herself: She knew the phone lines had been cut. Their cells disconnected. She even claimed to have seen the packages of sarin.

But who knew what David had done to her? She must have been too terrified to do anything but obey.

She certainly looked terrified now.

"Are you okay?" Amy asked redundantly.

Molly shook her head. *No. No, I'm not okay.*

"Come on." Amy opened up her arms.

Whatever was behind the north fire tower door would have to wait.

. . .

David Murphy had taken bullets before. Once in West Germany. Another time, the Sudan. Never a head shot, though. And this one felt fairly serious. Just the ricochet effect alone—the slug jarring his skull, transmitting aftershocks to the rest of his skeletal structure—was enough to make him want to roll over and go to sleep. Anything to stop the aching. He just felt . . . *wrong*.

Molly was a damn good shot.

Never would have guessed.

When his bosses sent her six months ago, David assumed he was being reprimanded. David loved salsa and wasabi; here was a woman who was plain vanilla yogurt. Nondescript hairstyle, mousy features, no build whatsoever. You could iron a shirt on her chest. David had carried on a bit with his previous charge, and it had gotten in the way—in the opinion of his handlers. It wasn't as if David had forgotten about the network of hidden cameras throughout the floor; he just thought his handlers wouldn't care.

David was wrong. They presented him with grainy black-and-white photos of a particularly steamy tryst on a lazy Tuesday afternoon. Dress pants were bunched up around ankles; skirts were hiked; lipstick smeared; hair mussed. His handler told him this was behavior unbecoming someone of his stature. Told him the object of his affection was being moved to a station in Dubai. Molly arrived the next day.

Sometimes, David thought about his previous charge. Thought about Dubai. They had built a fake ski resort right there in the middle of the desert. He wondered if she ever had the opportunity to enjoy it. He'd promised her they'd go skiing sometime.

But Molly didn't look like she enjoyed skiing.

She didn't look like she enjoyed much of anything.

His employers had a strange idea about staffing.

David had been brought in during the early, tentative days; his special blend of charm and ruthlessness carried him to the upper echelon of the fledgling intelligence organization—but not to a hiring position. That operation was always performed by other people. People David had never met.

David wished he would, someday. Just so he could slap them silly.

Look at Molly. Okay, okay, subtract the act of gross insubordination where she shot her own boss in the head. Still, she was trouble. David's charms were totally ineffective on her. She had no discernible sense of humor. It wasn't clear if her beard of a husband—some paunchy dork named Paul—was a real love interest, or if Molly skipped through Lesbos's groves. David was totally unable to handle her.

Oh, she listened. Textbook support personnel.

But he couldn't play her. That vaguely troubled him.

And look how it had all turned out.

David stared up at the ceiling and wondered how much longer he'd be conscious. Maybe it was his imagination, but he swore he could feel the blood throbbing out of the little hole in his head.

Yet, except for the paralysis that had washed over his body, he felt oddly normal. As if he could just snap out of it, and sit up. Which was *so* not going to happen.

David wasn't that delusional.

Amy ushered a shaking Molly into her office and closed the door. She needed to calm this one down *now*, even if Amy ended up calling David's bosses and had her hauled in for debriefing. Operations were one thing; this was a broken human being here. All Amy knew was that one minute, her boss of five years was threatening to kill everyone in the room, and the next, Stuart had keeled over, and the next, David's secretary of six months was shooting him in the head. It was too much.

She wished she had somebody calming *her* down.

Be the adult. Be the adult.

"Are you okay?" Amy asked. "Sit down. Let me get you some water."

"I'm okay," Molly said. She continued to stand, but looked around Amy's office nervously, as if bracing for a wild animal to leap out from behind a desk and pounce.

"Sit down, Molly. Nothing can hurt you in here."

"I know, I know. I'm okay. I promise."

Amy wished Molly would sit down and just drink some water already. Her office was hot. It was always hot. The windows faced the north, and the early morning sun always seemed to beat the cool air pumped from the building's ductwork. Fetching Molly a Styrofoam cup of water would give Amy a few moments in the chilly kitchen, a chance to wipe a paper towel across her forehead and neck and, more important, give her a moment to think. With David gone—and oh, how that was a weird euphemism to use, considering the man was lying in the conference room with a bullet in his head—Amy was technically in charge. And she didn't have a single idea what to do next.

The Department handbook didn't cover stuff like this.

She also wanted desperately to find Ethan. While he could act like a schoolboy, he was excellent in crisis moments. Whenever she had an office meltdown, she could walk over to Ethan's office, close the door, and sink into his blue beanbag chair—a ridiculous holdover since college. Ethan would ask her what was wrong, and no matter the answer, announce that it was time for "creamy treats." Some guys keep a bottle of booze in their lower right-hand drawer; Ethan kept Tastykakes. Ethan gave her the two things she needed to settle down: a patient ear and a hit of sugar, enriched flour, and partially hydrogenated vegetable oil.

But there was no time to find Ethan now. Because Molly didn't want any water, or to sit down.

"We need," Amy said, "to find a way to call in support."

Support: the euphemism for David's bosses. As David's second-in-command, Amy had been given the phone number and code key to use in case of emergency, such as David's untimely death. Backup would descend upon 1919 Market Street. Hard drives would be secured. Order would be restored. Only if Amy could find a working phone.

But Molly didn't seem to be listening. She lowered her face into her hands.

God, this couldn't be easy for her. She wasn't a high-level operative. She knew what they all did, to some degree. But Molly didn't know how dangerous this game could be.

Amy put a hand on her shoulder.

"You're going to be okay," Amy said, even though it was a blatant lie. The woman had pulled a gun out of a white box—it may even have been a cannoli box from Reading Terminal Market—and shot her boss of six months in the head. That was decidedly *not okay.*

Molly surfaced from her palms. "Amy?"

"Yeah, sweetie."

"I'm going to enjoy you the most."

Amy watched one of Molly's delicate hands shrink into a tight little fist. Then it smashed her in the eye.

She staggered back. Confusion set in before the pain. *Wait. What had just happened?*

Did Molly Lewis just punch her in the—?

Again.

And again.

Left hook, right jab. Classic boxer combo.

Amy's head buzzed with pain, now, finally, radiating from her skin deep into her skull. Her butt bumped up against the front of her own desk. She needed to keep standing. She needed to start defending herself. That much was sure. But what was going on here? Amy lifted a hand, but Molly slapped it aside and then jabbed her in the throat.

Amy started choking.

She slid to the side and put her hands to her throat, as if she could undo the damage manually. But Molly had done something. Something very bad. Amy couldn't even scream.

Two minutes before, Molly had been alone in David's office. Everyone had scattered to the rest of the office, to see if their boss's crazy talk was actually true. To see if the elevators would come. If the dial tone would be there. If their cell phones would work.

Of course they wouldn't.

Molly had helped David disable them all.

David, a week ago, promised, "You help me; you and I walk out of here. We've got new identities waiting for us."

Later, Molly had found the memo. The faxed hit list.

With her name on it.

Liar.

So she decided to cut a deal of her own.

Molly walked down the hallway and into David's office. In the corner, where the south-facing windows met with a solid oak bookcase, was a security camera obscured by the wood and drywall. It had been positioned so that it could scan not only the entire office, but the face of David's computer screen. David knew this. It was company policy.

Molly looked up at the security camera and flashed it a tight little smile. She held up her left hand, palm out.

And raised her index and middle fingers.

It wasn't a peace sign.

It was an announcement.

THE MORNING GRIND

Management is nothing more than motivating other people.
—LEE IACOCCA

Thirty-five hundred miles away . . .

. . . in Scotland, near the sea, in a quiet section of Edinburgh called Portobello, a red-haired man in a black T-shirt and neatly pressed khakis crossed the street. He was holding a pharmacy bag stocked with tissues and Night Nurse. He'd felt awful all morning. Maybe a solid dose of medicine would head it off at the pass. Summer colds were the worst.

This summer, too, was the worst. Freakishly warm for Edinburgh. Plus, there was a hot, greasy drizzle in the air, which did little to cool it. By the time he returned to the flat, he reckoned, his T-shirt would be soaked with sea mist and sweat, and he'd have to change. He kept only a small valise of essentials; he didn't bring piles of T-shirts like McCoy, his surveillance partner, did. The man packed like the Apocalypse was around the corner.

The red-haired man, who called himself Keene, had almost reached the bottom of the road when he bumped into a man walking his dog. Wee thing—the dog, that was. It had only three legs. The owner had two, but looked haggard, if finely muscled.

"Sorry, mate," Keene said.

The man just smiled at him. And not in a particularly warm way.

Keene stepped out of the way, then watched the little three-legged dog titter and bounce after its master. A lot of work, walking uphill in the drizzle with only three legs.

Upstairs, Keene embraced his partner. His lip brushed against the stubble on his cheek; he could smell the intoxicating aftershave. Then Keene told him about the dog.

"I've seen that dog," said McCoy. He was American. He'd barely turned to face Keene. Instead, he was focused on a bank of computer screens: a desktop and three laptops. "It creeps me out."

"I'm putting on some tea," Keene said. "Would you care for a cup?"

Some tea and Night Nurse might make the afternoon tolerable. Keene planned on asking McCoy to take over for the next few hours. Keene had been at it through much of the morning. His eyes felt like there were grains of sand floating around in there.

"No, but you can fetch me a can of Caley."

"Sure."

McCoy was a drunk.

"Did I miss anything?" Keene asked.

"You missed *everything.*"

"What do you mean? Nothing's supposed to be happening in Dubai for at least six hours."

"No, not there. Back in America. Remember? The Philadelphia thing?"

"Girlfriend."

"Right."

"What time is it there?"

"Half past nine. So far, our girl is doing exactly what she said. You should have seen the look on Murphy's face. I can run it back for you later."

"Sure," Keene said. *No thank you.*

Girlfriend, who until about thirty minutes ago was just another low-level operative, had contacted McCoy a few days ago with an intriguing proposal: Give me a chance to show you my talents. McCoy had been impressed she even knew how to find him. It was enough for him to kick her proposal upstairs and receive clearance to follow it up.

Girlfriend wanted a promotion. And she wanted to demonstrate how much she deserved it.

The employees in the office were slated to die anyway, she'd argued.

Why not let her try?

McCoy told Girlfriend: You impress us, we give you the way out and a new job. If not . . . well, nice interviewing with you.

Girlfriend accepted.

Keene, though, was more concerned with Dubai and this summer cold that seemed to be taking root in his head. It was never a good idea to focus on more than one operation at a time. That kind of juggling invariably led to mistakes.

But there was no stopping McCoy, who was enamored with this Philadelphia thing. So Keene had to pretend to be enamored, too. It made things easier.

Keene put on the kettle and took a green earthenware mug down from the cupboard. Wait. McCoy's beer. He opened the fridge and snatched a can from the bottom shelf. That was the extent of McCoy's weekly contributions to the pantry. Everything else he consumed was takeaway. Usually Thai or Indian.

He handed the can of Caley 80 to his partner, who was looking at one of the monitors with glee.

"Will you look at that," McCoy said.

On screen, Girlfriend—who looked a bit mousy, if you asked Keene—was holding up a peace sign.

"Number two, coming right up." McCoy popped the top of his beer, then started thumbing through a stack of papers on the desk. "You've got to love her style."

"Hmmm," Keene said. "As in Murphy was number one?"

"Right."

"Remind me again what this Philadelphia office does?"

"Financial disruption of terrorist networks. Or something like that. Bunch of geeks using computers to erase the bank accounts of known terrorist cells. I'm not too familiar with it myself. I'm a human resources guy."

"Oh, is that what you do?"

"Shhh. She's moving."

They watched as Girlfriend allowed herself to be led to another office. McCoy leaned forward and tapped some keys. A separate fiber-optic feed picked her up on the second screen. They watched another woman—a well-scrubbed, bright-eyed American with shoulder-length hair—try to comfort Girlfriend.

And then they watched Girlfriend start to beat the woman savagely.

"Ugh," Keene said.

"Oh, she's *good.*"

Amy couldn't scream, but that didn't mean she was giving up. She pretended to faint backwards, pivoting so she was facing her own desk from the opposite side. There. An orange-and-black *Philadelphia City Press* mug was loaded with Sharpies, ballpoint pens, and one pair of Italian forged steel scissors with black grips.

Behind her, Molly was closing the door. For privacy, presumably.

So she could kill Amy in peace and quiet.

Amy wrapped her fingers around the cold steel, then lunged out behind her. Molly stepped back; steel whisked against her blouse, ripping the fabric slightly. A smirk appeared on Molly's face. Amy growled—that was all she could do—and lunged again, but Molly sidestepped it, in the exact opposite direction Amy thought she would. By then it was too late to lunge again. Molly kicked Amy in the chest, which sent her flipping backwards over her own desk. Her fall was temporarily broken by her rolling chair, but it slid away and Amy crashed to the floor.

Run, Amy thought. Run away.

Regroup.

She scrambled to her feet and pressed her palms against her window for support.

The entire pane popped out of its frame.

Amy gasped as the glass fell away from her palms.

Down.

Down.

Down.

The glass dropped thirty-six floors, flipping and coasting and flipping again before shattering in the small street behind the 1919 Market Street Building.

McCoy smiled. "Hah. I didn't see her do that. I wonder when she did that."

Keene frowned. "Isn't that cheating?"

"No, no. She told us she would be doing a few hours of prep work, just like in a normal job. Nothing out of the ordinary."

"Smacks of cheating to me." Keene sipped tea. It soothed his throat, and the warmth—a good warmth—made its way up his sinus cavities. Did nothing for the dull throb in his head, though.

"No, she's *good*. Her target is in total shock. That window popping out was the last thing she expected."

They watched the monitor. Keene sipped his Earl Grey.

"Oh . . . *wait!*"

"What?"

"Now I get it. Why she sent me those employee performance sheets."

Keene took another sip of his tea. He wasn't about to sit here asking *What do you mean?* all afternoon.

That was one of the truly annoying things about McCoy. He loved to draw out everything. Instead of just coming out with it, he'd make cryptic statements designed to force you to ask "What?" or "Tell me!" or "Oh, really?" Well, McCoy could play with some other fool. He was either going to tell Keene what was on his mind, or he wasn't.

This time, it didn't take too much silence to goad McCoy into continuing.

"A few days ago, she sent me a bunch of paperwork. Résumés for her proposed targets, as well as their employee performance sheets. You know, the stuff bosses use to tell you if you're doing a lousy job or not, if you're getting a raise or not."

Keene said nothing. But inside, a little voice urged: *Go on, go on now.*

"I couldn't figure out why she sent me this stuff. I mean, we have everybody's info, and then some, already on file. This was junk we didn't need."

Yeah, yeah, yeah. Mmmm, this tea was good.

McCoy tuned in. "Hey—are you even listening?"

"Of course, love."

"Anyway, it just dawned on me right now, when that pane of glass dropped away."

"What?"

Keene silently cursed himself.

"She's playing on their individual weaknesses," McCoy said. "David Murphy would do some subtle mind-ops stuff during employee evaluations—that's what he used to do, psyops—and work it into his evaluation. Girlfriend here picked up on that. She's showing off."

Keene sipped tea, then said: "Some people will do anything for a job."

Amy was frozen; it was all too much to comprehend. The pane, gone. The pane of glass that shielded her not only from the temperamental seasons of Philadelphia—with its snow and humidity and rain and gusts—but also from her darkest impulses.

Amy had explained it to David years ago when he'd asked her what she feared the most. She'd answered honestly: losing her mind for three seconds.

David had tented his fingers, raised his eyebrows. "Care to explain that one?"

Specifically, Amy had said, "I'm afraid of losing my mind for three seconds near an open window. Because part of me might decide it's a good idea to jump out the window, just to see what would happen." If that did happen, Amy knew that she would recover her sanity almost instantly. Not in enough time to prevent her from jumping out the window, but plenty of time to realize her mistake as she plummeted at 9.8 meters per second—plenty of time to scream in horror before pounding into the concrete below.

"Interesting," David had said.

And now she was looking at it. An open window, thirty-six stories above the ground.

Would Amy lose her mind?

And would it be for three seconds, or longer?

Then, at the moment of truth, the moment she thought she may actually do it . . .

Fingers.

Gripping the back of her shirt, pulling Amy away from the window. Thank God. A hand, reached into the waistband of her pants, holding tight, and guiding her backwards. Deeper into the safety of her office. Away from the window.

"Oh God," she whispered, even though her voice was barely a murmur, and her savior was the same person who'd been brutally assaulting her just a few seconds ago. *Thank you.*

"You're welcome," Molly said.

Amy felt something tug at her waist. Her leather belt.

Slipping out of her pant loops.

Then she felt something wrap around her ankle.

Molly eased Amy back until her grip was secure, and she had enough room. Then it was time.

She looked up in the corner of Amy's office, where the camera was tucked away.

Winked.

And then she launched Amy out the open window.

Thirty-six floors above the pavement.

At the last second—and oh, how she hoped the fiber-optic camera in this office could capture this, her impeccable timing, reflexes, and strength . . .

At the last possible second she snatched the end of the leather belt. Grasped it tight, then collapsed down into a ball, wedging herself against the metal radiator that ran along the lower office wall. All would be lost if Amy's weight were to pull Molly right out the window.

But it didn't. Molly held the leather firm.

McCoy, eyes affixed to the laptop screen, said, "Wow."

In that moment, Amy knew she had lost her mind, lost it to the point of imagining that someone would actually throw her out an open window, thirty-six stories up. Because who would do that? Clearly, she had lost her mind.

Not to be recovered.

And it was nothing like she had imagined.

In all her dreams, a fall from a great height like this one was a nightmare, but one of only a few seconds. The crushing air, the blur of motion . . . it was all horrible beyond words. But it was finite. When she smashed into the ground, she would jolt awake.

Not this time. In real life, falling to your death felt like forever.

She felt like she would
be
falling
forever.

Molly didn't look, even though she wanted to. She used the scissors to secure the leather belt to the metal grille of the radiator; as long as Amy didn't jolt around, it should hold for a short while.

Taking a peek over the edge of the open window would be unprofessional. Better to seem aloof, as in: *I don't need to watch.*

The moment Amy Felton cleared the window, and was suspended—frozen—paralyzed—in midair, it was on to the next task. After all, she was being watched herself.

Molly was curious, sure. She wondered about the expression on Amy's face. Wondered if her calculations had been correct. But she cared more about what her special audience thought.

There'd be plenty of time to watch later.

On playback.

Jamie DeBroux

~~Amy Fulton~~

Ethan Goins

Roxanne Kurtwood

Molly Lewis

~~Stuart McCrane~~

Nichole Wise

. . .

Down the hall, Jamie stared at his two-way Motorola pager. It had sat in a front pocket of his leather briefcase for over a month, unused. As far as he knew, Jamie had never turned it off.

The day before the Fourth of July, he'd received a final page from Andrea:

GET HOME NOW, DADDY :)

Andrea's water had just broken. She'd been pulling steaks out of the freezer, hoping to thaw them in time for a little pre-Fourth grilling session. She craved meat—big fat T-bone steaks, specifically—throughout her pregnancy, and damn it, she'd be eating steaks right up until the moment the baby was born.

As it turned out, Jamie rushed home, gathered up Andrea and the emergency baby bag she'd packed a week before, and raced—cautiously—to Pennsylvania Hospital. The steaks ended up sitting out on the counter for the next day and a half. When Jamie arrived home, delirious with joy and exhaustion, he was smacked in the face with the scent of rotting cow flesh. Welcome home, Daddy.

The pagers had been Andrea's idea. Frustrated that she couldn't reach her husband at will—whenever Jamie had his cell phone tucked away in his bag, the thing was hard to hear—she went Motorola on his ass. Found a sweet deal on matching Talkabout T900s. Less than a hundred dollars for the two of them. Ran on a AA battery. During the last month of her pregnancy, Andrea *suggested* that her husband carry the T900 at all times. She suggested it like an umpire suggests to a batter that *he's out.*

Jamie's T900 was a royal blue; Andrea's hot pink. Totally out of character for Andrea. But pregnancy had done strange things to the woman.

So now Jamie stared at his T900, wondering if it had any juice left. He hit the power button, but no luck. The thing had lost its last volt probably right around the time the steaks had reached full ripeness.

But that was fine. All he needed was a single AA battery. And then he could text-message the cops or an ambulance or something. YEAH, OFFICER? MY BOSS JUST GOT SHOT IN THE HEAD. THINK YOU CAN SEND SOMEBODY UP? And get off this floor already.

Where did they keep batteries around here?

Amy Felton. She was always good for stuff like that.

There was a knock at the door, two quick taps, just as Molly was about to open it. She paused, then placed her hand on the sturdy silver knob. Opened the door an inch, then pressed the lock button. Then she opened it the rest of the way and quickly pressed her body into the space between the door and the frame. Whoever was there would notice the missing pane of glass, and the leather belt hanging over the ledge. The sticky August air was already flooding into Amy's office.

Molly bumped into Jamie, who took a nervous step backwards. He looked stunned.

"Jamie."

"God, are you okay? Is Amy in there?"

"No. She asked me to lock her office door while she went for help."

"She did? Where?"

"Come with me."

Molly charged down the hall, giving Jamie zero chance to

refuse. He followed her, just as she knew he would. He had a crush on her.

She remembered that night a few months ago, when the staff had been out drinking. Jamie had joined them, which was uncharacteristic of him. They talked; they flirted. He offered to walk her to her car. He wanted to say good night. She pulled back slightly, and that only drew him in further. His breath smelled like beer, and his button-down shirt like a thousand cigarettes. It was difficult for her to pull back, but she did. It wasn't the right time.

But now . . .

As she walked by one of the security cameras in the hall, Molly held her hands up in front of her chest. Five fingers on one hand, two on the other.

"Look at that," McCoy said, sitting in front of a laptop screen 3,500 miles away. "Number seven. She's going out of order. Now why would she be doing that?"

"Oh, I don't know. Maybe because the guy knocked on the door moments after Girlfriend hung his coworker out of the window."

"Yeah, I know that. But someone like Girlfriend could have easily handled this guy. Look at him. He's a cream puff. I got his file around here somewhere. She was saving him for last. Like dessert."

"Why?"

"You always take out the toughest targets first. Girlfriend identified the first woman—this Felton woman—as her most formidable target. Despite her fear of heights."

Keene sipped his tea. He was going to have to get up to pour another cup soon. "I've been thinking on that. Seems like a very sloppy move to me. You have the pane of glass shattering on the street below. No telling what that may have hit. There might be six schoolchildren down there, bleeding to death."

"Not likely. That bank of windows faces north, and there's nothing down below but a minor street used mostly by delivery trucks. Girlfriend was thinking ahead."

"Fine, I'll spot you the glass. But what about the target? Surely, somebody's going to notice a woman hanging out of a window, no matter how small the street."

McCoy smiled. "Again, not likely. This is Philly. You ever been there? I have, and the murder rate's out of control. Plus, the sun's strong today. A lot of glare."

"Be serious now."

"Seriously? I think this is Girlfriend showing off. It was a tremendously ballsy move. Because you're right—you can't keep that kind of thing under wraps for long. Somebody's going to look up and see that woman. It may take a minute. It may take an hour. But you can bet that somebody's going to spot her and start freaking out, and boom. That's where the clock really starts to tick."

His name was Vincent Marella . . .

. . . and he was reading a paperback thriller. He'd found it in the changing area. Someone had left it on a table with a few other books, the idea being that other employees of 1919 Market would bring in their old books and get a swap thing going. Of course, that never happened. Only the original guy brought in books. And that was it. Vincent guessed that there weren't many readers on the security staff.

The book wasn't bad, actually. It was called *Center Strike,* and was about a gang of high-class yet tough-as-nails thieves who tried to loot the gold stored in vaults beneath the rubble of the World Trade Center within forty-eight hours of the collapse. Completely ridiculous, Vincent knew. A red burst on the cover promised that the book was BASED ON ACTUAL EVENTS. Yeah. Right.

Reading stuff like this was both exciting and unnerving. Exciting because one of the book's heroes was . . . wait for it . . . a World Trade Center security guard, who also happened to be a Gulf War vet who single-handedly saved his platoon from a nutty Iraqi general who had held them captive in the desert.

It was unnerving because . . . well, Vincent was a security guard in a thirty-seven-floor skyscraper in a major American city.

He wasn't a Gulf vet—he'd grown up between wars. Too young for Vietnam, too old for the Gulf. And he'd never had anybody hold him captive.

Still, he'd seen some action. Not too long ago, in fact.

Vincent was in the middle of a flashback passage about the hero's gruesome torture in the Iraqi camp when a disheveled-looking guy dressed in a ratty T-shirt walked through the revolving doors. Guy was white, but his black T-shirt was emblazoned with a fake cereal box advertising CHEERI-HO'S, and the busty woman on that fake cereal box—with oversize lips, hips, and bust—wasn't exactly a General Mills mascot.

Vincent sighed.

It was Terrill Joe, your friendly neighborhood crackhead.

What was interesting was that this neighborhood—if you could call this corporate canyon of towers a "neighborhood"—had any crackheads at all. Center City West was heavily policed, scrubbed, swept, and kept nice and clean for the business set. It was a far cry from the area forty years ago, when it was full of broken-down storefronts and porno theaters on one side, and a huge monstrosity called the Chinese Wall on the other. Actor Kevin Bacon's dad was the city planner back then, and he decided to rip out the Chinese Wall—rail lines leading out of the city—and replace it with a corporate playground. By the 1980s, Bacon's dream had been fully realized. Concrete, glass, steel, and sheer height were the order of the day. If you wanted to see what West Market Street looked like in the 1960s, you had to venture up past Twenty-second Street. But even that was going fast. Condos were moving in, even though nobody was buying them.

Crackheads like Terrill Joe would have loved it back in the 1960s, had there been crack to purchase. Of course, back then, they would have just been hippies.

Vincent had no idea where Terrill Joe holed up at night. Couldn't be neighboring Rittenhouse Square—too fancy, even though Terrill Joe was the right shade of white. Probably some corner of Spring Garden, which lay to the north.

He thought about asking Terrill Joe where he holed up, but decided it wasn't worth it. It was tough enough getting him out of the building.

"Mr. Marella," he said. "You've got serious trouble."

"Every day," Vincent mumbled.

"Huh?"

"What can I do for you, Terrill Joe?"

"You gotta take a look around back."

"Do I."

"You'd better. Otherwise it's your job."

Terrill Joe's skin was a spiderweb network of broken veins. His teeth were like tombstones in a graveyard that had been bombarded with short-range missiles. And the stench rolled from him like a tsunami, engulfing countless innocent nostrils. In short, Terrill Joe was an absolute wreck.

Usually, Vincent's MO with Terrill Joe was to get him out of the building as soon as humanly possible, lest he disturb the tax-payers. He saw no reason to change his MO now, even though it was a humid, swampy mess outside.

"Show me," he said.

There were two entrances to 1919 Market. The main entrance faced Market, and across the street was the symbol of Philly financial strength: the stock exchange. The place took itself so seriously, it was pretty much licking its lips after 9/11, thinking Wall Street would migrate southeast by a hundred miles or so. Yeah. Like that had happened.

The other entrance faced Twentieth Street, which faced another corporate tower. Terrill Joe led him out the Twentieth Street side.

"What's the deal?"

"You see, you see."

Yeah, I'll see, I'll see.

The crackhead led the security guard around the back to the small alley between the corporate tower and the apartment building behind it. It was too small to have a name—it was only ten feet wide. Maybe a real street had run through this spot at some point. Not forty years ago, certainly. Then, the Chinese Wall dominated. Whatever street had existed before then had been obliterated by years of paving and repaving and demolition and construction. The object lesson: If you're not careful, they can take away your name.

"Lookit that."

Vincent saw what the crackhead was worried about. Shattered glass, on the dark asphalt of the nameless alley.

Where had that come from?

Vincent craned his neck up, even though he knew it was a silly gesture. Like he'd be able to see if there was a single pane of glass missing from one of the thirty-seven stories.

"You see this happen?"

"See it?" Terrill Joe asked. "Thing nearly cut my head off comin' *down*."

"How far up, about?" He squinted. The sun was blazing this morning.

"*Real* high up."

"Yeah?"

"Yeah."

He squinted for a little while longer—the sun was bright, shining over the top of the white building—then turned to look at the apartment building on the other side. More than likely, the pane of glass had fallen from that side.

Still, he had to check.

Which meant a grueling floor-by-floor check on this side of the building.

Thanks, Terrill Joe.

"You want a smoke?" the crackhead asked.

"Those things'll kill you."

"Like I want to live forever?"

His Saturday, ruined by a crackhead. Typical. But what really pissed him off was that it'd probably be at least an hour or so before he got back to *Center Strike*, and he wanted to know how the torture thing turned out.

Thirty-six floors above, Ethan Goins was sprawled out on an uncomfortable slab of concrete with a pen tube sticking out of his throat.

He was breathing out of it. And he was thankful for it. Don't get him wrong.

Pens were wonderful.

He *loved* pens.

But still: *He was breathing out of the plastic tube of a ball-point pen*. Even an eternal optimist had to admit that life for Ethan Goins had taken a serious downturn in the past fifteen minutes.

Once Ethan had heard Amy's voice, and he'd confirmed that there was actually hope of rescue from this friggin' fire tower, the decision had been clear. He needed to open his throat.

There was pretty much only one way he knew how to do that.

Granted, his imagination may have been limited by his time in Iraq. Maybe that experience prevented an easier solution from popping into his head. Some quick and simple way of opening up his throat, so that air could make its way into his lungs and bloodstream and muscles and brain.

If there was an easier way, it wasn't coming to him. Blame his oxygen-starved brain.

Pen to the throat it was.

Ethan worked quickly so he didn't have too much time to dwell on it. Fished the pen out of his bag, pulled the tip and ink stem out of the pen, yanked the neck of his black T-shirt so it wouldn't get in the way, and then started feeling for his Adam's apple, and then the cricoid cartilage, and back up to the cricothyroid membrane. Bingo.

Do it, Goins, do it fast.

He wished he had any kind of blade to make an incision. He wished hard. But he knew the contents of his bag, and there was nothing even close. His car keys, maybe, but by the time he sawed open an incision, it might be too late.

Ethan had dots appearing in front of his eyes as it was. So enough messing around. He knew his target: the valley of flesh on his neck.

He knew there would be no do-overs, no second chances.

He had to strike powerfully and cleanly.

First, though, he had to shatter the tip of the pen on the

concrete landing. A flat tube would do nothing to his throat . . .
except hurt.

Ethan jammed it against the ground. The plastic chipped as
he'd hoped.

There.

Nice and jagged.

Ready to go.

He imagined the air he'd be breathing through that pen tube.
Sweet, cool nourishing air. His for the taking, all for one little
stabbing motion—

Now!

That had been fifteen minutes ago.

Ethan was still alive, and breathing sweet, nourishing air
through the pen tube in his neck.

At first, the pain had been fairly astounding. It was probably a
good thing he'd been unable to scream. But the shock to Ethan's
nervous system was far worse. He'd quickly drifted into a semi-
catatonic state, most likely his body's way of defending itself. It
wasn't every day the body's right arm decided to do something
as foolish as take a ballpoint pen, pull the ink stem out of it, then
jab the tube into the throat area. If Ethan's body were the
United Nations, then his right arm had become an unstable terrorist state, one that had lashed out—without warning—against
a neighboring country. The right arm could say all it wanted
about the stabbing being in the throat's best interests—*It was
sealed up, Secretary General; I had to destroy that throat in order to save it*—but to the remainder of the body, this was an in-
comprehensible act of aggression. The body imposed sanctions.
The body condemned such violence. The body decided to shut
down.

For a while.

Now Ethan was on the concrete slab of a landing, regaining his
senses, pondering his next move.

Calling for help: pretty much out.

Climbing back up the stairs and opening the door to the thirty-sixth floor: Um, yeah, right. He'd had enough of the chemical agent for breakfast, thank you very much. Ethan's luck, he'd figure out a way to disarm the thing, then realize at the last second he was wrong, and then have to spend the next ten seconds scrambling for a spork so he could scoop out his eyes to stop the poison from reaching his brain. No thanks.

He wasn't even sure what that chemical was. It didn't taste like ricin.

So that left down. Thirty-six flights of down.

Are you down?

Ethan was down.

Down to the lobby, *down* to a security guard, where he'd have to put it *down* on paper. Unless a game of charades would be faster. Though it would be tricky to convey the events of the past thirty minutes with a few simple hand gestures.

How do you say "chemical nerve agent" in American Sign Language, anyway?

Worry about communicating later, Ethan told himself. Focus on climbing down this fire tower. One concrete half flight at a time. With a pen tube bobbing up and down in a hole in his throat, like a throat cancer patient leading an orchestra.

Down, down, down.

This, among other reasons, was why Ethan hated working on Saturdays.

Molly led Jamie down the hallway, past the conference room, then down another short hallway and through the main lobby.

A desk of deep oak dominated the room, along with a brass-plated logo of Murphy, Knox & Associates affixed to the wall. Jamie never walked through the lobby. Never had any reason to, really. The side entrances led him straight to the hallway closest to his office.

"Did you say Amy's down here?"

Molly said nothing. Kept right on walking.

That didn't surprise Jamie. Molly had always been an odd duck. Her social awkwardness put him at ease, actually. Whenever they were gathered in a meeting, Jamie could count on Molly to make some kind of weird nervous mistake, or refuse to make eye contact with any other employee, save David. This was good, because it made Jamie look like less of a geek. It was probably why they got along so well. Two fellow inmates on the corporate island of misfit toys.

"Look, Molly," Jamie said. "All we need is a double-A battery, and we're pretty much saved. No matter what Amy has in mind."

Jamie had no idea why Amy would be down this end of the hall. It didn't make sense. This part of the floor was populated by empty offices and cubicles, a remnant of Murphy, Knox's go-go years. Or that was the way David had explained it. The company had been buzzing during the dot.com boom, only to succumb to postmillennial downsizing. Now, the only people who ever used this side of the office were the occasional auditors who passed through from time to time, and building inspectors, who insisted on updating it with the latest in OSHA requirements, even though nobody used it.

Without warning, Molly stopped. Turned to the left. Opened a door. Ushered Jamie inside. Closed the door behind them.

Then she did the strangest thing.

Molly looked into his eyes, with a soft, almost doting expression. It wasn't a sexual look—no *C'mere big boy and I'll show you a good time.* It was more, *Come here, my sweet friend, and let me give you a hug.*

It reminded him of a night a few months ago. A night after a long drunken evening . . .

"Um, Molly?" Jamie asked. "Why are we in here?"

Molly didn't reply. She held out her hand. It was small and pale, with thin, elegant fingers. Her breath smelled good. Pepperminty.

Before Jamie knew what he was doing, he reached out and took her hand, as if to give her a handshake.

He felt her fingers slide against his skin. Molly's fingers danced over his, searching. Then she latched on, and—

Jamie fell to his knees, crying in pain.

His thumb and middle finger were *on fire.*

What was she doing?

OH GOD.

More pressure now, more agony, nowhere to hide.

STOP OH GOD PLEASE STOP.

Jamie may even have thought he said this out loud.

Keene fixed himself another cup of tea.

He heard McCoy in the other room: "Will you look at this!"

McCoy, again with his Philadelphia people.

They should be focusing on Dubai.

Keene and McCoy shared operational space, and more often than not, operations. But this Philadelphia thing was all McCoy. As a "human resources man"—his words, not Keene's—he liked to dabble in new talent, build his little network within the larger networks. Having "his" people in various places all over the organization increased McCoy's power exponentially.

This was how Keene paired up with McCoy in the first place. A series of e-mails, sent back and forth between San Diego and Edinburgh, hinting around the edges. You never come out and say what you do. You sense it in each other.

A few months later, a chance meet-up in Houston had worked to their mutual benefit. Similar adventures in Chicago, and then later, New York City, had been successes as well. So when it came time for a series of operations that needed special attention, it was McCoy who had suggested Keene to his bosses, and from that, thousands of dollars' worth of equipment had found its way into a Portobello flat.

The primary operation, as Keene saw it, was this Dubai deal. It was still in its infancy, but needed coddling.

Philadelphia was little more than a distraction, but McCoy was engrossed with it.

"C'mere and look at this. Check out what our girl is doing."

"Aye."

If Keene didn't, McCoy would only continue to pester him.

Might as well engage him.

Would do him good to pay attention, probably. If McCoy were to be believed, they could be working with Girlfriend in the near future.

The pain was so blinding, Jamie found himself detached from his surroundings. He was aware that Molly was moving behind him, sending fresh waves of agony up his arm and into the hot pain centers of his brain. Jamie's hand and arm felt like a thick mass of rubber, alive with agony, able to be bent any way his torturer wished.

His torturer—his friend Molly.

His office spouse.

Suddenly, he was being lifted up. Jamie was startled to discover that his legs could support some of his weight.

Molly had positioned herself behind him. He could feel her body heat, her chest pressed up against his back. The long sleeves of her blouse brushed against his bare forearms. They'd never touched before, except for the occasional handshake or shoulder pat. If he wasn't in so much agony, he might have been aroused by the touch of her unfamiliar body.

She was a lot smaller than Jamie, but that worked to her advantage. She could tuck in behind him, do what she wanted, and Jamie would have no prayer of reaching around and stopping her.

Not that he knew how to do something like that.

Molly nudged him to the left, left, left, pointing him to a corner of the empty office.

"That's it, Jamie," she whispered.

"Whyareyoudoing*this*," Jamie said. His voice was raspy. Wheezing. Desperate. It startled him to hear it.

"Shhhhhh, now. The pain will stop soon."

Keene said, "What's she doing?"

"Holding him up for us to see."

"Like a slaughterhouse employee showing off the chicken."

"That's exactly right."

"She going to slice his throat, hang him up by his feet now?"

"I wouldn't be surprised."

"Does it matter that I'm vegetarian?"

"I don't think she cares."

Molly hurled Jamie to the floor.

Jamie caught himself on one hand—the numb one, unfortunately. His arm was too weak to support his body weight, so his face hit floor. Sucked in air and dust from an industrial carpet that hadn't been vacuumed in at least a month.

He saw that Molly was slipping off her shoes, delicately sliding them into a corner of the office, where they'd presumably be out of the way. But for what?

What was she doing?

Jamie pushed himself up to his knees, then reached out his good hand to the desk. He'd pull himself up, bolt, and leave it to the guys with the cozy white jackets with the buckles and straps to figure out. Molly had lost her mind; that much was clear. Had she lost it after she shot her boss in the head, or was it a good while before that? Who cared? Jamie needed to get out of this office. Off this floor.

Home to his family.

But as he reached out his hand, Molly grabbed it. Yanked it toward the ceiling a few inches.

Then pressed two of his fingers backwards in such a way that it paralyzed him completely.

She did this with one hand.

"Ow," Jamie said, more out of surprise than pain.

Molly looked at him and smirked. She mouthed something to him, and applied more pressure.

Okay, now it really, really hurt.

"Oh God please let go. I can't move."

She mouthed something again.

Maybe Jamie was losing his mind, because he could have sworn she mouthed: *Just play along and don't pass out.*

But aloud, she said: "Tell me everything you know about the Omega Project."

"What?!"

And now Molly pressed her fingers against Jamie's, and Jamie found himself making a hideous sound that tried to accomplish three things at once:

Suck in air.

Express pain.

Beg.

He'd never made a sound like that before, never thought his vocal cords were capable of such an animalistic cry.

"Tell me," she said loudly, as if announcing it to the whole office, "about the Omega Project."

"I don't know . . . what you're . . . *talking about*."

Molly shook her head, as if she were disappointed.

Then with her free hand—again, Jamie couldn't believe his entire body was incapacitated by one soft, slender hand—she reached over and unbuttoned the cuff on her blouse. She was the only one in the office, aside from David, who wore long-sleeved shirts in the humid Philadelphia summer. As Molly rolled up her sleeve, Jamie saw why.

A thick silver bracelet was strapped around her wrist. It looked like a series of metal dominoes linked together, side by side, enveloping her delicately muscled forearm. Molly tapped one of the silver dominoes, then flipped open a compartment on the bottom. She pulled something out.

Then she showed it to him.

A silver blade. Nothing too long. It was shaped like a triangle, with one long end wrapped in black electrician's tape.

Jamie recognized the blade. It was an X-Acto blade. Common office supply, especially in the newspaper business. He'd done paste-up at his college newspaper for a few years. Nicked his fingers with X-Acto blades endless times.

Now Molly pressed the sharp edge of the blade to the pad of his thumb, like a teacher touching a piece of chalk to a blackboard.

"The Omega Project," she repeated.

Keene asked, "The Omega Project?"

"No idea."

Keene turned a laptop around, closed the video feed, opened up a new window, and started typing. One window led to another in a furious progression, with Keene typing a series of keywords and passwords and search terms.

"Nothing," he mumbled.

"Strange. I've never run across anything with a name like that. It's so . . . 1970s. We wouldn't give an operation a groaner like that."

"*Bloody* strange."

Then McCoy's face lightened. "Wait, wait," he said. "Hold off on that search."

"Why?"

"I think she's messing with his mind."

"And ours, too. So there is no Omega?"

"Remember, she's auditioning. Maybe she's just showing off her interrogation techniques."

"Even if her subject knows nothing?"

"Even better. She has to take it all the way."

"She's sick, mate," Keene said.

"She's awesome. Hand me that file, will you?"

Jamie tried to squirm away, but each movement yielded fresh agony in his arm.

"What are you doing?" Jamie asked. He could feel the tip of the blade on his thumb. Maybe it was his imagination, but the blade felt like it was sinking into his flesh, deep enough to scrape bone. God. Was she actually stabbing his thumb?

"Tell me about the Omega Project," she said aloud.

Then Molly squinted and whispered: "*I know you don't know anything, Jamie. Don't pass out.*"

"Why the hell are you asking me then?"

"Wrong answer," Molly said.

Then she cut him, dragging the blade down the length of his thumb, across the thick muscle at the base, and out before she reached the vulnerable veins of the wrist.

Jamie howled. He tried to move, but couldn't. He couldn't see the damage to his thumb, because his palm was facing Molly, who was now placing the bloodied tip of the blade to his index finger.

"Tell me about Omega," she said again.

Then she whispered: *"Stay awake."*

Stay awake? Jamie couldn't see his thumb, but he imagined a Ball Park Frank on the grill, skin burst and curled open, exposing the meat beneath.

God, what will make her stop?

Jamie tried to move. Bolt forward. Knock her off balance. Anything.

But he was paralyzed.

She pressed the blade deep into the tip of his index finger.

Only now did he realize that Molly was holding his left hand. Jamie was left-handed. He held pens with his thumb and index finger. He grabbed the adhesive strip on Chase's diapers between his thumb and index finger. He ran his fingertips down Andrea's chest, feeling her soft skin and bumpy edges around her nipple, and it was one of his favorite sensations, and now lost to him forever because—

—because Molly was ripping his index finger down to the palm.

She asked him more questions. Maybe it was the same question. *The Omega Project.* Whatever that was. The Alpha. The Omega. Omega Man. Early Man. Dead Man. But Jamie couldn't hear, because he was in shock by then—dazed and incoherent and searching for some other part of his body where he could hide out for a while. Away from the pain of his burst hot dog fingers, and the warm blood—his blood—running down his forearm, racing around, dripping from his elbow.

Maybe she was on his middle finger now. He thought she might be. Because it felt like she stopped halfway down. Because one of her own fingers pressed down at the base of that finger, which was partly how she'd paralyzed him, and maybe she was going to finish off the hand and slice off the tops of his fingers and put them in a little Ziploc baggie for later and ask him again about the Omega Project on the way to the ER. . . .

"I guess you don't know anything after all," she said, or maybe Jamie fantasized it.

Molly let him collapse to the carpet again.

He could move again, if he wanted.

He didn't want.

"I'm proud of you," she whispered. He watched her stockinged feet walk around his body, trying to avoid stepping in the blood.

He didn't want to listen to her voice anymore.

"But we're going to do just a little more," she continued. *"Try not to pass out."*

He heard Molly's words but tried not to extract any meaning from them. But that was difficult. Words were everything to him. He had been a writer—was still a writer, even if it was toiling over meaningless press releases for financial services that made absolutely no sense to him.

It was impossible to deny her words had meaning.

Try not to pass out.

Which was an incredibly frightening statement. Because "Try not to pass out" meant there was more pain coming. Probably a great deal of it. And that didn't sound good. Jamie thought they'd explored his personal threshold for pain quite thoroughly.

It was exactly one thumb, one index finger, and half of a middle finger.

So when Molly lifted him to his feet again, wrapped a well-muscled arm around his torso, and rested his weight on her own body, he thought:

I'm in for more pain.

And we're going to work on that together.

But then the blade was in her other hand, and this time she had a fist curled around the taped-up part, and the blade was pointed down like a dagger. Her supporting arm loosened, and Jamie slipped down a bit. Her arm caught him under his right armpit and extended around his neck—tight. Almost choking him.

The blade touched Jamie's chest, right through his shirt. Pierced the skin like it had pierced his thumb.

And then the blade whisked down his chest.

Oh God.

This time she was going to kill him.

"Ugh," Keene said. "Not sure I'm in the mood for an evisceration. It's almost supper."

"Shhh," McCoy said.

"What is she doing?"

"Don't know."

"She's not cutting his chest. Not that I can see."

"No, she's not."

"What, is she pretending?"

"Hang on a sec."

McCoy had the Girlfriend file on his lap. Which showed how much he was engrossed in this operation. Usually, he'd store his can of Caley between his legs. He flipped through a few pages.

"She flashed me a seven, right?"

"I believe so, mate. I can roll back the recording if you like."

"No, no. We both saw it. Seven is this guy. Jamie DeBroux. Media relations director. Formerly, a journalist. He received the lowest risk assessment."

"Which explains the fingers."

"Yeah . . . hey, you're right. I didn't think of that. That's brilliant."

"Look. She's still slicing at him."

"Still no blood?" McCoy asked, but slid himself closer to the laptop nearest him and punched in a few numbers. The same scene popped up on his monitor.

"No," said Keene. "Either she's playing around with him, or she has the worst aim I've ever seen."

"What the devil is she . . ."

Then McCoy smiled. He was like a kid at a birthday party who'd blasted apart the piñata with one whack of the stick. Candy and toys rained down all around him.

"I *love* this girl! Oh, man, I want to be her baby daddy."

Keene looked at him. There was no way he was asking "What?" again. He stone refused.

"When we meet, I will fall to my knees and worship her blood-caked feet. Oh man, I am crushing so hard right now!"

Keene wasn't going to do it. Not dignified.

On screen, Girlfriend continued to feign stabs at her quarry. Only now she had him on his knees, and was swiping her hooked blade across the space directly in front of his throat. His eyes. His abdomen. His genitals. Vicious, sharp little movements, leaving little margin for error. If the quarry were to so much as sneeze, he'd be ripped open in a flash.

The quarry, this DeBroux guy, was trembling. Hard to tell if it was fear or spasms of pain. His injured hand hung limply at his side, and blood dripped from his savaged fingertips in a Jackson Pollock pattern.

McCoy slapped Keene on the arm. "You know what she's doing?"

No, I don't, Keene thought. He's waiting for me to say it. He wants me to say it. He needs me to say it.

Oh, this is childish.

"What?" Keene asked.

McCoy said, "She's running us through her résumé."

Jamie was in the strange position of being close to death, expecting death, and slowly coming to terms with death, but unable to actually die.

The moment he saw the blade again, he knew it was going to enter his chest. An atom bomb of fear detonated in his heart.

He thought of Chase.

Chase and that cartoon duck in little boy pants.

Although he imagined it did, the blade didn't seem to be cutting his chest. It whipped over the surface of his shirt above ever so slightly, then slipped away and plunged toward another spot on his chest. This failed to enter his body, too.

A flurry of motion followed, almost too quick for Jamie to comprehend, but with every stroke he expected that this would be the one, the blade would penetrate his flesh and his life would rapidly come to an end.

Even on his knees a few moments later, the blade dancing across his throat and face now, so fast, he actually felt the wind from Molly's frenzied movements.

But the blade never penetrated.

This, more than anything else that had happened this morning—the gunshot, the sliced fingers—broke Jamie DeBroux's mind a bit.

. . .

McCoy pointed out what he could. Keene was still a little mysti-
fied.

"That's right out of the *Solthurner Fechtbuch*," McCoy said.
"And oooh. A little *jung gum* in there, too."

"Why isn't she taking him out?"

"Because he's number seven. She doesn't need to."

"So why go after him at all?"

"To show off. She already lost one of her targets—number
five, that McCrane guy. The one with the champagne?"

"Right."

"That means she needs to make it up somehow. She promised
that she'd demonstrate a full array of her techniques. She promised they'd be surprising yet economical. Wants us to know she
could tear people apart any countless number of ways, from the
undetectable to the flashy. First, she did a straight-on interrogation. Now, she's being flashy."

They continued watching the monitors for a while.

"Won't they find evidence of these . . . mutilations?"

"Nah. Bodies were to be burned up anyway. Doesn't matter."

Keene sighed, then turned away from the screen. "Aye, she's
overdoing it."

"Maybe, but I like to watch her work."

"She should just kill him."

Jamie DeBroux wished she'd just kill him already.

And then a funny thing happened.

She stopped.

For the third time that morning, Jamie collapsed onto the
carpet. Through Molly's legs, he could see that the door to the
office had opened.

And there was another pair of legs standing in the doorway. Bare legs. Black flats.

"Busy, Molly?" a voice said.

He tried to see past Molly's legs, but his view was obscured. The voice sounded familiar, though.

It sounded like

"Nichole Wise, code name Workhorse."

"That's interesting," Keene said. "I didn't realize we did the whole gay nickname thing."

"We do."

"I was being facetious."

"But you know who else does?"

"Well, the CIA."

"The motherloving CIA."

"Interesting. They send her to monitor the Philadelphia operation?"

"No. They've got a crush on Murphy, and they're jealous he left them. In fact, I don't think they're aware we're behind his operation. Probably better that way."

"Does Girlfriend know about her?"

"She hasn't said as much. If she's figured it out, it'll be all the more impressive."

"Murphy's office is full of wonders, isn't it?"

"It's what makes this line of work so much fun."

Keene could see why McCoy got wrapped up in this sort of thing. The people assets. It could become as addictive as an American soap opera. Not that he watched those things. Who was screwing who. Who had a secret alliance with who else. You could work for a company—or the Company, as it were—for years and not unravel every sticky web.

"Think your girl can handle it?"

"From the looks of it, she can handle everything."

"Care for a little wager?"

"Stop talking. I think Girlfriend is about to kill Workhorse, and I don't want to miss it."

ONE-ON-ONE

If you're attacking your market from multiple positions and your competition isn't, you have all the advantage.

—JAY ABRAHAM

Nichole Wise, code name Workhorse, had been waiting for this moment for, oh, a little less than six months. One hundred and seventy-eight days, to be exact. Ever since "Molly Lewis" started working as David's assistant. The snotty little priss. Nichole knew she wasn't a civilian, as they'd all claimed.

That little demonstration in the conference room only confirmed what she'd suspected for months.

She was one of *them.*

One Murphy didn't tell the *other* operatives about, for some reason.

Nichole had been recruited a year after 9/11. Those were heady times. *Let's scramble up some terrorist nest eggs,* David had said, and in that moment, Nichole could be suckered into believing he was a patriot. But she knew better. She knew David Murphy was up to something else, and used this line about an "ultrasecret wing of the intelligence community" as a ploy to dupe otherwise good people into doing his bidding.

Some agents may have seen this as a babysitting gig, but not

Nichole. She was keeping tabs on one of the most notorious operatives the Company had ever known. One who had suddenly retired a few months after 9/11, then opened up a "financial services" corporation.

We can smell a front company a mile away, Nichole's handler had told her. *We want to know who he's fronting.*

Nichole had nodded.

We want you in there, and we want you to stay in there until you find out.

Whatever he had cooking on the side—and Nichole's bosses were fairly sure David Murphy had *something* cooking on the side—she would be there to assess and act, if necessary.

So when Murphy had called them in here on a Saturday morning, she *knew* something big was breaking. But it frustrated her to no end that she had no idea what it might be.

And that would be a failure.

Whatever Murphy had going, she should have been on it from the beginning. This completely blindsided her.

She'd installed an undetectable key logger on Murphy's machine a few days after she started, and changed the gear every month. She knew every e-mail he sent, every Web page he browsed.

She'd recorded every closed-door conversation Murphy ever had.

She used compressed air, a digital camera, and many long nights with Photoshop to read his sealed mail.

She'd collected every shredded bag of crosscut papers and reconstituted them in her suburban apartment, one bag at a time, one long weekend at a time. She'd used tiny paperweights to hold them in place and worked one piece at a time. Many nights she'd dream about strips of paper.

She entered into a clandestine, sex-only relationship with the mail guy—and every mail guy henceforth—even though many of them had a devil-may-care attitude toward personal hygiene.

She'd even burned through countless cheap wristwatches, placed under the back tire of Murphy's car—oh how relentlessly old school *that* was—to fastidiously track his movements.

Over three years of clandestine operations, she'd earned the sobriquet "Workhorse" a dozen times over.

And nothing.

"Keep watching him," her bosses told her.

She did as instructed, only occasionally pausing to conduct other operations now and again. She was too valuable to waste on David Murphy full time.

That was when Nichole began to grow paranoid. Perhaps she was missing something when she was conducting her other ops.

Maybe Murphy knew about her, and conducted his other business when she was otherwise engaged. Just to make it look like he was being a good corporate choirboy, heading up a successful private business.

Maybe he had a way around her key logger.

Maybe he switched out her surveillance tapes.

Maybe he purchased bags of shredded nonsense from another company, and switched out his own shredded documents for a ringer.

Maybe he was on to the watches. An old-head like him probably would be.

Maybe he was just messing around with her head.

If that was the case, one thing was for sure: For six months now, Molly Lewis was helping him.

Her surveillance of David Murphy had become increasingly frustrating during the past six months, and it was too much of a coincidence that Murphy had hired Molly right around the same time. The moment Nichole first shook Molly's hand, the bad juju alarms went off in her head. She immediately hunted for evidence, had the Company screen Molly's background hard, but nothing came up out of the ordinary. Born in Champaign, Illinois, to a conservative Catholic family. Attended a year of UI, agricultural college. Dropped out to marry an actuary named Paul.

But the only evidence she could find of any kind of intelligence background: the slightest hint of a Russian accent.

Which would be kind of weird coming from the lips of an Illinois farm girl with a maiden name like Molly Kaye Finnerty.

But Nichole swore it was there.

She wished she could confide in someone, ask if they heard it, too.

The only other evidence: her surveillance tapes. Pre-Molly, Nichole's secret recordings of Murphy's offices yielded innocuous office banter, phone conversations. But post-Molly, the tapes yielded literally nothing. Blank hiss. It was as if someone had waved a high-powered magnet over the tapes. Nichole switched to digital recording devices, but the result was the same. Even though she knew Murphy wasn't sitting in his office all day in silence. The man loved to talk on the phone. Nichole had listened to countless hours of voice, piped through her ATH-M40fs Audio-Technica headphones.

So why dead air?

Molly listened to the blank tapes in search of an audio clue. An electronic pop or spike. Something to indicate the device that had wiped them clean.

And then she heard it.

Or she swore she heard it: *Zdrastvuyte.*

Impossibly faint, at the edge of human hearing.

Zdrastvuyte.

Formal Russian for "Hello."

The more she listened, pumping up her playback equipment

to maximum volume, the more she swore she heard two more syllables after the greeting.

Nee-cole.

Zdrastvuyte, nee-KO-ool.

It was all beginning to prick at Nichole Wise's mind . . . until the day David Murphy made his next civilian hire: intern Roxanne Kurtwood. In Roxanne, Nichole saw a clear path to sanity.

Murphy's organization was strange in that it blended operatives and civilians. Operatives ran the joint; civilians supported them.

Roxanne deserved more than "support" status. She was smart, versatile. Ivy League. From a family of Pakistani doctors. She had a flexible moral code. All that good stuff that makes for a good op. And not a trace of Russian in her speech.

Nichole decided: Roxanne would be *her* girl.

Nichole decided to recruit her slowly, bring her into the ocean one inch of water at a time. She hadn't given Roxanne a hint of this, but quietly laid the groundwork. She hadn't proposed this to her CIA handler yet, either. But he knew they were always looking out for new talent. She suspected they'd approve. Then they'd have two sets of eyes on Murphy. It would be hard for that snake to wiggle around two sets of daggers plunging into the grass, trying to pin him down.

Roxanne: her partner-in-training. Her savior.

And something even more important—something Nichole hadn't known for years.

A friend.

Of course, it figured that she was dead.

Jamie DeBroux

~~Amy Fulton~~

Ethan Goins

~~Roxanne Kurtwood~~

Molly Lewis

~~Stuart McGrane~~

Nichole Wise

. . .

After Murphy was shot in the head, and everyone decided to split up, Nichole had taken Roxanne by the wrist. "This way."

"But . . ."

"Trust me."

Nichole told Amy they'd check the elevators to be sure, but that's not where she led Roxanne. First they headed to Murphy's office, because whatever was going down, a burn of his office was probably next. It was the tradecraft thing to do. Molly's betrayal was something Nichole had *not* seen coming. Every theory Nichole had about the Illinois farm girl went spinning down the toilet the moment she pulled a Lee Harvey on the big boss man. Molly hadn't been hired to cock-block Nichole. She had wormed her way into Murphy, Knox, and was in the process of her own little hostile takeover of the company and all its assets.

But *whom* did she work for?

David's own bosses?

Another intelligence agency?

Another country?

It killed Nichole that she didn't know the answer.

"Where are we going?" Roxanne asked.

"Toward the elevators," Nichole said.

Sure, they were headed to the elevator bank, but only as a shortcut to Murphy's office. Out one side entrance and in another, a quick left, and they'd be in. Nichole would bar the door—no, wait.

First she would recover the pistol she'd stashed here and moved periodically over the past five years. Her Heckler & Koch P7. Eight 9 mm rounds. Not the most desirable weapon in the world for a firefight, but it would do its job here.

Because she was going to give the HK P7 to Roxanne, and then barricade them in Murphy's office.

Nichole would instruct Roxanne to shoot anything that tried to come through the door. Use all eight rounds if you have to. Then Nichole would rip apart the office, gather what she needed, then do a burn herself. She'd get Roxanne out of there, make it outside, call for Company extraction. Pray she wouldn't lose her job for missing something this catastrophic.

What if, after three years of undercover investigation, it came out that David Murphy was working for foreign terrorists?

"Nichole, the elevators are this . . ."

"Never mind. I've changed my mind. There's something . . ."

But when she opened the door, she saw a blur of Molly Lewis shooting down the hallway, headed right for Murphy's office.

So much for mourning the boss.

Okay, change of plans. First, map out an escape plan. Then go back and deal with the Russian farm girl.

"Follow me, Rox."

"What? What now?"

Poor Roxanne. She'd seemed so carefree last night at the Continental. Bummed out about having to report to work in the hot city in the wee hours of a Saturday morning—for members of Roxanne's generation, 9:00 A.M. was indeed the wee hours— but still, able to separate herself from that and have a good time anyway. Cosmos and tapas. Flirting with boys. Laughing about people at work.

Now she woke up to have her boss threaten to kill her, a coworker die, and another coworker shoot her boss in the head, JFK-style.

And now her best friend (Nichole hoped, anyway) was leading her willy-nilly through the halls.

She needed Rox to keep it together.

"You have to trust me," Nichole said. "I know what's going on here, and I know how to get us out of it."

Rox, God love her, looked her in the eye, like a Girl Scout reciting an oath, and said, "I trust you."

"We're going to the other side."

The half of Murphy, Knox that had lain fallow since 2003.

"First, the kitchen."

For the past few weeks, Nichole had stashed her HK P7 in a white casserole dish in the kitchen on the other side of the office. Hardly anyone used the refrigerator over here. Even if someone did use this fridge, nobody was desperate enough to open up someone else's casserole dish.

"You're not seriously going to eat that, are you?" Roxanne asked.

Nichole pulled out the dish, peeled off the plastic top. A layer of cold peas was on top of a watertight Ziploc bag. Her fingers found the edge of the bag, and the cold peas went racing over the kitchen counter as Nichole unearthed the HK P7.

"Oh my God."

Nichole removed the pistol from the plastic, yanked back on the slide, slapped a round in the chamber, tucked the pistol in the back of her waist. She wore her capris with just enough give for moments like these. It had been far too long since she'd had a moment like this. The adrenaline felt good cascading through her blood.

"Oh my God, you're going to kill me."

"No, darlin'," Nichole said. "I'm one of the good guys, and we're going to get ourselves out of here."

Murphy had said he put the elevators on bypass, and rigged the fire tower with nerve agents. Murphy was certainly capable of such things. But what about the air-conditioning ducts?

Ah yes, air-conditioning ducts. Favorite of action movies everywhere across the land. When you're trapped in a room and need to escape in a hurry, simply yank off the metal register—it wouldn't be screwed in tight or anything—and shimmy on up in there, even though modern air ducts are designed to carry air, not adult human beings, so even if you were able to fit yourself into the duct, you'd probably fall right through the bottom at some inopportune point, probably land on a cubicle and impale yourself on a No. 2 pencil. But that's why we love action movies, right?

Life isn't an action movie, though.

And Nichole didn't want to use the air ducts to escape.

She wanted to use them to call for help.

Nichole moved down the hallway until she found what she was looking for. The air-return vent, which was about the size of a hardcover novel turned on its side.

"Give me your purse."

"Why?"

"Rox, please."

"Okay, okay."

Roxanne never went anywhere without her bag—even 9:00 A.M. Saturday morning meetings. And she never went without a full-size bottle of her signature scent: Euphoria for Women by Calvin Klein. Roxanne had been trying to convert Nichole for weeks now, offering her wrist for a sniff often and irritatingly. Nichole didn't do perfume. She preferred a clean, freshly scrubbed scent. Irish Spring, if possible. Fancy scents make you easy to track.

But now, Nichole was glad for Roxanne's perfume.

Because she was going to spray an ungodly amount of Euphoria into the air-return vent.

Nichole had read about a lawsuit years ago: In a nine-story law firm, a junior partner decided to play a prank on a coworker who had been caught going to a strip club. He bought a bottle of cheap perfume from a street vendor, then sprayed it all over his buddy's office. On his seat. On his desk. On the carpet. In the corner. Enough to make the place smell like a lap-dancing stripper for at least a few days. Then the junior partner closed the door.

The problem was, the building's HVAC system picked up the cheap perfume and redistributed it all over the building. The air-conditioning system wasn't enough to strip away the scent, and soon, the building was overcome with *eau de stripper.*

A secretary was allergic. Her throat closed up on the way to the hospital.

The junior partner's career ended with a one-two punch of criminal and civil lawsuits.

Nichole didn't want to kill anybody with Euphoria, but if it attracted the attention of building security, they'd have a better shot of making it off this floor alive.

She uncapped the perfume and felt something brush up the base of her spine.

Her HK P7.

God, Rox, no . . .

"Don't move," Roxanne said, hands trembling. She backed away from Nichole slowly. She had the pistol pointed at Nichole's head.

"This is not what you think," Nichole said. "I'm CIA. Listen to me, Roxanne: *I'm CIA.*"

"David wanted to kill us all, and now you're going to poison us all."

"Rox, you're making a huge mistake. Please put the gun down."

"I'm not stupid! I heard him talking about nerve agents!"

Nichole showed her the perfume bottle. "This is yours, Roxanne. Your Euphoria."

"I slept over last night! You could have switched it!"

"Honey, you can't put a chemical nerve agent in a perfume bottle."

Well, you could, actually. But Nichole needed to calm Roxanne down. Tell her what she wanted to hear. Get her gun back.

"Then put the perfume down."

"This is our way out of here."

"God, Nichole, don't make me do this. *Please* don't make me do this. But I'm not going to let you kill us all. I'm not! I don't want to die in here!"

Everything positive that Nichole had seen in Roxanne—her initiative, her resilience—was now distorted in a fun house mirror. How could she have thought about recruiting someone who could snap so easily, who'd abandon rational thought in a matter of minutes?

Roxanne was still her friend, but she was all wrong for this line of work.

Now Nichole had to do something regrettable. She had to incapacitate her best friend. It would hurt Rox, and it would kill Nichole to do it, but she needed Rox safe and out of the way for now. She could be stashed in one of the empty offices until this was all over. Maybe then they'd have a chance of repairing this breach of trust.

So Nichole pretended to put the perfume back into the purse, but snapped her arm up and blasted it right in Roxanne's eyes, then slapped the gun down, wrapped her fingers around it, pulled the gun away, dropped the perfume, and then followed up with a chop to Roxanne's face, right between her nose and lip—an incredibly painful blow that would bring her to her knees. Nichole would use the opportunity to cut off her air and render her unconscious for at least an hour.

But Nichole had misjudged the chop.

And she had kind of, accidentally, sent fragments of bone into her best friend's brain.

Nichole sat there for a while, crouched down next to her friend's dead body, pondering her next move.

Pondering how she was going to piece together the broken

shards of her career as an undercover intelligence operative, which had shattered spectacularly—and quite possibly irreparably—in the past thirty minutes.

That's when she heard footsteps, way on the other side of the room.

Somebody was walking into the dead wing of Murphy, Knox. Some *bodies.*

A male voice said, "Look, Molly. All we need is a double-A battery, and we're pretty much saved. No matter what Amy has in mind."

"You busy?" Nichole asked now.

Molly turned. She had a twisted little smile on her face. She parted her lips, the upper one beaded with perspiration. She'd been having fun in here with poor Jamie. There was a lot of blood on the floor. God knows what kind of torture she'd inflicted on him. Then she saw his hand, and had a pretty good idea.

Nichole should have charged in sooner. That would have been the nice thing to do. But those harrowing minutes she'd spent, crouched down next to Roxanne's body, listening to Jamie scream and beg—they'd been essential. Nichole Wise wasn't one to strategize on her feet. She needed a few minutes to get her game on.

And now she was ready for the Russian farm girl.

"Zdrastvuyte," Molly said.

Formal Russian for "Hello."

It *was* her on the tape.

But Nichole didn't let it shake her. She replied: *"Kak delah?"*

How are you?

"Kowaies Kateer," Molly said.

Ooh, Arabic now. Little Russian farm girl got herself an edu-mah-cation.

Nichole asked, *"Min fain inta?"*

Molly ignored the question, and shot back her own: *"Sprechen Sie Deutsch?"*

"Natürlich," Nichole replied. *"Mirabile dictu,* wouldn't you agree?"

"Quam profundus est imus Oceanus Indicus?"

"La plume de ma tante."

Jamie didn't know what Nichole and Molly were talking about, everything sounded like gibberish to him—but he knew one thing. Nichole had no idea what she was facing.

"Nichole," he gasped. *"Run!"*

Then he started to crawl forward, using only his right hand, skin burning on carpet, his eyes scanning the empty office for anything remotely resembling a weapon. . . .

There were many ways to go about this, Nichole thought as they bandied about the languages. She had run through two different scenarios while crouched down next to Roxanne's body.

Molly Lewis had the slender frame of a Russian gymnast— short and skinny. She was probably well trained in various forms of hand-to-hand combat. Now Nichole saw that Molly had this cute little X-Acto blade with a taped-up handle. She was probably like a surgeon with that thing. She'd certainly done a number on Jamie DeBroux's hand. It had to go.

Nichole, meanwhile, was built like a WNBA player, or at least a decent guard on a women's college team. She also had her fully loaded HK P7 shoved in the waistband of her capris.

Option #1: Pull the gun, blow the Russian farm girl into the back of this wall, soak the drywall with her blood.

But then she wouldn't have the chance to gather some potentially career-saving intelligence. So an instant execution was out.

Sure, she could shoot Molly in the leg, but the woman could go into shock very easily. No intelligence there, either.

Option #2: Sudden blinding force.

Pummel the Russian farm girl until her eyes blacken and her spine nearly snaps in half. Smash her ribs so badly that every breath becomes a session of exquisite agony. Cripple her, but hold her back from the brink. Nichole needed her conscious. Pliable. Only then would Nichole have a chance of keeping her job, dim as that prospect may seem at the moment.

Nichole liked Option #2 the best, but it wasn't as if Molly gave her a choice.

She was already charging with her baby blade.

On screen, Girlfriend jabbed her blade forward.

McCoy smiled. "Look at that."

Her opponent, a tall big-boned blonde whom the paperwork had identified as Nichole Wise, slapped the blade aside with her right hand, then followed up by smashing the heel of her palm into Girlfriend's nose. Girlfriend was visibly stunned. She dropped the blade. Took a few steps back.

"Ah," Keene said, sipping at a fresh cup of tea. "Will you look at *that*."

"Shut up," McCoy said.

Nichole was surprised how fast Molly dropped the blade. She thought it would be more of a fight. But so what.

Nichole wrapped her left hand around Molly's throat and used her right to grab the material of her skirt. She pushed hard, slamming Molly's head against the doorframe. Nichole pulled her back, then pushed forward even harder, aiming higher up the wall. Molly's head ricocheted off drywall again.

Then Nichole hurled her across the room, smashing her compact little frame against the opposite wall. Some drywall shattered on impact. Dust exploded from the surface. The floors seemed to jolt beneath her feet.

On the return throw, Nichole put Molly through the window overlooking the office, shattering glass and wrapping Molly's body in the aluminum slats of the venetian blinds.

The Russian farm girl rolled ten feet through glass and bent aluminum before coming to a dead halt.

Eat it, Molly Kaye Finnerty, Nichole thought. Her arms were already sore. It had been a while since she'd gone to the gym.

On the floor, Molly didn't move.

Oh hell.

She didn't do it again, did she? Accidentally kill someone?

This would *not* be good.

Nichole thought about her cousin Jason, who was four years older, and liked to inflict all manner of playground tortures on any younger cousin he could catch at family gatherings. That is, until the day Nichole—all of eight years old—grabbed Jason's wrist, twisted his arm behind his twelve-year-old back, locked the elbow, then pushed. She pushed up hard, hard as she was worth, dislocating Jason's shoulder.

Nichole's father said, "Sweetie, you've gotta learn to control that temper of yours. You're stronger than you think."

I hear you, Dad.

But any concern was short-lived. The moment Nichole stepped through the shattered window, glass crunching beneath the soles of her black flats, Molly came to life.

She sprang up, like an unbreakable industrial coil had been fused into her spine.

She stood erect, like nothing was wrong, even though she sported cuts over her arms and face, with some glass still poking out from the flesh. But Molly acted as if the shattered glass, broken drywall, and bent aluminum didn't exist. Hands at her sides. Hair still parted in place. Lips still deep red, glistening with moisture.

She smiled at Nichole. Raised her eyebrows, as if to say, *What else you got, big girl?*

McCoy let loose a "Hooo-*hah*!"

Which annoyed Keene. He'd seen, *hated* that Al Pacino movie.

"Big deal. She's standing up."

"Uh-uh," said McCoy. "My baby is Cool Hand Luke."

"I don't know what that means."

"You wouldn't."

Nichole instantly decided that her dad had been exaggerating that day, that her cousin was nothing more than a little pansy.

Because Nichole thought she'd given that Russian farm girl a serious pounding, and yet there she was. Standing. Grinning. Taunting.

But that didn't stop her from charging forward, grabbing Molly by her throat and crotch, and starting the punishment all over again.

The floor plan of this unused section of Murphy, Knox was relatively simple. Closed-door offices lined three sides, with a series of supply closets along the fourth. In the middle of the floor were drywall sections that divided the space into cubicles and, toward the middle, a space for two photocopiers and four printers. Five years out of date. Unplugged. Unsupported.

What interested Nichole were the closed office spaces. Each with their own window, reaching from two feet from ground level up to the ceiling. Privacy granted with aluminum venetian blinds mounted on the inside.

Nichole smashed Molly's body through the closest available window.

The crash was spectacular; the force behind the throw was so great that Molly took glass and aluminum blind with her as she rolled across the carpet and bounced off the opposite wall.

Nichole stepped through the broken window.

"How you feeling today, Molly," she said. "Everything okay?"

Nichole heard the sound of spitting. Russian farm girl was finally feeling it. Good. She needed answers, and Nichole was already tiring of throwing her through plate glass windows.

"Just relax down there. We're going to do some talking. Whatever language you prefer. We could even do Farsi."

Molly planted both hands on the carpet, then pushed down against the floor and snapped up into a perfect standing position. Facing Nichole.

Smiling.

No hesitation this time. Nichole wrapped both hands around Molly's neck and slammed her back against the wall.

"You want to talk, *puta*?" Molly said, curling her lips into another hideous smile.

Nichole would admit it. She lost her mind for a moment.

She screamed and hurled Molly through the window again. Molly tripped over the bottom frame of the window and rolled across the hall and into a cubicle. Within a second, she had popped up again. But this time Nichole was ready. She hopped through the jagged window frame, planted her feet, pivoted, and leveled a roundhouse kick at Molly's face that—if Nichole's training sessions were any indication—would fracture her skull upon impact. Nichole was through screwing around. She needed to *hurt* Molly.

But Nichole's foot never had the chance to connect.

Because Molly launched up in the air, flipping backwards over the wall of the cubicle like a dolphin at a waterpark.

Nichole's foot slammed into drywall instead.

. . .

McCoy was practically orgasmic. "Oh! Did you see that? *Oh!*"

Keene had a difficult time containing his surprise. That *was* an incredibly impressive move. And he had watched a lackluster video feed. Imagine what it must have looked like in real life.

The audio, however, was crystal clear. Murphy had equipped the office with omnidirectional mikes in pretty much every corner. The man clearly wanted to hear if his operatives tried to stifle a fart. So Keene heard the thud of the kick slamming into drywall, and it was like a wrecking ball accidentally dropped on a slab of sidewalk.

"I'm so in love," McCoy said.

"Want me to pull it out of your pants for you, give it a few tugs?"

"Would you?"

"Pervert."

"Tired old queen. Okay, quiet now. This is getting interesting."

McCoy tapped a few keys. The view on two of the monitors—McCoy's laptop and a freestanding monitor in front of Keene—flipped to a new vantage point. Within an office, looking out a window missing a blind.

Girlfriend's back was to the camera.

Nichole leaped over the drywall. No fancy flips. She just swung her legs over, eyes forward at all times. Molly was waiting for her. Still smiling. In the six months that Molly Lewis had been employed at Murphy, Knox, Nichole couldn't remember a single time she'd seen Molly smile. Perched behind her big cluttered oak desk, she'd appeared to be perpetually overworked, nervous, or constipated.

A smile on Molly now was unsettling. Kind of like seeing a

comatose patient spontaneously curl her lips into a rictus of imaginary bliss.

"Going to throw me through another window, *Nee-cole*?"

Nichole responded by kicking her through another window.

Sometimes, the best thing in a fight is to resist the urge to get creative.

This time, though, Molly caught herself before plunging through the stress-fractured glass. She regained her balance in a second, curled her right hand into a fist, then drove it into Nichole, just below her left breast.

The moment she took the punch, Nichole knew something was wrong. A single blow shouldn't hurt this bad. It shouldn't send her heart racing. It was the first punch Molly had thrown, and it threatened to send Nichole to her knees.

Wait. Update on that. It *did* send Nichole to her knees. Why couldn't she catch her breath? What was wrong with her?

Suddenly she was aware of Molly's face in hers.

"*Does it hurt?*" she whispered in a heavy Russian accent.

It wasn't going to end now.

Not like this.

Because Nichole still had a fully loaded HK P7 tucked in the waistband of her capris.

Nichole reached behind, wrapped her hand around the grip.

Molly either guessed or knew what was coming. She executed another perfect back flip—both palms up and over and planted on the carpet—and then smashed her feet through the already spiderwebbed glass, her body following behind.

Nichole swung the pistol around and started firing.

BLAM!

BLAM!

BLAM!

Glass shattered completely.

Drywall burst into chunks.

The recoil knocked Nichole back, off her knees and onto her butt, but she continued to blast away.

BLAM!

BLAM!

BLAM!

That was it, because Nichole felt a sledgehammer blow to her chest, and then she stopped breathing.

Jamie jolted when he heard the gunfire. Three bursts of gunfire, followed by another three, then a barely audible *gasp*.

Forget about the blood. Forget about your burst hot dog fingers. Get out there. It might be Nichole who's hurt. She saved you. You need to return the favor.

It wasn't the most dignified thing in the world, but Jamie had little choice. He crawled out of the empty office on his elbow and knees. Standing up would make his head a bobbing target above the cubicles. He'd heard gunfire, but had no idea who was taking the shots. Last he saw, Molly had a gun in the conference room. The one she'd used to shoot David. Jamie wasn't going to survive having his fingers carved up by a psycho secretary only to catch a stray bullet in the head. That would be anticlimactic.

He took some comfort in knowing that he hadn't completely lost his sense of humor.

Jamie crawled down the short path to the edge of the cubicles. The plan: Stop there, poke his head out, look down the long hallway.

He made it there, holding his sliced-up, burst–hot dog hand away from his vision as much as possible. He couldn't look at it. Not yet.

He looked around the corner.

He saw legs.

Bare legs, terminating in a pair of flat black shoes. One of the shoes was half off, hanging from the toes.

God, that was Nichole. She wore capris, no pantyhose. It was the psycho Molly who had dressed up for a hot August morning in the conference room. Long-sleeved blouse and everything. Nichole was bare-legged.

So Nichole was down for the count.

Crap.

Where was Molly? Did she still have that gun?

Think, Jamie, think. Because as much as your hand kills, it'll be nothing compared with the guilt over letting someone die. No matter that it was Nichole Wise, who'd probably looked at him only once in his year of employment, and dismissed him as a nonentity. Nichole was innocent. And no matter how much of an ice princess she'd been, she *did* distract Molly. She'd saved him.

Was Molly still down there? Waiting for him, with either a gun or her blade?

Nichole's foot twitched. Her shoe fell off completely. Rolled to one side.

Screw it.

Jamie used his elbows and knees, braced against the floor and the side of a cubicle wall, to make it up to his feet. He limped down the hall as fast as he could. "Nichole," he said aloud, figuring if Molly was waiting for him, perhaps she'd be lured out at the sound of his voice. And he'd have a prayer of ducking into an open office or empty cubicle. Not that he knew what he would do after that. Not against someone who could paralyze him with two fingers. But he was making this up as he went along anyway.

"Nichole," he repeated.

Jamie reached her, and leaned his back against a section of drywall next to the shattered window.

There was no sign of Molly.

But Nichole was unconscious.

Maybe even dead.

"Nichole!"

Jamie walked over and dropped to his knees, felt the side of her neck with his good hand. No pulse in her carotid artery. He put his ear to her mouth. Nothing. He wasn't sure how he was going to do this without it being agony, but he knew what he had to do. CPR. He'd learned it in a class, a month before Chase was born. Andrea had insisted. Now, he was faced with the real thing.

Jamie ripped open Nichole's blouse with one hand. Saw that she wore a white lace bra, low-cut. He reached under her neck, tilted her head back. Pinched her nose. Pressed his lips to hers. Pushed air down into her lungs. Her mouth tasted like cigarettes. Pumped her chest—yes, using his bloodied, shredded hand, and her bra was soon stained with red. Breathed into her mouth. Pumped her chest. Felt for a pulse. Breathed in her mouth again. For such an intense act, it was devoid of all sensuality.

The third time around, he revived Nichole.

Her eyes fluttered open. She saw Jamie, but seemed to have trouble focusing on him.

For a moment there, Jamie could have sworn she was about to hit him.

"Are you okay?"

Nichole's chest rose up and down, working hard to suck in air. "Fine."

Her fingers danced over her stomach, looking for something. The sides of her blouse. She found them, and covered herself.

Jamie leaned back against the wall of the cubicle. His mouth tasted like cigarettes.

. . .

Thirty-five hundred miles away, McCoy frowned.

Tapped some keys. The view changed on the second screen. Tapped more keys. The view changed on the third screen. Then the laptop.

He cycled through as many cameras as he knew, fanning out from that unused part of the office.

"Where is she?"

MIDMORNING BREAK
(WITH PEPPERIDGE FARM COOKIES)

Your best teacher is your last mistake. —RALPH NADER

Vincent Marella hit the floors one by one, starting with twenty-three, focusing on the north side. Vincent knew he wouldn't be that lucky and find a pane of glass missing on twenty-three. Or twenty-four. Or twenty-five. Twenty-six, twenty-seven, or twenty-eight. Nahhh. Because then, it would be a quiet weekend, and heaven forbid something like that actually go down on his watch.

Weekend staff at 1919 Market was kept to a minimum. Just four guards—three on at all times, while breaks and lunch were rotated. There wasn't much downtime. Somebody always needed help. Not much difference there between corporate security and hotel security—always undermanned and underfunded. Often, Vincent could barely read a page uninterrupted. He did most of his reading on breaks, which never lasted long enough. Three up, one down. At all times.

To check out the shattered-glass thing, Vincent put Carter on the desk and had Rickards check floors eight through twenty-two, starting with twenty-two and working his way down. Floors one through nine were lobby and garage, so that meant there were only twenty-eight floors to check. One at a time.

By the time Vincent reached twenty-nine, he had settled into a rhythm: Punch STOP on the elevator control panel. Pray the floor had a single tenant. If so, pop the master key in the double security doors, enter through the lobby, and make a counter-clockwise sweep of the floor, checking every window on the north side.

On one floor, it was easy; there were no offices partitioned off, just cubicles. But the other floors used their prime window space to reward employees with private offices. Some had large windows covered with aluminum blinds. Very few people kept their blinds up—most preferred privacy on the job. Which meant he had to key into every single office. Sometimes the lock would stick, which would piss him off.

Ah, weekend work.

He knew he shouldn't complain. He was lucky to have this gig after flaking out last year. In fact, he'd been out of work from Halloween through Presidents' Day of this year, trying to get his act together. A few prescriptions, a couple of sessions with an occupational therapist—not fully covered on his insurance, by the way. Nothing helped.

His teenaged son, whom Vincent saw only on weekends, gave him the best advice of all, "Just chill, Dad."

So he tried to chill, best he could.

After a good long while of chilling, Vincent saw some improve-ments. His heart stopped racing for no reason. He stopped hearing phantom noises. His dreams weren't as horrifying as they used to be.

A year ago, he'd been employed as a security guard on the night detail at the Sheraton, a reasonably expensive hotel on Rittenhouse Square, the richest slice of real estate in Philadel-phia. The Sheraton had since closed. But one hot August night, a year ago to the month, Vincent had been called up to the seventh floor to check out a suspected domestic dispute. These things happen, even in a nice hotel. Before he reached the door, though, some ape in a suit tackled him, pounded the crap out of him. Vincent put up the best fight he could—he fought mean and sloppy, and this kind of approach had served him well in bars over the years. But it didn't matter to this guy. Next thing he knew, there was a big fat ape arm around his neck, and he was plunging into darkness.

Vincent woke up in bizarro land. His kid read these Japanese manga things, which you flip through from back to front. That was how life felt after he had been assaulted. Back to front. Nothing made much sense. Maybe it did to others. Other people who knew how to read this stuff.

As it turned out, the ape who'd attacked him was believed to be part of some terrorist cell—I know, right? Vincent would say whenever he told friends this story, which wasn't often. The DHS guy who showed up, somebody with a Polish name, thanked him for his bravery, slapped him on his back, and disappeared into the night. Vincent checked the *Inquirer* and *Daily News,* but never saw any follow-up. The hotel manager gave him a few days off, told him to shake it loose.

Vincent had a hard time "shaking it loose."

Eventually, the Sheraton shook him loose.

You go through life thinking you know your place in the natural pecking order. You know which creatures are easy pickings, and you know which ones outweigh you. Keep your head down and beat a steady path between the two, and you'll make it out all right.

Problem was—and this was a first for Vincent—somebody who seriously outweighed him had broken him.

Forget outweighing him—the thing that attacked him was of a different species entirely.

All of a sudden, the universe seemed way too friggin' whimsi-cal. The threats too great. The chances for failure too large.

It had taken him until Presidents' Day to work up the courage to apply for another job. Security was all he'd known for fourteen years; it wasn't as if he could go and open a flower shop in Manayunk. A pal recommended 1919 Market: all corporate tenants. Whiny, self-absorbed people, but no crazies, like you get in a hotel. Even swank ones like the Sheraton.

By Easter, Vincent Marella was on weekend-day and weekend-night detail.

So now here he was, on a miserably hot August day, checking every single window on the north side, all because a crackhead saw broken glass in the alley behind the building.

Up on thirty now.

Hit STOP. Go to the double security doors. Pop the mas—

Wait.

What was this on the door? Looked like a small dent, right near the handle. And a black friction mark. Vincent felt a cold tingle in his spine. He had a feeling he was going to find himself a broken window on this floor.

He couldn't help himself. Before he unlocked the security door, Vincent put his ear to it. Listening for another ape.

David Murphy was thinking about popcorn.

This August marked the fifth anniversary of Murphy, Knox, and he wanted to let the whole building know it. To be perfectly honest, he didn't care who in the building knew it. But a gift needed to be sent anyway. After consulting with the right tech guys—a team of chem-lab geeks he'd worked with back in Bosnia—he'd cooked up the perfect gift. A five-gallon tin of popcorn, divided into three sections: salt and butter, cheese, and caramel.

David was looking up at a row of those tins now. He had even more in his office, and at least a dozen stacked behind Molly's desk.

He'd sampled some of the popcorn. The cheese was a bit too orange, and a bit too cloying—not to mention vaguely reminiscent of a foot. The caramel stuck to his teeth, and wasn't so much sweet and caramelly as it was dark and syrupy. The salt-and-butter variety . . . now that was something he could get into.

Not that he did. He sampled only a few handfuls to convince himself that yes, this tasted like the kind of popcorn office denizens would get into, keep around the office for a while. They'd probably skip the cheese and caramel, though. But what was it Meat Loaf once sang? One out of three ain't bad? Something like that.

David hired a company to insert the popcorn and trifold cardboard divider; he supplied the tins himself.

The exterior of the tin featured a wraparound skyline of Philadelphia, with the text in a hunter green oval on two sides:

MURPHY, KNOX & ASSOCIATES
PROUD TO CALL THE CITY OF BROTHERLY LOVE HOME . . .
. . . 5 YEARS RUNNING!

Molly had written that. She had been good at those things.

Before she shot him in the head.

Yesterday, dozens of popcorn tins were delivered to every single tenant of 1919 Market Street, from floors thirty through thirty-seven. This included three law firms, an accounting office, a local lifestyle magazine, the private office of a state supreme court justice, two philanthropic concerns, and a few other random businesses that didn't mean much to David.

If any tenants in floors twenty-nine or lower were to have felt slighted, David was prepared to cheerfully reply: *Ah, you see, the delivery service could only do so much in one day. The rest were to be delivered on Monday. Hope you don't mind waiting!*

There were no more popcorn tins to be delivered, though. He'd ordered only enough for the eight floors at the top with some left over for special clients.

Was this a loose end? Would a nameless researcher for a congressional investigatory commission check the order later?

Like it really mattered.

Even though David was paralyzed, lying in a pool of his own blood in the conference room, he imagined himself smiling at the stack of popcorn tins on the small table against the wall. Six little popcorn tins. The one part of this morning that hadn't completely gone to hell.

Whatever Molly had planned, David hoped for her sake she was going to finish it up quickly.

Maybe she'd come back and do the right thing. Finish him off.

Which would be perfect.

There was no ape on the thirtieth floor.

Nothing even remotely simian. And more important, no broken windows or missing panes of glass. Vincent enjoyed a few deep breaths of relief. The scuff on the security door had been nothing. Probably a late-night FedEx guy, banging his steel dolly into it.

Nothing to worry about.

He knew he was probably still freaked out by his little adventure at the Sheraton. Being choked into unconsciousness could do that to a guy. But he also knew it was partly his boy messing with his mind. His fifteen-year-old conspiracy theorist.

For weeks now, the boy had convinced himself that the 9/11 attacks on the World Trade Center were actually the work of the U.S. government—an elaborate stage show that cost thousands of lives, but won those in power a blank check to protect their business interests in the name of "the war on terror." He told his boy to get the hell out of here, but the boy, as usual, had a way of chipping away at his old man, one piece of evidence at a time. He'd be sitting there at Vincent's home PC, watching something intently, and of course, he would have to check it out, because what if it was porn? It was his paternal obligation. He would walk over to the monitor, though, and the boy would be pointing excitedly at the screen. "Watch this, Dad," and before Vincent knew it, he was watching one of the two towers fall. He didn't know which one—north or south.

The boy pointed at the side of the falling building. "Did you see that?"

"No—what? And hey, what are you watching this stuff for?"

"Look closer." The boy rewound the video a few seconds, then clicked the little triangle. "See that?"

"See what."

"The puff of smoke, shooting out of the sides as the building pancakes down."

"I guess."

"That's a sign of a controlled demolition, Dad. The government brought those buildings down on purpose. They knew a plane hitting the top couldn't do the job, so they put in a little insurance."

"Get the hell out of here."

Vincent heard himself speak those words, and realized that they were coming straight from his own father. Only his father would not be finding his boy Vincent poring over a conspiracy video on the Internet. He'd find him in the back shed with a copy of *Swank,* and his ironworker dad would curl it up, beat Vincent with it, and then say "Get the hell out of here," before confiscating the magazine for personal use.

If only it were that easy.

So he had been hearing a lot of this crazy stuff recently—every weekend, when his boy came to stay. He got interested despite himself. Poked around a few articles the boy had printed out for him. It's what made him grab that copy of *Center Strike* from the tiny book collection in the security lounge.

It also made him think way too much about the building he was paid to protect.

There were taller, more important buildings in Philadelphia than 1919 Market, that was for sure. Any terrorists thinking about attacking a building would most likely shoot for Liberty One and Two, Philly's gleaming blue answer to the World Trade Center. Or City Hall, which at one time actually was the tallest building in America . . . for about seventeen minutes. Or the obvious symbols of American freedom: Independence Hall and, right across the street in a shiny new pavilion, the Liberty Bell.

In comparison, 1919 Market was neither architecturally nor historically significant. No government offices, unless you count that state supreme court justice's pad.

So why had he been so freaked out?

Vincent decided he had to tell the boy to lay off the 9/11 stuff for a while.

What Vincent Marella didn't know was that there *were* four explosive devices tucked away above the acoustic panels on the thirtieth floor. Two on the south side, one on the west, another on the north. One of the south-side devices was hanging ten feet from where he stood.

The scuff on the security door, though, was *not* the result of a last-minute break-in.

That really had been a FedEx guy.

In actuality, the explosive devices had been planted five years ago, shortly after David Murphy signed a ten-year lease on his portion of the thirty-sixth floor. David kept the trigger close at hand, at all times.

David liked to be prepared for all eventualities.

Even if the office were to be breached someday by a well-meaning law enforcement agency, they would find no such explosives on the thirty-sixth floor. Above, or below it.

No one would think to check six floors below.

Not until it was too late.

And when it came time to close up shop—like today—it was simply a matter of providing the right kind of accelerant. And spreading it on floors thirty-one through thirty-seven.

The kind of accelerant that could be melted into popcorn tins, and distributed to the companies on those floors.

MURPHY, KNOX & ASSOCIATES
PROUD TO CALL THE CITY OF BROTHERLY LOVE HOME . . .
. . . 5 YEARS RUNNING!

The model David had in mind was One Meridian Plaza. He'd read about it before basing his company in Philadelphia. On February 23, 1991, a fire broke out on the twenty-second floor, engulfing and eventually gutting the eight floors above it. The building did not collapse, but remained a hulking shell of itself for more than a decade before city officials finally authorized its destruction.

A simple fire. Eight floors of destruction.

With the right kind of accelerant, it was more than enough to destroy the existence of Murphy, Knox.

Except in the minds of the fine people who enjoyed its free popcorn from time to time over the years.

Vincent Marella had no way of knowing any of this. This did not make him a bad security guard. In fact, the only piece of physical evidence that David had left behind, five years ago, was a tiny black tube of wire sheathing, cut from the wire when he patched the devices into the building's power lines. David had missed it when he did a quick sweep of the rug to make sure he had left no traces.

Two days later, a vacuum cleaner from housekeeping had scooped it up.

It was now at the bottom of a floating landfill somewhere near South America.

Piece *that* together.

Vincent's two-way beeped, snapping him out of his daydreams. If there *were* any terrorists hiding up here, that would have completely given away the game. Gotten his ass killed.

"What's up?"

"You'd better come down to sixteen, Vincent." It was Rickards, who'd been checking the lower half of the building.

"What's going on?"

"Got a guy down here you should see."

"Let me guess. He has cuts all over his hands from pushing through a window."

"No," Rickards said. "He's unconscious and he's got a pen sticking out of his throat."

Nichole wasn't sure what was worse: the fact that Molly had dropped her on her ass with one punch. Or that a drone like Jamie DeBroux had to revive her.

People in the world were divided into a few simple categories. The large majority were drones, buzzing about their daily lives, completely unaware how their contributions fit into the larger hive. They could be frightened into collective action quite easily—a terrorist threat or environmental disaster or flu epidemic. Some of these were even real. But most were engineered by the queens, or put into action by the workers.

Nichole and Molly were the workers.

People like David Murphy were the queens.

Nichole liked to believe that she was on an equal playing field with other workers. Sure, there were workers more powerful or gifted in some ways, but they were all still workers.

Molly, however, had been an extraordinarily tough worker.

Nichole was stunned by her ability to take a severe beating and still remain standing. She almost felt bad that she had to cheat at the end. But it was the only scenario available to her. Nichole knew she was mortally injured. And she knew Molly must be stopped.

"Where is she?" Nichole asked now. She sat up and felt incredibly dizzy.

"Who? Molly? She's gone."

"What?"

Nichole tried to get to her feet faster than she should have. The floor spun. But she had to look, see for herself.

The office where Molly had fallen was empty. Shattered glass was all over the floor, along with chunks of drywall and dust. Nichole counted bullet holes. Two in the window. One in the metal radiator. Another two in the desk. And one on the right wall, a wild shot (probably her last, Nichole thought) that probably sailed three feet over Molly's head. Six shots fired. Six shots accounted for.

None of them had struck the Russian farm girl.

Nichole cursed and pounded her fist into the nearest available wall. Which happened to be the outer wall of the empty office.

A jagged shard of glass that had been hanging for its life at the top of the frame now fell, bursting against the frame below, and sending pieces over Jamie's legs.

"Hey," he said.

Nichole looked down and saw that she was missing a shoe. She carefully stepped over to it, shook out the glass, and replaced it on her foot. Then she recovered the HK P7 from the floor and tucked it in the back of her pants again.

"Come on," she said.

"Where?"

"Off this floor."

Nichole was lying, though. She needed to go to David's office to recover any intel she could. Only then could she think about escape. If it came to it, she could pry open the elevator doors and make their escape down the shaft. Unless David had rigged those, too.

"Can you give me a hand?"

Nichole sighed. Drones. She held out her hand, then felt a panel of her shirt open wide, giving Jamie a clear view of her bra. Her bloodied bra. She withdrew her hand. Jamie had reached out by then, and when Nichole withdrew, his hand grabbed air. He slammed back against the cubicle wall.

"Ouch," he said.

Nichole didn't pay him any mind. She was looking down at her ruined shirt.

"What did you do?" she asked.

"I had to rip open your shirt to give you CPR."

"You couldn't do it over my shirt? What, were you hoping for a cheap feel?"

"I wasn't thinking about that," Jamie said. "I was trying to save your life."

Nichole looked up the hall. "I guess I should be grateful my bra is still on."

"Hey, it wasn't like that."

"Sure. I remember it from my CPR classes. Step one: If the victim is female, rip open her shirt."

Nichole looked to see if there was a single button left standing. There wasn't.

"Come on," she said, "let's go."

Jamie slowly pulled himself to his feet.

"Where's everybody else? Do you think Molly's going after them, too?"

Nichole considered this carefully. How much to tell him? After all, Roxanne's dead body was just a few feet away, around the other end of the cubicles. She would have to lead him around to David's office the long way—and hope they didn't encounter Molly.

At least she had two rounds left in the HK P7. If she was given another opportunity, she'd do it point-blank style.

Press the barrel right up against Molly's forehead and squeeze.

Nichole looked at Jamie—disheveled, bloodied, battered, but still a drone.

Silence, for now, was the best policy.

"Follow me," she said.

They found the three essentials in David's office: bandages, booze, and a battery. AA, even. Just what the Talkabout T900 needed.

Unfortunately, the T900 had been crushed.

On their way back, Jamie had scooped it up from the floor of the office where Molly had tried to filet him. The plastic screen was gone. Now the unit refused to turn on, even with the new battery, which Nichole had found in one of David's desk drawers.

"Let me see it," Nichole said.

Jamie didn't argue. He handed it over and sat down on the floor with the first aid kit Nichole had found in David's desk. Standard company issue, purchased at OfficeMax. Six hundred sixteen pieces, with the ability to serve up to a hundred people.

Handy for mornings like these, when your boss and coworker go bananas and try to shoot, slice, and poison you.

Meanwhile, Nichole was replacing the battery door on the back of the T900. She had opened it up and reinserted the batteries, just in case. She pushed a few buttons. Nothing happened.

"This thing is shot," Nichole said.

"Told you."

"Did you land on it, or something? *Damn* it."

Okay. Jamie couldn't put it off any longer. He had to do what he could to patch up his hand. At least something to make the bleeding stop until they made it off this floor. If he had his way, he'd wrap the fingers in gauze and slip a black leather glove over the whole thing, like Luke Skywalker wore in *Jedi.* Even better: Convince the Rebels to replace his hand with a cybernetic part. Start over.

Jamie looked at his fingers.

Oh, God.

He couldn't look at them.

They throbbed hard, as if to remind him: *We're here. We're damaged. We're here. We hurt. Fix us. Fix us now.*

Jamie pulled some gauze from the kit and tried to wrap them blind, using as much tape as possible. If Andrea were here, she'd yell at him for not using disinfectant. Of course he could argue that it wasn't worth worrying about infection. When Jamie looked down, he could have sworn he saw bone.

"What are you doing?"

"Wrapping up my fingers."

"You're not doing a very good job."

"I'm new at this."

"Give me your hand. We don't have much time."

Nichole looked down at Jamie's mangled fingers and said, "Oh, God."

"Yeah."

"I'm not going to be able to stitch anything. There are no stitches in this kit."

"That's fine. Whatever you can do."

"I'll tape it best I can, try to sterilize everything with this Scotch I found in David's desk. You can get it looked at later. Okay?"

"Seriously, whatever you can do."

"Want a drink first? It's Johnnie Walker Black."

"I'm okay."

"I think you're going to regret that decision in about ten seconds."

Nichole got to work. Jamie looked up at the ceiling tiles, and listened to peeling and tearing sounds of tape. He didn't want to know the gory details. Better that he pretend she was expertly stitching up the flesh of each finger, so perfectly, in fact, that a few days later he would be able to flex his fingers and *ping! ping! ping! ping! ping!*—the stitches would pop out, and he'd be completely healed. Even though he knew there were no stitches.

"Here we go."

"You haven't started yet?" Jamie asked.

"Brace yourself."

Jamie kept his eyes transfixed on the off-white ceiling tiles, imagining that the dimples in the material were craters big enough to hide in. He heard the quiet hollow *thoooomp* of a corktop being removed from a bottle.

"Cheers."

There was no way Jamie could have prepared himself for the agony that washed down over his mangled hand. The old pain—the pain that caused the horrible gashes in the first place—was like a memory of the beaches of heaven compared to this NEW PAIN. The burning-acid molten-flesh drilled-bone torture of NEW PAIN.

"Shhhh now."

Nichole held his wrist steady while the rest of his body writhed violently. Jamie shrank and floated up into a big crater on the ceiling.

A few minutes later, he opened his eyes. The light was harsh. He was back down on the floor.

Riiiiip.

"You passed out," Nichole said.

"Urrrgghhhhh," Jamie said.

"Don't throw up. I'm halfway done."

She continued working.

Passing out didn't erase a single memory. There was no blissful moment of, Hey now, where am I? Why is this tall woman fussing over my hand? Why is she only wearing a bra? Jamie remembered everything. Nothing had changed. Except that he felt like he needed to throw up.

"Nichole."

"Yeah."

Riiiiip.

"Do you have any idea why David wanted to kill us this morning?"

She didn't reply.

"Did he lose his mind?" Jamie asked. "I think that's the theory I would prefer. The stress of the job, he goes postal . . ."

"That what you believe?"

"No."

"Me neither."

Riiiiip.

"That's because you know what's really going on, don't you? That we're actually some kind of secret intelligence agency."

"If you don't already know, then you're not supposed to know."

"Jesus, Nichole, c'mon!" Then he added a faint "Ow." She had pressed down hard. Maybe even on purpose. "I almost died this morning. Along with everybody else. I deserve to know."

"Trying to concentrate here."

"Can you at least tell me if we're working for the good guys?"

Nichole looked at him with a lifted eyebrow.

"You know? The U.S. government?"

She returned to her tapework.

"Reason I ask," Jamie said, "is because if we are the good guys, then how come David Murphy was allowed to come in this morning with orders to kill us? That's not something the good guys do, is it? Especially to people like me, who until about an hour ago had no friggin' idea we actually worked for the government?"

"*You* don't work for the government," she said.

Jamie would have stormed out of the office had Nichole not been taping up the remains of his hand. This was not right. This was not fair. Guy in the military, he gets a draft notice, gets told, yeah, you might get a ball blown off in another country, or come home in a flag-draped box. *That's how we roll, Private.* Guy puts on a police badge, same deal, only you take your risks in your own backyard. Death's unlikely, but certainly possible. You know walking in.

But Jamie wasn't a cop or a solider. He was a public relations guy who thought he was working for a financial services company, and did so because of decent pay and medical benefits. He didn't sign on for anything else.

This was not right.

This was not fair.

Not to his wife and baby, who right now had no idea what was happening up here.

This was the horror of 9/11, or at least, the horror Jamie imagined whenever he thought about what it was like on one of those burning floors of the towers. The horror that your family will never know what happened in your last minutes alive. Like you were already dead.

He felt eyes. Nichole was staring at him.

"I've been thinking about what to say to you," she said. "Because I *do* want you to live through this. And the less you know, the better. Trust me on this. I can't speak for the rest of this company, but I'm one of the good guys. I may be the only good guy here. You probably saved my life, so I'm going to try to save yours. Fair enough?"

Jamie swallowed. His mouth tasted like death. "Yeah."

"David is a bad guy. David sealed this floor and tried to kill us. Molly stopped David, but now *she's* trying to kill us. That makes her a bad guy, too. That's all we need to know."

"Okay."

"Our strategy is simple. We avoid Molly, and we try to make it off this floor alive."

"I'm hoping you know how to do that."

"Yeah," Nichole said. "We ask David."

She showed him a syringe.

"That wasn't in the first aid kit, was it?" Jamie asked.

Thirty-five hundred miles away, Keene asked: "Find your Girlfriend yet?"

McCoy grunted, then drained the rest of his Caley. He walked back to their tiny kitchen for another can. Keene was going to have to think about fixing supper soon. Whenever McCoy reached the six-pack point, he became ravenous. And he was especially cranky when he was hungry.

Keene took over, cycling through the cameras on the thirty-sixth floor, spending barely a second on each office. In the conference room, the boss was still on the floor, the blood around his head looking like an oddly shaped pillow. The corpse of his faithful employee, McCrane, was situated across the room. Kurtwood's dead body was still in the hallway of the abandoned section of the office. The still-alive DeBroux and Wise were in the head office. But no Girlfriend.

Where could she be?

Keene hoped she wasn't dead. Otherwise, McCoy would be insufferable for weeks.

Girlfriend was doing her hair.

She had no choice. Six shots had been fired, and she had twisted and rolled and managed to avoid every single one . . . except one. A lucky shot, most likely fired when Nichole Wise really started to lose control, and was firing blind. Because there was no possible way that had been intentional. That kind of shot was the stuff of military snipers, not workaday Company watchdogs. Wise didn't have the precision.

The bullet had sliced through the air, then the glass, then more air, and then her cheek.

It had gouged a bloody trail high across her cheekbone, and it had carried enough ground glass to make it hurt.

The pain didn't matter, though. Her appearance did.

After cleansing her face and the wound, she reached behind her head and pulled the clips from her hair. Her hair was quite long. Paul had liked it that way. She kept it up and away from her face during the workday. Home, alone with Paul, she let it down. Home alone with Paul, she'd often wander around the house without clothes. It left him quite powerless, even if he thought he was in control.

Now she let some of her hair fall down in a wedge over the right side of her face; the rest was clipped up behind her head. She used hot water to smooth out her hair, tease some of the drywall dust and blood and ground glass out of it. After a minute of grooming, it looked passable. This was not a look she'd ever used before. Perhaps this was a good thing.

At the end, she was going to have to look presentable.

That would be the final exam.

Boyfriend would see it.

And, God willing, Boyfriend would give her the promotion she so desperately craved. No. *Needed.*

Good thing Boyfriend couldn't see her now.

She had wanted him to see the pain she endured—that was part of the interview. But not the aftermath. A good operative was super-resilient, able to bounce back from any form of punishment. Most American operatives didn't have much of a threshold for pain.

This would distinguish her from much of her competition.

She kept bandages and liquid skin in her right bracelet; tweezers and a simple stitching kit in her left. She used them now, working quickly and efficiently. Time was against her. She'd already wasted a minute on her face and rearranging her hair.

Her black skirt was fine—the color masked the blood—but her pantyhose were ruined, sliced open in a dozen places by the sharp glass. They had served her well. The pantyhose weren't ordinary; you couldn't buy them in a plastic egg in a department store. They were a special order, reinforced by woven Kevlar. Her legs had scratches and cuts, but no major gashes.

Her blouse was similarly reinforced. The worst damage she'd taken had been to her left forearm. She had rolled up her sleeve to access her bracelet.

Perhaps she should have rolled her sleeve back down.

Like the pantyhose, the blouse had to go. She wore a sleeveless shirt over her bra, one that didn't look strange when paired with a skirt. It would do for the remainder of the interview.

Her legs and feet were bare, but she could easily recover her shoes before she departed.

Her hair now covered her face.

Glass had been plucked out; flesh taped, bonded, or sutured; clothes wiped clean.

Girlfriend was ready for the remainder of the morning activities.

She allowed herself the luxury of staring at herself in the bathroom mirror for a few moments. She was deep within the offices of *Philadelphia Living*. She'd stolen a key from the publisher two months ago. She'd followed him to a bar called The Happy Rooster—how appropriate, that name. He had been drunk and had stumbled off to sing karaoke. She slipped her hand into the bag, secreted the key, and disappeared into the shadows before he'd reached the second chorus of "Afternoon Delight." In the meantime, she'd kept the key in a compartment in her right bracelet. She was glad it had finally been of some use.

Now she looked at herself, and was stunned by the passage of time.

Ten years ago, a much scrawnier, timid version of herself would have been looking back from the mirror.

A little girl, so eager to please.

Now she was different.

She was a young woman, much stronger, much bolder.

But still, eager to please.

Some things cannot be beaten from your soul.

Girlfriend spoke to herself in Russian. Mumbling, really. Nonsense rhymes. Things she would say to herself when she was a girl.

That was enough now. No more indulgences.

Number three was still missing. He had never shown up to the meeting, yet there was evidence he had arrived at the building.

Number three might still be hiding on the floor.

Or, Ethan had been clever enough to find a way out of David's traps.

BACK TO WORK

Twenty floors down, somebody finally spotted him.

Well slap him and call him Susan. Weren't security guards supposed to keep an especially keen eye on the fire towers? You know, as a potential security risk? Glad to know the Department has been in such safe hands all these years. Then again, that was probably the point. A heavily armed, man-heavy, hard-core, SWAT-style building security team would be kind of a red flag to the enemy. And what was the use of running a cover business if something like that blew the cover?

Still, Ethan knew there were fiber-optic cameras up and down the friggin' tower. Even the lowest of the low-rent sky-scrapers had 'em. He waved, then saluted each with a middle finger, on the way down. Hello, asses. Notice me.

Every couple of concrete staircases, he collapsed. He didn't know if it was the nerve-agent blast or the pen tube in his throat or the remnants of that friggin' French martini worming its way through his mind. But Ethan felt like hell.

So he collapsed.

He didn't feel bad about it. As long as he fell on his back, no worries. If he ever pitched forward, however, they'd find a hung-over twenty-something with a pen tube sticking out through the back of his neck. That would be a tough one to explain to his parents.

Ethan'd told them he was in law school.

For seven years now.

Maybe they didn't know how long law school took.

By floor sixteen, however, everything changed. Ethan felt an awesome weight on his head and shoulders. His eyes felt heavier than ever. When he started to pitch forward toward a cold slab of landing, it took every last bit of strength to buck himself backwards. Must . . . land . . . on . . . back. . . .

Absurd, wasn't it, how your most basic needs could change within an hour?

Must . . . eat . . . Big . . . Mac.

Must . . . land . . . on . . . back . . . so . . . pen . . . tube . . . doesn't . . . kill . . . me.

Ethan's wish was granted.

He landed on his back.

And gurgled loudly before he passed out.

Maybe it was just his nerve-agent-riddled imagination, but as he drifted into unconsciousness—and Ethan knew this was go-ing to be one of those long-haul blackouts, not one of those wimpy pass-out sessions that lasted only a few seconds—he thought he heard footsteps pounding toward him. A fist on a steel door. Someone saying, Is anyone in there? The faint sound of a metal door latch twisting to one side. Another footstep, fainter still, on the concrete landing above.

And the final bit of sensory input, just before Ethan grabbed the heavy black curtain by the corner, folded it up over himself, and rolled over to one side:

You'd better come down to sixteen, Vincent.

. . .

Molly flipped open the compartment on her bracelet that held the ear receiver. She flipped the micro-size ON switch, then pushed it into her ear canal. The receiver was pretuned to pick up all internal radio contact. She didn't expect to hear anything useful, but it was possible that Ethan had made it out of the building and was calling for backup. If so, she'd hear the security chatter. Not a huge worry. She'd just have to speed the assignment up. Hope that her reaction time would impress Boyfriend.

She'd been wearing the ear receiver for only a few minutes when she heard:

You'd better come down to sixteen, Vincent.

Static.

What's going on?

Static.

I've got a guy down here you should see.

Static.

Let me guess. He has cuts all over his hands from pushing through a window.

Static.

No. He's unconscious and he's got a pen sticking out of his throat.

Ethan.

The scream made sense. Ethan must have felt something was off, and tried to flee early. Probably had enough sense to avoid the elevators—they were easier to control or sabotage or both. But he didn't have enough sense to realize that a man who would sabotage an elevator would do the same thing to a fire tower. That miscalculation had earned him a blast of weaponized sarin.

Molly knew the effects of sarin; she'd briefly trafficked on behalf of an Afghan warlord years ago. And Ethan probably had enough sense to know what was happening. Probably felt his skin burn and his eyes bleed and his throat start to close, and he had been smart enough to attend to his throat first. Bleeding eyes will hurt—but a lack of air will kill you.

Look where that got him. On the sixteenth floor, surrounded by building security.

Ethan Goins was supposed to have been seated in the conference room with the others. She had arranged everyone in order: Ethan was third. First, David. Then Amy Felton. And then Ethan, the hired muscle. She had even checked to make sure that Ethan was on the floor. His office door was open. His computer on. At the time, Molly had assumed Ethan stepped out to use the men's room.

And he had.

The men's room . . .

. . . on another floor.

It all clicked into place. The thirty-seventh floor was currently unoccupied. A mayoral candidate based his headquarters there until a dismal showing in the May primary bounced him out of the race. Now there was nothing but office partitions and rented desks that needed to be picked up and restocked. There were also two restrooms—men's and ladies'—on the thirty-seventh floor. Unlocked. Free to anyone in the building who preferred a little privacy when attending to bodily functions.

Like Ethan.

He must have been on his way back down—the fire tower staircase was the easiest way between two floors—when David had engaged lockdown, as well as the sarin packages. Ethan had opened the doors. Ethan had received a wet surprise.

Poor Ethan.

Actually, screw Ethan. He was to have been third. This was not the way it was supposed to have unfolded.

Now building security had discovered him.

There was a good chance he was already dead. Sarin is nasty. Hard to shake the effects, even if you are tough enough to perform a self-serve tracheotomy.

But what if he were alive?

Ethan knew a lot. If he regained consciousness, he could ask for a pen and paper. Another pen, that is. Then he could make the remainder of the morning considerably more difficult.

Molly needed to make it to the sixteenth floor as quickly as possible.

Vincent waited for the elevator. He was more than a little relieved. Rickards had the culprit, who was unconscious. Vincent wasn't sure what this "pen in his throat" stuff was all about. Rickards wasn't a confrontational guard, and even if he was, he wouldn't attack somebody with a friggin' Bic.

Whatever. He knew this guy he caught had to be responsible for blowing out a window on the north side. Mystery solved. He and Rickards could escort the guy down to the lobby, call the Philly PD, ask for an incident report, then boom. Back to the world of *Center Strike,* where there were bigger problems than a blown-out window and a dude with a pen in his throat.

Molly flipped open another compartment on her bracelet. She removed a pair of plastic wraparound safety glasses. She unfolded the arms, and then the bridge, separating the two lenses from each other. The hinge in the middle snapped in place with a hollow click. She aimed the lenses at her face, holding them a few feet away. It was *Hamlet,* minus Yorick's skull. If Yorick wore plastic wraparound safety glasses.

She waited for the camera buried in the frame and lenses to come online. Then she held up her free hand and showed the lenses three fingers.

Always have backup technology.

Straight out of Murphy's beloved Moscow Rules.

"Hey, mate," Keene said. "She's back."

McCoy had ducked out to take a leak or throw up or just stare at himself in the bathroom mirror. You never knew with McCoy. Once, Keene had caught him rubbing an issue of *Vanity Fair* around his neck and under his chin. Free cologne, he explained. Then he'd gone out and blown an absurd amount on a bottle of single malt.

"And I know you'll want to see this."

Keene heard the toilet flush.

Ah, taking a piss.

"McCoy! Your girl is back online!"

A meaty head popped out of the door.

"What?"

Molly placed the glasses on her face and then made her way to the north fire tower. Had to be that one. It was the closest to the active side of the office. No reason for Ethan to select the other. He'd be going out of his way to visit a bathroom.

Now it was time to outrun a sarin bomb, perched over a doorway.

Molly had faked a marriage to an actuary for three years. She figured she could pretty much handle anything.

It was all about the speed. Blast through the door, make it down the first concrete staircase, then vault to the left, hands on the landing, and flip down the next staircase. And so on. Hope she made it clear of the dispersal cloud fast enough. Even a little bit in her lungs could slow her down. Take root there. Potentially ruin the operation.

The door latch. That was the problem. She couldn't hold it down and flip through the door at top speed at the same time.

She ran through the gear in her wrist bracelets. Wire. Blade. Hooks. Heroin. USB key. Poison.

Wait.

Wire. Hooks.

She fished out the gear, tied off the hook, looped the wire around the flat door latch, pulled it to the right, freeing the bolt from the strike plate, then sank the hook into the drywall to the right of the door. She let go. The wire held. All she needed was for it to hold for five seconds.

Five seconds was a generous amount of time.

Molly leaned up against the opposite wall, then launched herself through the doorway. Steel banged against the cinder block. As she sailed through the air, hands outstretched in front of her, she heard a *beep beep* and a pneumatic *hisssssssss*.

The device had been placed above the doorway, some kind of delivery nozzle pointed down—just as she thought it might be. She imagined the nerve agent coating the backs of her bare legs, her heels . . . but no, that wasn't possible, she'd moved too fast. She was fine. She was *fine*. Her palms slapped the concrete landing below and she regained her balance and immediately twisted to the left, planted both feet on the ground, then flipped backwards down the flight of stairs, her outstretched palms waiting for the harsh slap of concrete so she could twist her body to the right this time, and then feel the concrete beneath her feet again, and flip backwards again. . . .

This was just a vault and floor routine, she told herself. Just like 1988.

Only, no rubber foam or plywood or springs. No music. No padding on the perimeters. No choreography.

Simply cold, unforgiving concrete.

She could do this.

And her glasses were going to stay on her face the whole routine.

Because she wanted them to see *everything*.

McCoy, who was finally out of the bathroom, squinted at one of the laptop monitors. He settled into his chair.

"She's stunning, isn't she?" McCoy said, pulling the zipper up on his jeans and trying to find the buckle to his black leather belt.

"I'm dizzy," Keene said.

"How is she taping this?"

The image on the monitor was a Steadicam nightmare: a shaky, floor-over-ceiling-over-floor blur of motion, with a cinder block wall doing a violent 180 every so often.

"Cameras in her spectacles. I saw her put them on. She showed us three fingers before proceeding."

"Three fingers," McCoy repeated.

"But what is she doing? She came blasting through that door like someone was after her with a gun. Now she's trying to qualify for the Olympics by flipping down a bloody fire tower. Strange way to make a getaway. She's not even finished her operation."

McCoy wasn't paying attention, though. He kept his eyes on the monitor and searched the table for the thick file Girlfriend had sent him. "Number three, number three," he said. "Yeah, that's Goins."

"Odd thing was, she took time to set up the door handle before going berserk."

"Huh?" McCoy said.

"I said, she took—"

"Oh," McCoy said, then paused. "Oh, that's right. You were out buying your little bottle of nursemaid—"

"Night Nurse."

"Whatever. You missed the part of the meeting where JFK there told his employees that he'd rigged the two fire towers with sarin."

"Murphy's a paranoid guy, isn't he? Why not just lock the damned things?"

"No better lock than a weaponized nerve agent. So my little Girlfriend there is trying to outrun death. That cloud of sarin is only going to make its way down the fire tower. She can beat it, but she can't stop it."

Keene stared at the monitor.

"Fine, sure. But what's she running towards?"

"Why," McCoy said, "number three."

Ethan Goins was having a weird sex dream about Amy Felton. He had them often. They'd become so familiar, part of his brain probably believed he *did* share a sexual history with Amy, even though that was not the truth. Amy clearly wanted it, and so did Ethan. Usually when he had too much to drink.

But office romance was suicide in a line of work like theirs. It would be discovered in a flash. Picked apart. Exploited. Most likely by David himself. It was only when Ethan carpet-bombed his liver after work—take, for example, his recent adventures with the French martini—that he started to think that work didn't matter so much.

And Amy did. Very much.

The most they'd ever done, physically, was hold hands beneath a small Formica table in a crowded bar on Sansom Street. They'd gone out with a gang of four from the office: Ethan, Amy, Stuart, and some intern Stuart was trying to nail. Stuart was too busy trying to make out with the intern's right ear to notice Amy slide her hand over Ethan's, her fingers seeking purchase in the space between his. Ethan gave her a look like, *What's the deal, Felton?* She pulled his hand beneath the table and held it there, his hand cradled in hers, until Ethan became dead certain Stuart was on to them, and he excused himself to go to the men's room. Stuart never nailed the intern. Ethan and Amy never touched in quite the same way again.

This sex dream he was having was a little bit different.

Amy was wearing an oversized hotel bath towel, which quickly slipped off.

Only problem: She was working for an imaginary boss, some Alpha Chi thickneck with just the right amount of facial hair at all times. He was wearing a bath towel, too. His was not so oversized. It kind of slipped off.

Ethan, for some inexplicable reason, was standing in the hotel room with the both of them.

(Even now, Ethan knew he was dreaming—in fact, he knew he was passed out on the gray concrete landing in the fire tower with a pen sticking out of his throat. But the idea of Amy Felton in a hotel bath towel was too much of an attraction. He wanted to stay here and linger for a while.)

Naked Alpha Chi guy said to her, "Want a poke before my meeting?"

Ethan felt true panic. He didn't know what Amy was going to say. To his relief, her reply was friendly—

Tempting as that sounds, you have a meeting to attend, she said, in his dream.

—and curt.

Then Alpha Chi guy disappeared, and Amy was on the bed, and her towel was now slipping off again. She looked at Ethan. Ethan looked at her breasts, which sloped to perfect pink tips. He'd never seen them before—yet, in dreamworld logic, they seemed as familiar as the front door to his apartment.

She put her hand on his face, and said to him: "Look at me lovingly."

In the real world, somebody was touching his face, then his wrist.

Ethan knew what it was; he wasn't delusional or in some kind of fugue state. Somebody—probably a building security guard—had found him passed out and bloodied in the stairwell. The guard probably saw the pen and freaked, and was trying to find a pulse.

But Ethan wanted to keep thinking that Amy was still touching his face, imploring him to look at her.

Where was Amy?

Was she all right?

"Buddy! Are you awake, man?"

Oh yes, I'm awake. I'm back in my chemical-nerve-agent-dosed body with my bargain-basement tracheotomy. I could be spread out on a bed with Amy Felton, sans hotel bath towel. But no, I'm here. Trying to resist the urge to reach up and feel your tits.

Ethan even opened his bloodied eyes to confirm it.

I'm here, dude.

Molly flipped and twisted until all of reality was reduced to a simple series of events: concrete slapping her naked palms, concrete slapping the bottom of her bare feet. Again. And again. Somewhere, in another part of her mind, she ticked down the floors as she completed them. She didn't focus on the numbers.

She knew her mind would warn her when she was close. She focused on the concrete.

If the security guards beat her to Ethan Goins, and they'd already moved him, all was lost.

She would have let an employee escape. Operation failed.

And her mother was as good as dead.

The elevator arrived and Vincent Marella stepped in and started to push *16*. But his finger hung in the air, the slightest bit of space between the tip of his index finger and the white plastic square that would light up if he applied enough pressure.

C'mon. Push it.

C'mon.

Okay, fine. He was willing to admit it to himself. He was stalling.

He knew the call was completely different from the one he'd taken over at the Sheraton a year ago. There, it was like: Calm down a domestic disturbance. This was: dude down in the stairwell, pen in his throat. Completely different.

But the terrors were back.

With, as they say, a vengeance.

"This is stupid," he said aloud. He pushed the button.

As the elevator descended, he felt like his stomach was already a few floors below it.

Molly landed on the security guard. Or more precisely, on his back. Her feet jackhammered into him. The guard's face smashed up against cinder block. His eyes fluttered. The rough surface of the wall gouged at his cheek as he slid down. Molly quickly regained her equilibrium. The judges may have dinged her a few points, but it was still a competitive dismount.

Ethan couldn't believe what he was seeing.

Molly Lewis. David's quiet little assistant, flipping down a concrete staircase and stomping a guard into unconsciousness.

Then again, look at him. He could endorse a check with his throat.

Molly checked the guard, made sure he'd gone bye-bye, and then turned her attention to Ethan.

My God, she was here to rescue him. Who would have thought.

He tried to let his eyes do the talking: *Look, Molly. You see the pen. You probably know my deal. So you'll need to kick-start the conversation.*

Ethan had once sat next to Molly at an impromptu lunch; David had discovered this new Indian place down Twentieth Street and dragged whoever he could to try plates of biryani and seafood korma and chicken tandoori. Ethan had made exactly three attempts to initiate a conversation with Molly, and all three were about as welcome as the seafood korma was to Ethan's lower intestinal tract. (Sue him; he had a sensitive stomach.) Molly just wasn't about talking.

Apparently, she was all about flipping down concrete staircases and knocking out security guards.

"We've had a security breach upstairs. You were locked out when it began; David is dead. He placed me in charge before he died."

David? *Dead?*

But wait. Amy was second in line.

Ethan put his hand on Molly's forearm. He needed to find a way to ask about Amy.

It was as if Molly could read his mind. "Normally, Amy Felton would be in charge, but she's the one who killed David. Right now, she's missing."

No, no. That just wasn't possible. Amy? Killing *David?*

"The entire floor is on lockdown, but when I realized you were missing, I made it past the sarin bomb—which I believe was planted by Amy Felton to keep us trapped—and made my way down to you."

Amy? A traitor?

No. No way.

I was just out with her last night, drinking French martinis, doing our usual dance of sexual frustration. I would have seen it in her eyes.

Ethan was suddenly bursting with questions. It was maddening that he couldn't articulate a single one of them.

He needed to take Molly to a quiet room, away from building security, grab a legal pad and a pen—one with actual ink in it, unlike the one sticking out of his throat—and grill her. Gather the facts before acting. One thing was clear, though. They needed to operate privately. No outside interference.

The world was crashing down around the company, and if Amy was out of commission, he had to take the reins.

"Building security must *not* be involved," Molly said, as if reading his mind. "David was explicit about that."

On cue, there was a short and sharp rapping sound. Coming from the door at the top of the staircase. The entrance to the sixteenth floor.

Somebody knocking.

Building security, getting involved.

Vincent should have just opened the door right away, but the fear was back big-time. C'mon, Vincent—your goddamned partner is behind that door, guarding some loser who broke a window and tried to stab himself in the neck. Do your job and relieve him. Relieve him *now*.

But Vincent was still worried about the ape.

That ape was going to follow him around the rest of his days. Cage the ape. Do your job.

Molly needed to move *now*. One missing guard was enough. Two would send red flags up all over the building.

Okay, let's hoist Ethan up. Brace him against the wall.

Wait.

That was all wrong. Anybody coming in through that door would see Ethan's reddened eyes, the throat wound.

Turn him around. Support his weight. Think of something. *Now*.

Could the people watching the scene through her eyeglasses tell that, for the first time this morning, she was panicked? Was her face shaking?

She leaned forward quickly and whispered, "Play along," in Ethan's ear. She said it as a confidence booster. To let the men watching know that she had this under control.

Even though she didn't.

Another factor: the sarin. If Ethan had been dosed with it, there was still a risk of inhaling it. Her throat would close up.

There was only one option.

Molly sucked in enough air to inflate her lungs, but not to the point of bursting. Then she picked Ethan up from the concrete landing. He did not protest, even as she heaved him over her right shoulder.

Then she did the same with the unconscious guard, only over her left this time.

A three-way.

Paul would have found this kind of thing kinky, were he still alive.

She moved to the side and planted a foot on the first step going down.

. . .

Vincent opened the door and looked down the stairs.

Nothing. No sign of Rickards.

Wait.

Scratch that.

There was a sign. On the landing. And not a good sign.

A sign like blood.

Vincent opened his mouth, then thought better of it. What if Rickards were in trouble? Calling out his name wouldn't do any good. It might embolden the creep who had a gun to his head.

Listen to him. Gun to the head. Vincent didn't know what was going on, and already he was assuming the worst. That blood on the landing was probably from the guy with the pen in his neck. Most likely, Rickards hadn't wanted to wait. Maybe the guy was seizing. Maybe he carried the guy down to the fifteenth floor, caught an elevator there to head to the lobby, get the guy help.

So why hadn't he radioed him to say that? Rickards knew he was on his way.

Because he had a gun to his head, that's why.

Stop it.

Vincent reached for the two-way strapped to his belt. Unsnapped it.

Molly was five steps down when she heard the snap. And a footstep on concrete.

What was the snap?

Not a gun being unholstered. A nightstick being removed from a belt? Guards at 1919 didn't carry them.

Then it bumped against her cheek. It had been hanging from the unconscious guard's belt.

The radio.

Which came alive in a burst of static.

Thirty-five hundred miles away, McCoy tried to do some math.

"Number three's a big guy, probably close to two hundred pounds. And that guard looked like he was at least that. Jesus, Keene—she's hoisting over four hundred pounds of *man* on her shoulders. Is that even possible?"

"Apparently not. Look."

The view from the glasses froze in place. Then, Ethan Goins—number three—came into view. He was being placed on a concrete step. He looked confused.

"What's she doing?" McCoy asked.

"I don't think number three knows, either."

Vincent heard the return squawk of Rickards's two-way. It was directly below him.

"Andy!" he shouted, then started down the staircase, wrenching the lead sap from his duty belt. 1919 Market didn't arm their guards. It freaked the suits out too much. They didn't like the idea of working in a police state.

All he had was a sap. The weakest kind, too: flat sap with lead shot and no spring in the shank.

No match for somebody, say, with a gun to Andy Rickards's head.

Molly handed Ethan the radio, hoping he'd understand. She held up an index finger. One minute. I'll be back for you in one minute. Maybe she could get this guard stashed.

Ethan nodded.

Above, someone shouted, "Andy!"

Molly continued up, guard still slung over her shoulder. She had a decision to make. It was coming down to her mother's life, or these security guards.

Of course, there was another way.

It would be violating her orders. It would be putting the operation at risk—somewhat. Early on, when she had first contacted Boyfriend, she asked about operational priorities. They were given: sanctions first, experimentation second. By continuing to pursue the experimentation, she was putting the sanctions at risk.

If they were really watching—Boyfriend and his minders—then they'd have to understand why. And they'd have to approve.

Molly stopped midstep, then bench-pressed the guard off her shoulders and flung him down to the next landing. Her back cried out in relief. She wanted to collapse to the staircase and hoped the spasms would go away.

But there was no time for that now. She walked back down a few steps and knelt next to Ethan, who was looking at her with wide-eyed wonder. He was probably wondering what she was doing. Wasn't she supposed to be stashing the guard somewhere while he distracted the other guard?

"Ethan," she whispered. "I want you to know something." She gently placed her hands on the sides of his head.

Maybe she could salvage part of the experiment, after all.

Maybe that would count as extra credit.

A voice behind her said, "Miss, step away from that man."

The flat sap in his hand was useless, Vincent realized.

Not because he was squaring off against a gun. But because it was a girl.

A young girl.

In a skirt and long hair and bare feet, she didn't look more than twenty-one. Hell, Vincent's son would be dating girls like this in a few years.

Here she was, doting on her fallen man—and yeah, Rickards was right. The guy did have a pen sticking out of his neck. What was that about?

But in an instant, Vincent had a pretty clear picture of what was going on. The shattered glass, Rickards's message, these two kids, this fire tower . . . all of it. It was a low-budget office burglary gone wrong. Plain and simple. She probably worked here, in an office on the thirty-first floor or higher. Just a secretary, or an assistant or something. She was certainly dressed like it— skirt, blouse. Got by on a little better than minimum. Lived with her parents maybe. Dated this dopehead here—a real sweet-heart no-account type. One day, Dopehead decides he needs cash to score ecstasy, or maybe finance a deal of his own, talks his young girl into helping him break into her office. Steal a few laptops, raid the petty cash, whatever. Maybe it was heavier than that. Maybe she had the combo to a safe.

But somewhere along the way, something bad goes down. Something spooks Dopehead; he accidentally shatters a window. She freaks. They fight. He has a seizure, because he's an X-poppin' Dopehead. She knows enough to know she has to open an airway. She gives him a quick-and-dirty tracheotomy, saves his life. The unthankful creep makes her carry him down the fire tower steps, hoping to get away clean. They run into Rickards. She pleads for help. Rickards calls Vincent. Vincent agrees. The girl, desperate, pushes Rickards down the steps, still hoping they'll be able to get out of this one without her parents finding out.

And there's Rickards now, still out cold, at the bottom of the landing.

And here they are, Girlfriend and Dopehead, realizing they're done for.

"Miss," he says in the most reassuring tone he can muster, "I really need you to step away from that guy so I can help him."

Detain him.

But yeah, help him.

Dopehead deserves jail time, but he doesn't deserve to die.

Molly ignored the guard, because what she had to say to Ethan was important.

"Amy's hanging for her life outside her office window," she whispered. "She's waiting for you to save her."

Molly pulled back slightly. She wanted the fiber-optic camera in her glasses to capture everything—his reaction, her words. Maybe it would still prove useful.

Maybe these few seconds of video would be enough to get her back on track with Boyfriend.

Ethan's reaction was worth the effort. He seemed to rage against his own body. Blood seeped out of the hole in his neck, and there was a phlegmlike rattle in there. He was actually trying to talk.

"Miss, please, step away and let me help him."

Molly continued, "I'll let her know you were too busy to come up."

Ethan wasn't sure if this was another dream, because none of it made sense. What made it seem like a dream was the fact that it centered around Amy. But it all felt real. His fingertips were pressing down on the smooth concrete.

And it was the wrong woman. It was *Molly* here, touching him. Molly's bare hands, touching his cheeks. Now caressing his head, her fingers sliding behind his skull, stroking his chin with her palm.

Molly?

Molly *Lewis*?

A second before she pulled and pushed at the same time, Ethan realized this wasn't about sex.

It was about snapping his neck.

Jamie DeBroux

~~Amy Fulton~~

~~Ethan Goins~~

~~Roxanne Kirkwood~~

Molly Lewis

~~Stuart McGrane~~

Nichole Wise

. . .

The girl did exactly as Vincent asked, stepping back away from Dopehead. But something was wrong. Dopehead's head lolled to one side. It might have been his eyes playing tricks, but Vincent thought he saw him seize his girlfriend's hands on his face.

"Move away," he said. He needed to get in there, do CPR. Vincent wasn't quite sure how you did that with a sloppy tracheotomy thrown into the mix—what, do you press your thumb down on the hole in the neck? But that didn't mean he wouldn't try.

The girl stood up and seemed to be moving away.

Right until the moment she turned on Vincent. One of her hands grabbed his neck and drove him back into the cinder block wall. She squeezed *hard*.

For Vincent Marella, it was the worst possible kind of déjà vu. A little over a year ago, in the Sheraton. Wide awake, knowing what was happening to him and powerless to do anything about it. His mouth open, silently screaming for air that would not come. Consciousness being stolen from him, one oxygen-deprived brain cell at a time.

Good evening, kids, his strangler had said. He had been talking to the couple in the room. The people who had later disappeared. All because Vincent had been choked into unconsciousness, and had failed to protect them.

And it was happening again. Not by a muscular thug, but by a young girl. A girl who looked like a mild spring breeze would blow her over.

But her grip was steel. Vincent was already seeing gray spots dancing in his vision.

Then he remembered the sap.

He'd snapped it back onto his duty belt, hadn't he?

He had.

Grab it. Unsnap it. Forget she's a girl. She's trying to *kill* you, Vince. Unsnap it and get to work. Do your job, already.

Vincent unsnapped it.

Molly did not see it coming.

She had been paying half attention to the security guard, waiting for the loss of oxygen to knock him out. She kept the other half of her attention on Ethan's corpse, wondering where she could stash the body while she finished the rest of the operation. But wait; she couldn't do that. The fire. The fire was supposed to burn up everything, *including* the bodies, and if he were down here, he could be discovered. Fingerprints could be lifted. And someone with enough incentive could—

Her face felt like it exploded.

It exploded again, this time from the opposite side. Her cheekbone shattered. Her broken camera glasses flew off her face, skittered across the concrete and down three steps, landing facedown.

The security guard had a sap.

The potential skull fractures didn't worry her as much as the idea of trying to look presentable at the end of her operation. Her long hair could cover the slash trail of a bullet. It could not cover a battered face.

A battered face would not impress her employers.

Molly squeezed tighter. The guard twitched and then smashed the sap down on her forearm, numbing it instantly from the wrist to the shoulder. But she refused to let go. Molly tried to snatch his weapon from him, but the lead cracked her knuckles.

Then he brought it up again at her face, savagely. Her lips burst. A tooth shattered in her mouth.

She squeezed even tighter, careful not to kill him. Even though she wanted to. But security guards weren't part of the operation; such a sanction would be seen as sloppy.

Oh, but the urge was strong. She hadn't felt this kind of bloodlust since . . .

Since 1996.

The Olympic Games.

The bitter sting of loss.

Molly Lewis—whose birth name was not Molly Kaye Finnerty, but Ania Kuczun—tried to resist her basest instincts and stick to the operation.

Ania Kuczun not only would have crushed this man's windpipe in a matter of seconds. She would have severed and mailed his head, in a plastic-lined box, to the man's family. She would have researched and found the person who cared about him the most. She would have sent it cash on delivery.

Ania Kuczun had spent many years trying to become Molly Lewis.

She couldn't give it up now, when it mattered the most.

The life of Helen Kuczun depended on it.

Thirty-five hundred miles away, the monitor showed nothing but an extreme close-up of a concrete slab. Then, gray static.

"What's going on?" McCoy barked. He slapped the side of the table, as if that would do something.

"I'm trying another camera."

"Damn it! Tap into building security. You can do that, can't you?"

"I don't know. I'm not a tech guy."

"Get a tech guy!" McCoy caught himself. "I'm sorry."

"It's fine," Keene said, "but I'm not finding anything. What we have are access codes to the cameras on the thirty-sixth floor and not much beyond. Guess we never thought we'd need anything else."

McCoy cursed.

Vincent Marella felt his skin burst with sweat and his muscles start to flutter. He assumed this was it. In his last conscious moment he thought about his boy, and all his wild conspiracy theories. If he could be with him one last time, Vincent would place his hands on the boy's shoulders—which he remembered his own father doing to him, when it was about something important. And Vincent would tell him: *You were right.* The deck is stacked against the common man, and God bless you for asking the right questions. Keep asking them as long as you can.

Then Vincent was out.

Molly, Ania, Girlfriend. She answered to them all.

But as the guard fell to the floor, she took a few steps back, and she heard one name the loudest: *Victim.*

She felt like a victim, once again. No matter the personae she created. No matter how hard she trained. No matter how many things she learned. At her very core was the word imprinted on her DNA: *Victim.*

Bruised.

Battered.

With another busted lip. Swallowing her own blood. Feeling it burn a hole in the lining of her stomach.

Stop it. Take stock of yourself.

Ania rested on the lower step, next to Ethan's body. Her tongue found another shard of tooth; she pulled it loose with her tongue, sucked the blood from around it, then spit it at the wall. It bounced from the cinder block and landed on the guard's chest. There you go. A souvenir.

From Ania.

Forget Victim; she could reclaim her birth name now. Molly Lewis was dead. She was dead the moment she poisoned her husband, mixing the potato salad while he slept. And "Girl-friend"? After this grievous setback, she wasn't sure the name still applied.

Ania Kuczun lives.

EARLY LUNCH

You can't get a pay raise when you're angry. People will react to the negative energy and will resist you.

—STUART WILDE

Thirty-five hundred miles away, McCoy walked away from the monitors and opened the fridge. It was an American-style fridge—oversized, with a ridiculously large freezer. Neither McCoy nor Keene had ever frozen anything. It contained one item: ice cubes. McCoy scooped some out now and put them in a rocks glass, then filled it with single-malt Scotch. He put the glass to his mouth and drank steadily, as if consuming a sports drink.

In the living room, Keene stared at his partner. He hated seeing him disappointed.

Keene wanted to go over to him now, try to untangle the tight knots of muscles in his back and shoulders. That was where the stress hit him.

But Keene knew better, from experience. Best to leave the man alone.

"I'm going out for a bit," he said. McCoy didn't seem to hear him. He was busy pouring himself another Scotch.

How about you drink a Scot instead? Keene had once said, in a light moment.

Now was not the time for that.

Keene took his valise with laptop and cell, along with notepad and paper. He could work on some of the Dubai operation in a secluded booth at the pub just as well as he could in the apartment. He didn't need to start surveillance for another hour and a half.

The barman nodded to him, brought him a bag of crisps and an ice-cold orange juice. Keene was probably the only Scot within ten miles who didn't touch alcohol or red meat. He liked to keep his mind clear, his body lean. When he first started in his line of work, back when he had another name, he told himself that the drink was necessary; it kept the darkness contained in a lockbox. Slowly, he realized that the alcohol only strengthened the darkness—emboldened it. Eventually, the alcohol locked him inside the box, along with the darkness. He didn't need that again.

When Keene first met McCoy, it had boggled the man's mind.

"You're a Scot? And you don't even drink beer?"

Keene shrugged.

"So much for a drunken shag," McCoy had said.

Their relationship was a complicated one.

Keene tried to work on some of the trickier details of Dubai, but his mind kept wandering out the pub door, down the block, and four flights up. To McCoy, and his "Girlfriend." He wondered idly: Why did he pick that code name?

What puzzled him the most, however, was the former operative known as David Murphy.

McCoy had told Keene about him some time ago; Murphy was famous for stopping a 9/11-style plot a full two years *before* the original 9/11. Clinton was still in the White House; the United States was still reeling from Columbine. The plan was a hybrid: suicide bombers in twelve American cities, armed to the teeth, with bombs jacked into pulse-checking wristwatches. The bombers were told to choose the most crowded location. Reveal weapons—preferably assault rifles. (The jihadists had been paying *careful* attention to Columbine.) Take out as many people as you can, stopping only to reload. When law enforcement or armed civilians come to take *you* down, rejoice in Allah, for the watch will tell the bomb your pulse has stopped, and the bomb will do *its* job on the police and emergency technicians.

Anyway, Murphy caught wind of it through an informant, arrested one would-be bomber, then extracted the entire plot—along with names and addresses—through a method of interrogation that still had not been revealed.

In uncovering the plot, Murphy erased many, many sins.

After 9/11, Murphy had joined an organization without a name. Some wags called it "CI-6." This was a joke—a mutant blend of CIA and MI-6. Neither intelligence organization had anything to do with it, or knew much about it beyond rumor. CI-6 was another beast entirely. The blackest pocket of the blackest bag—in no visible way was it attached to any official budget line of any government.

The way Keene had heard it, CI-6 had started as a joke in the crowded upstairs bar at Madam's Organ on Eighteenth Street in Washington, D.C.

The more the story was retold, the more the details were simultaneously obscured and embellished. One current version had it that the whole thing started as a bet, much like the Vietnam War. But this much was certain: a person of political influence met up with a person of lobbying influence, had way too many pints of Pabst Blue Ribbon one night—hell, it was a blues bar, what were you supposed to do, sip Johnnie Walker Black among the civilians?—and started talking about what to do about all these goddamn terrorists. Though in the smoky haze, the word was pronounced *terrizz*. As in, *We gotta stop the got-damn terrizz.*

On a car ride to a houseboat party on the Potomac, a loose plan was formed. Secret financing secured. Types of operations determined.

"It'll be like the CIA and MI-6 got drunk and went to bed together, then didn't tell anybody the next day."

Hence, CI-6.

Pickle your brain in enough Pabst, it'll seem funny to you, too.

There was no official name for the covert offspring of that drunken evening.

Those parents weren't around to see their child take its first step; the political fixer found himself caught up in a Capitol Hill scandal soon after and was drummed out of the city posthaste. The lobbyist, too, was caught in the vacuum pull of the tidal pool. But other men were in place to handle the birth, education, and development of this fledgling life-form. The baby grew fast.

The baby grew so fast, it quickly forgot its parents.

The baby grew so large, it forgot parts of itself, like a toddler running through an antique shop. Such a baby doesn't realize that swinging its arms out willy-nilly will shatter rare teacups and serving plates. All of that is boring anyway. The fun thing is to *run*.

Guys like David Murphy were a vital part of the baby.

On the outside, Murphy had surprised his fans within the conventional intelligence world by retiring and starting a financial services company. Like, what?

He called it Murphy, Knox.

Even the name was a gag: Knox=NOCs, CIA slang for "non-official covers." Murphy and his NOCs.

Murphy had quickly become a key player in CI-6.

So had Keene, once he saw how useful he could be. How much more power he could wield working for an outfit like this.

But what was Murphy mixed up in that, suddenly, he had to

wipe out his front company? Along with more than a few of his employees, including several operatives?

This was the problem with the baby that was CI-6. An invisible structure meant a hazy sense of self. Lack of accountability.

Could a guy like Murphy just go and wipe out his own front company on a whim?

Sure he could.

But why?

And did everyone else know about it?

McCoy wouldn't be much help in this department. He was too distracted by Girlfriend. He was more about recruiting—"nurturing talent," he was fond of saying—than running operations. Keene couldn't complain; it was how they'd met. Keene had liked being wooed. But now, he worried that his man didn't have his eye on the full picture here.

Keene fired up the laptop and hit the phones. Told the barman to keep the OJ coming.

David was imagining he was inside a Wawa, and he was browsing the aisles, and he had an unlimited operational budget.

He was able to procure microwaveable hamburgers, Italian submarine sandwiches—Philadelphians called them "hoagies"—tubs of cottage cheese, ooh, cottage cheese. That suddenly sounded good. If he could get himself up off this floor, and take care of everything that needed taking care of, he'd fix the elevators and ride down to the lobby and walk out to Twentieth Street. Just a block south . . . okay, two half blocks south, if you counted the stupid little side street below Market . . . there was a Wawa, right at Twentieth and Chestnut. He sneaked down there at lunch, sometimes. A man in his position was expected to dine at one of the Market West hot spots. Truth was, he hated those places. Gimmicky names, nine-dollar cheeseburgers. He preferred to buy lunch in some common place, bring it back in a brown paper bag, feast behind his closed office door. And Wawa was one of his favorites. The refrigerated dairy section was along the right wall. He could see the stacks of 2 percent cottage cheese, blue plastic containers, stacked in the middle. Oddly enough, the whole-milk cottage cheese was too cloying, while the 1 percent skim version was too acidic. Two percent was perfection. Perfect chunky creamy goodness . . .

Someone touched his face.

"I know you're still there."

A female voice.

Someone he recognized. Sort of.

"I'm going to bring you around. But a bit of warning: This is going to hurt."

Hurt?

Hurt was fine.

As long as he woke up to a blue plastic container of Wawa 2 percent cottage cheese, already open, white plastic protective layer already peeled back, white plastic fork gently shoved into the side.

And crackers. Plenty of Nabisco saltine . . .

Nichole held the adrenaline shot two feet above David's chest, then stabbed down and thumbed the plunger.

A supersize dose of epinephrine—the so-called fight-or-flight hormone—pumped into David's heart and made a lightning tour of his circulatory system.

The reaction wasn't immediate. It took a few seconds.

But soon David was spitting blood and convulsing.

Then he said, ". . . *crackers*."

Jamie realized that he'd been holding his breath for a full minute.

Nichole didn't waste a second. She flung the empty syringe across the conference room and placed her left foot on David's throat. She applied enough pressure for him to start squirming slightly, even though he was still in the process of regaining consciousness.

"Tell me everything," she said.

"Can't . . . breathe . . ."

Jamie touched Nichole's shoulder. "Hey, you might want to ease up—"

Nichole slapped Jamie's hand away. "Don't." Then, she said to David, "Everything, or I snap your neck."

"Ffffffine."

Nichole eased up. Slightly. As far as Jamie could tell, neck-snapping was still a distinct possibility.

Jamie was still stunned, despite all that had transpired in the past thirty minutes. If you had called him at home yesterday and told him that he'd be seeing Nichole with her foot pressed against David's neck in the conference room, with Stuart's dead body lying in the corner, Jamie would have laughed. Okay, part of him would have hoped it was true. But most of him would have laughed.

Now here it was. Everything took on that harshly lit look of surreality. The hyperreal. The couldn't-actually-be-true-but-here-it-was.

Nichole was saying: "Who ordered this? And why?"

David smiled, which was creepy, because his eyes were still closed. "Who do you think?" he asked.

More foot pressure. David winced.

"I'm not asking about what I think. I'm asking about what you know. Tell me now and I'll get you the medical attention you need. Refuse and I'll be the last thing you see."

David swallowed. "I used to masturbate to your face."

A grim smile flashed on Nichole's face; then she removed her foot and straddled David's body. Both hands on the sides of his head. She turned him so they were face-to-face. Her thumbs were at his throat.

"Who is it, David? Who wants us all dead?"

"You're looking at him, big girl."

Nichole shook her head. "You report to somebody."

"At least I'm not a mole."

"Who do you report to?"

"A mole with a wet hole. Nee-COLE."

She dug her thumbs in deeper. David gasped, but he continued speaking anyway.

"You're out of your league, Nichole. Why do you think it's been so hard for you to penetrate me? But I bet I could penetrate *you*."

"Tell me about Molly."

"Oh. Yeah. Her."

"Who is she?"

"Your guess is as good as mine."

"Liar."

Nichole removed her hands, then paced around the conference room.

"What about the lockdown? Tell me how to reverse it."

"Since you're giving orders," David said, "let me give you one of my mine. A Big Mac. Two patties, special sauce, lettuce, cheese, all of that good stuff."

Nichole drove a fist into his face.

It was an audacious move, David thought—punching someone in the face who's already been shot in the head.

A bullet, lodged in the skull, could easily loosen and work its way into brain tissue, making him a drooling side of beef on a conference room floor.

Perhaps Nichole didn't care.

Maybe the crack about the "hole" was a step too far.

Maybe it was his Big Mac order.

Thing was, David wasn't trying to be difficult. Well, maybe a little, but it was mostly the truth: He was absolutely ravenous. He'd been starving for months now, the hunger inside him mutating into a constant, sentient, insatiable thing. Telling his stomach no would be like telling his lungs not to crave air.

He didn't know how or why it had begun, but he realized that something was amiss when he drove home after work one night, pulled into a Bertucci's off Huntingdon Pike, ordered two large pizza pies, fully loaded, along with three orders of garlic-and-butter breadsticks, then transported his bounty to his kitchen table and methodically consumed everything—every shred of dough, cheese, sun-dried tomato, shiitake mushroom, red pepper, black olive, and crumbled sausage—within an hour. No TV. No newspaper. No thoughts about the workday. Nothing to distract him but the pizza and breadsticks.

And at two in the morning, David had risen from his bed and eaten six Snickers bars he'd stashed in the freezer.

This had been in early June.

Since then, his binges had come at unexpected times—along with his sex binges. Always with hookers or strippers, in his car or the champagne rooms of allegedly upscale sex clubs. David had to call his bank to ask that his ATM max withdrawal be raised from seven hundred dollars to a thousand dollars. He never knew when the urge would overwhelm him, and somehow, seven hundred dollars just didn't go far enough in the champagne rooms.

Nobody at work suspected; his employees didn't usually make the rounds at suburban delis, chain restaurants, or brick-oven pizza parlors—or downtown strip joints or fetish clubs.

You couldn't tell by looking at David, either. His frame was still finely muscled and compact—essentially the same as the day he entered freshman year at Penn. His metabolism, always efficient, had shifted into overdrive to accommodate the influx of calories.

His penis was raw, but even that seemed to heal quickly.

David began to suspect he was losing his mind.

It had been known to happen in this kind of business.

By late July David decided to purge himself of the hunger. It was stress-related, he'd decided, and he needed to detox his body and mind. After a few quiet inquiries, he settled on an ayurvedic spa in southern India, where a radical panchakarma treatment might be what he needed to shake the cravings. He'd booked the flights and the package and told Amy Felton to take care of things; he had suddenly been called away. It was monsoon season in India. Tourists avoided areas like south India this time of year, but for David's purposes it was perfect. The harsh conditions were what he needed. As well as dinners of rice gruel. Intense early morning yoga sessions. Forced vomiting. Leeches. Pummeling. Herb steam baths. And finally, shirodhara, in which warm oil was poured over your forehead in a slow, steady, and potentially maddening stream. It was the panchakarma version of Chinese water torture, and it was exquisitely painful.

Fourteen days later—the required minimum stay—David emerged from the resort trembling but hopeful.

On his way home, he made a pit stop in Austin, and ate five pulled-pork sandwiches along with fries and enough frosty pints of Shiner Bock to require an extra night's stay in an airport hotel to sleep off his drunkenness. In the morning, he consumed four egg-and-bacon breakfasts, with croissants and extra-strong coffee.

His hunger was bottomless. Hopeless.

A few days later, he'd received instructions.

And then he understood.

Somehow, his body had anticipated all of this. His labor of

five years, building Murphy, Knox, needed to be destroyed. And he, along with it.

So it made sense. His body was merely trying to experience every last sensory detail it could before his eyelids closed a final time, and the heavy black curtain covered his face, and the data bank that was his brain flickered into nothingness.

Whether or not Nichole Wise cared if he lived or died, there was something more important. He didn't care either, beyond finishing this final operation.

And the longer David kept them here, on this floor, the more likely that would be.

His need for one last success was as sharp as the hunger.

Ania's palms and soles still burned and ached from racing down to the sixteenth floor of the north fire tower. But that was nothing compared with the pain of the return trip to thirty-six.

The events of the past thirty minutes had taken their toll on her body, already weakened from the soft years of living as "Molly Lewis." She'd tried to maintain her core strength, and she had, to a large degree, thanks to regular visits to the franchise gym closest to their home. Paul had been very supportive, renewing her membership every year for Christmas, even though he'd allowed his own waistline and chin to lie fallow. In bed, he constantly complimented her body—its compactness, its suppleness. Paul would suggest positions, and she'd agree to them, just for the exercise. The trick was having him hold steady. Often, it was over before her heart rate even peaked. But this meager regimen was no match for the long hours in front of the plasma television, or the constant barrage of carbs and sugar and fat that were the main ingredients of the meals Paul preferred. Pizza. Chinese take-out. His beloved Polish potato salad.

As a result, her battle with Nichole Wise—not so much a

battle as a chance to flex muscles she hadn't used in a long while—left her more winded than she would have expected.

And the abuse she'd taken in the past ten minutes—hurtling her body down endless sets of concrete staircases, hoisting two male bodies on her shoulders, snapping a neck, enduring a beating with a lead sap—had weakened her severely.

Ania, what has become of you?

Ania, potential Olympic gold medal winner?

Ania, whose body was both the source of her greatest pain and the key to her escape?

But walking up the south fire tower stairs with the corpse of Ethan Goins over her right shoulder, endless staircase after endless staircase, every weakness pronounced itself.

She'd made her way across the elevator bank to the south tower—away from the sarin. But it didn't make the flights up any easier.

Perhaps the worst thing about it was how Ethan's head rocked from side to side, like a bowling ball in a sack slung over your shoulder. Gravity pulled it one way. Then another. Then an entirely different way. It was unpredictable.

Ania took comfort in what would happen once she reached the thirty-sixth floor. If those watching had been satisfied with her performance on the landing, then there was not much left to accomplish.

She needed only to release the belt buckle holding Amy Felton in place, and drag her back into her office. She suspected she'd be dead from fright. If not, another neck snap, and she could finally join her beloved Ethan.

David was in the conference room, paralyzed, awaiting final interrogations. There were three questions she needed to ask, and then she could end his life, too.

And then it would be time to collect Jamie.

Most likely, he'd passed out, and was still in the empty office where she'd left him. If he'd wandered away, he'd find nothing but horrors. Either way, she would find him somewhere on thirty-six, docile, awaiting rescue. *Her* rescue. Repairs to his hand would need to be made, but that wouldn't take long. Ania had made clean, precise cuts down the lengths of his fingers. When they'd healed, she'd kiss the scars. Her lips would be the first sensations he'd feel. She'd encourage him to write again. Write what he wanted. Not press releases.

In Europe, he'd be free to write whatever he liked.

She hoped he'd get along with her mother.

Nichole decided to start with the fingers. Maybe he was paralyzed for real; maybe he wouldn't feel a thing. But she'd make him tell her what was going on. Whoops, David, there goes your ring finger. And most of the pinkie. Want to try for a thumb? After a while, he had to start caring.

And start telling her how to bring this floor out of lockdown.

"God, what are you doing?"

Jamie, the drone. Watching her hold the gun to David's hand, placing the barrel at the spot where the index finger met palm.

Jamie, cradling his own hand protectively.

"You can't do that," he said.

"You want to get out of here, don't you?" Nichole asked. "I need him to start giving me answers."

She pulled the trigger.

Almost at the same time Jamie said, "No!"

David appreciated the concern from Jamie; he really did. But there was no need. He was more or less numb from the neck down.

As a result, his body was vaguely aware of the loss. A finger was nothing to take lightly. Especially his index finger—one of the more useful digits of the human hand. But it wasn't as if David could move his hand anyway. He told his body this, and his body shrugged and said, Hey, it's your body.

David gritted his teeth and pretended to be in some kind of pain. He even winced. Showmanship to the end.

What did the Moscow Rules say?

Use misdirection, illusion, deception.

"It's your thumb next," he heard her say.

Sure, that would be natural.

Maybe she planned on doing all ten fingers, which would be wonderful. The more time Nichole spent torturing him, the less time she had to make it off this floor. That was the only thing he cared about now; everybody staying on the floor until the explosives did their job.

"Two seconds to decide, David."

His glanced at his hand, and saw Nichole had a gun pointed at the base of his thumb this time. She was bringing out the big hurt early. It was best to start with a small finger, because when you feel how bad it hurts to lose, say, a pinkie, the pain of losing a thumb or index finger seems unfathomable.

But hey, it was her show.

David was finished being her mentor.

Meanwhile, Jamie looked sick to his stomach.

"Jamie," he said, "if there's still champagne and orange juice on the table, I suggest you mix yourself a drink."

David would rather see Jamie fall asleep than burn up alive. Or worse—try to leap from the windo—

BLAM!

Ah.

The thumb.

. . .

Thirty-five hundred miles away, McCoy finally figured out how to tap into the building's security cameras. There was nothing of interest in the north fire tower. He found what he wanted in the south tower.

Girlfriend.

Dragging the corpse of Ethan Goins up one flight of concrete stairs after another, which had to be a real pain in the ass. But McCoy knew—and Girlfriend knew—that leaving his body in the fire tower wouldn't work. It needed to be on the thirty-sixth floor. Burned up with the rest of the bodies. That was the operation.

He also knew Girlfriend must be bitterly disappointed—she'd had other plans for Mr. Goins.

She must be a little worried. Her audition, so far, was more than a little shaky.

And she had started out so strong.

The arrangement had been simple: Execute Murphy, then demonstrate her skills on those present. One by one, over the course of an hour or so. Nothing terribly fancy, but demonstrating her varied abilities, knowing she was being observed on the network of fiber-optic cameras covering the office.

If Girlfriend's demonstration was impressive enough, she would receive the tools to escape the floor. Everything above thirty would burn. She would be extracted from the city, and given her reward: a promotion.

The pay hike wasn't enough to retire to a life of coconuts and limes and backrubs on some tropical island, but it was enough to change your perspective on life. Many people coveted leadership positions within CI-6, even though the agency had no official name or structure. Faith in CI-6 leadership was much like the nation's faith in the American dollar: powered by sheer will and absolutely nothing tangible like a congressional mandate. (Hah!) Still, the power and resources available to leadership were astounding.

For Girlfriend, ascending the ranks had more practical appeal. A promotion meant she could choose her location. In this case, Europe. She desperately longed to return to the continent. McCoy had enjoyed reading her screeds about the state of the American city, particularly Philadelphia, encoded in their communications over the past few months. *They murder the young here,* she once wrote. *But most people care more about the sports teams.*

It also meant she could afford to take her mother out of the assisted-living hellhole in Poland and put her somewhere to die with dignity. Maybe even prolong her life by a few months, or as much as a year.

Girlfriend wasn't about the coconuts and backrubs.

Or was she?

That was the puzzling thing about the events of the morning. It had gotten off to a rocky start, with one of David's younger reports . . . who was it . . . ah, Stuart McCrane, actually drinking the poisoned mimosa with little to no prompting. Stuart must have been a Boy Scout or an altar boy.

Then there was Ethan Goins, who had failed to report to the conference room on time.

In her defense, Girlfriend had tried to salvage the situation at the last minute:

Should I look for him?

No, no. We can start without him.

Are you . . .

I am.

Once Stuart was dead, it was too late to search for Ethan. The operation had begun.

This had radically altered Girlfriend's operational plan. She'd been saving Stuart and Ethan for later. In fact, she'd ranked the direct reports, from hardest to kill to easiest:

1. Murphy
2. Felton
3. Goins
4. Wise
5. Kurtwood
6. McCrane
7. DeBroux

Murphy had been the real worry. Miss your opportunity with this guy and watch out. Girlfriend would have spent the rest of the morning running throughout the office, ducking and hiding, fighting for her life. And, most likely, would have lost.

McCoy should know.

So killing Murphy instantly was a necessity. Girlfriend had to lay the groundwork for weeks to pull off that kind of surprise. And she did.

Not only that, but she'd pulled off a daring move that strained credibility when it was first pitched:

I will shoot him and paralyze him. Not kill him.

And right before the end, I will interrogate him.

He will tell me everything.

The last part remained to be seen, but as far as McCoy could tell, Murphy *was* paralyzed, and not yet dead. Props to Girlfriend.

And at that moment, Girlfriend's prospects seemed bright, despite the McCrane and Goins snafus.

Girlfriend immediately proceeded to Amy Felton, and carried out her neutralization as planned.

McCoy liked that one a lot.

Tip to employees everywhere: *Never tell your boss you're afraid of heights.* Especially if he's the kind of guy who'll write it down on a performance review.

But then came the problem: Ethan was missing. He was supposed to be next. In fact, the whole thing with Amy Felton *depended* on Ethan being next.

Big bad Ethan was sweet on Amy.

Aw.

Ethan Hawkins Goins, former Special Forces, had carried out some of the grisliest and most creative executions of Afghan warlords in the early days of Operation Enduring Freedom. His skill under extreme duress had brought him to the attention of CI-6. A loner by nature, he happily joined, using Murphy, Knox as a cover between operations. Ethan was a fierce warrior. Physically, Girlfriend was no match for him.

The thing was, Amy Felton looked a lot like the high school girlfriend who'd dumped Ethan's butt senior year, right before going off to Ivy League school in Rhode Island. McCoy even had someone in research dig up a yearbook; the resemblance *was* striking.

What was funny about the nonaffair—painstaking surveillance had revealed that Ethan and Amy had never kissed, let alone done the deed—was that both assumed such an affair would be against the "rules." As if an agency that didn't officially exist could have a policy on employees dating each other?

Such a situation, however, could be seen as a source of weakness.

Girlfriend, too, had glommed this from one of David Murphy's performance reviews.

The way to break through Ethan's defenses, Girlfriend reasoned, was to show him his beloved hanging upside down, thirty-six stories above the sidewalk.

Stun, then kill.

Then finish off Felton.

With Ethan gone, though, weakened by the sarin blast in the fire tower, dispatched by Girlfriend in a spectacularly uncreative fashion—did anyone snap necks anymore?—that plan was gone.

Girlfriend, though, was clearly trying to salvage what she could of the plan. Maybe she wanted to show off Ethan's limp body to Amy, right before she killed her. Maybe she thought that would count for something.

McCoy leaned back in his chair, thinking about that.

Would it?

Ania reached the south fire tower landing on thirty-six on the verge of collapse. Then she remembered: the sarin bomb.

Oh, the work never ends.

She had not planned on going near the sarin bombs. They were Murphy's idea of fun, not hers.

And she thought her plans would circumvent the need to deal with them.

Not so.

Ania dropped Ethan's corpse on the landing and flipped open a compartment on her wrist bracelet and removed a tiny pair of spring-loaded scissors. She'd found them in a freebie corporate gift—a Swiss Army "card," slim enough to fit in a wallet, but illegal to carry on airplanes—that had arrived at Murphy, Knox. It had been intended for Murphy; she kept it for herself. It came loaded with miniature versions of useful, simple tools. Toothpick. Nail file. Pen. Scissors. Her bracelets were full of ordinary tools like these. They tended to be the best.

It was difficult to see the device from her perspective. Ania rarely thought her height was a problem—until situations like these. There were no stepladders, no boxes. She had to improvise.

Ethan, from shoulder to hip, would be just about the right height.

She dragged him across the landing, propped him against the metal door, then leaped onto his shoulders. There was the slightest moment of adjustment, of balancing. Then she stood tall. Perfectly poised. Ethan's shoulders felt bony beneath her feet.

For a moment, she imagined Ethan's corpse coming to life, grabbing her by the ankles, and flinging her body down to the concrete steps. Then he'd be on her, teeth gnashing at the flesh of her throat, breath hot, and eyes closed.

Even as a child, Ania suffered from an overactive imagination. It was what she possessed instead of toys. Now, she reassured herself: Ethan would not be waking up. She had snapped his neck cleanly. Thoroughly.

Focus on the task at hand, Ania.

She gave the device a proper examination. It seemed fairly simple: wires running to a power source, another to a sensor on the door, and a few others probably meant as decoys.

But there, on a yellow wire, David Murphy's perverted sense of humor manifested itself. Printed on the side of the wire: CUT ME.

Murphy delighted in mind games. His performance reviews were just one outlet. Every casual encounter in the office turned into a psychological battle in miniature. Murphy's tools were the cruelest of all: questions designed to both raise your defense and open a weakness simultaneously, forcing you to defend a position or statement while sowing the seeds of doubt in your brain. Over the course of the past few months, Ania had detected a pattern:

There was no pattern.

The correct answer was, almost without fail, the most obvious one. And the ones that weren't obvious actually revealed themselves to be obvious later, with a little hindsight.

You went scrambling around, trying to outrun him, outthink him, and usually the right answer was your gut instinct, the first answer on your lips. The one he tricked you out of.

Ania wondered if the same would be true with these wires. Was the CUT ME a note to himself? Or did he expect someone to make it out here and try to disable the device, and knew that a message like CUT ME would drive that person mad?

Thirty-five hundred miles away, McCoy turned his attention to the other monitor. The one showing the increasingly weird scene in the conference room. Where Nichole Wise was torturing her boss by shooting his fingers off, one at a time.

Such a waste.

In the second monitor: Wise was straddling Murphy, contemplating another finger. It was hard to tell, but it looked like it was two fingers gone: index finger and thumb. Murphy wouldn't be snapping his fingers to the oldies ever again.

Meanwhile, speaking of the digitally impaired, DeBroux was standing in the corner, clutching his injured hand to his chest. Another of Girlfriend's clumsy little dismounts.

Her own weakness.

Girlfriend was supposed to save him until the end. Like, hello, #7 on the list? Instead, she sliced open his fingers, distracting her from Wise, who was able to exact some punishment before being taken down. Even then, it was only temporary.

The impromptu torture of DeBroux also prevented Girlfriend from dispatching #5, Roxanne Kurtwood. Granted, she was a low-level target, but she was supposed to have been used for the audition, not accidentally neutralized by her own partner.

All told, Girlfriend could boast only one and a half kills out of a potential seven: Ethan (and that was a sloppy, old-school kill) and Murphy, her first. Time was running out. And one of her remaining targets—the one she had failed to kill—had access to two weapons. Not exactly a résumé-builder.

Maybe Keene was right. He did fall in love way too fast.

Ania held her breath, closed her eyes, and then cut the wire that read CUT ME.

Not that these measures would do a thing to protect her from a burst of weaponized sarin. It was human reflex. Over the years she'd learned to keep many things under control, but sometimes, humans needed to flinch. She allowed herself the luxury.

The device did nothing.

Murphy, again.

She leaped from Ethan's shoulders. Without her to balance it, the corpse slid off to the right, his head smacking against a red water main before spinning around and face-planting onto the concrete slab.

Sorry, Ethan. One more stop before you can rest and await your cremation.

Inside your girlfriend's office.

That was the only way to salvage a small part of the original plan. Haul Amy Felton back inside, and allow her to gaze upon the corpse of her beloved. Wait for the reaction, which would be captured on the fiber-optic cameras.

Ania hoped she had enough left in her for a decent scream.

Then . . . execute her. Whatever method came to mind would be fine. Maybe Felton would kill herself when confronted with the corpse of her beloved. Wouldn't that be something?

It was coming down to the end, anyway, and thanks to Ethan's adventures in the fire tower, security was blown. She needed to wrap up.

Prepare for travel—herself *and* Jamie.

Then move on to the conference room, and complete her final transaction with David Murphy.

Ania opened the fire tower door quickly, scanned both sides of the hallway. Clear. She propped the door open with her foot and dragged out Ethan's corpse.

She was too weak to heave him over her shoulders again. Her trapezius muscles had been worked beyond failure; even Paul's kinky demands had not been enough to keep her body in the shape she desired. Another reason to leave America, and its slothful lifestyle, as quickly as possible.

Just a little longer now, she told herself. Down the hall, through the door, a quick left—and if all was clear—three doors down to Amy's office. Then no more carrying bodies. No more physical exertion, beyond strapping the escape gear to her body.

And plucking David Murphy's eyes from his face.

Crushing his skull.

Running her fingers through his brains.

Hearing the sound of the boom, hot and furious, below them all.

Keene was on his second glass of orange juice when his source called back.

"Working on a Saturday, are you?" said a male voice with a Geordie accent.

"Oh, is it Saturday?"

"Funny. I have what you need."

They were speaking through a VoIP connection, scrambled and rescrambled a half dozen times between their two locations.

Ordinarily, VoIP was about as a secure as a college sophomore with two roofies at the bottom of her pint glass. Unless, that is, you had encryption and cryptographic software not available to the general public. Which could make VoIP remarkably secure, especially when considering that most intelligence agencies would no sooner tap a VoIP connection than tap a set of two soup cans and string.

Keene was a bit of a VoIP fanatic. It was his favorite way to communicate, short of encrypted e-mails. He *hated* cell phones.

"Shall I send you a research packet?" his source asked.

"Yes. But how about some highlights."

"Now?"

"I'm insanely curious."

"Fine. Your boyfriend there . . ."

Keene chuckled.

"What?"

"Nothing. Just your choice of words. I'll tell you later."

"You say that as if we'll ever be in the same room again."

"So bitter. Please continue."

"Your man? He's not telling you everything about Philadelphia."

"Really."

"If someone gave the order to dismantle that company, it didn't come from us."

"The orders mentioned a bit more than *dismantle*."

"I know."

"Who could authorize something like that?"

"Who couldn't?"

Just as Keene had suspected. You try keeping a chain of command together in an organization that didn't exist.

"What else can you tell me?"

"This will all be in the research packet, but it appears that our company in Philadelphia flew a bit too close to the sun."

"How so?"

"Financing something they really shouldn't have. A kind of weapon and tracking device rolled into one."

"Which we didn't authorize."

"It didn't come from us."

Damn it.

"Look," his source said, "if you're planning on going to Philadelphia, don't. There are already alarm bells going off. If I were you, I'd stay by the sea."

Keene thanked his source, made vague plans about meeting up for a drink in Ibiza one of these years. "Sure, Will, I'll be here holding my breath while booking the plane ticket online," his source replied. Keene pressed the cold glass of orange juice to the side of his face. He felt feverish.

Ania dropped Ethan in front of Amy's door. Inside her bracelet was a master key for every office on the floor. She'd made it her first day of work. Turned out to be relatively useless. For an intelligence organization, people here had a funny way about not locking their doors. Too many of them were probably raised in the American Midwest.

Mainline Protestants. Way too trusting.

Once inside, she dragged Ethan's body into the office, closed the door behind her. Locked it, just in case, even though there was nobody left on the floor to check on her. Unless Jamie had regained consciousness.

Even if he had, that would be fine. This could be part of his education.

Ania walked over to the window. No point in arranging Ethan's body if Amy had already died of fright. She gripped the leather belt. It lifted far too easily.

Ania peered over the edge of the window.

Amy was gone.

. . .

The conference room door slammed open. Amy Felton staggered inside and dropped to her knees.

"Where is she?"

"Amy?" Nichole said, lowering her pistol. "Where were *you*?"

Jamie was just as surprised. For a moment, he forgot about his throbbing hand and considered this new development. Good God—Amy was still alive. Had anyone else made it, too? Like Ethan?

"Where is she?" Amy repeated, and this time it was a bit of a shriek.

"Who?"

"That bitch."

"She got to you, too, huh?"

"We need to kill her. *Now.*"

Amy was pale and trembling, but also looking like she could tear a person in half—the long way. She leaned against the conference room wall and allowed herself to ease down it, gently touching down and placing her palms against the floor. Her fingers clutched at the carpet.

Nichole left David and, pistol still in hand, approached Amy.

"We need to show our cards," Nichole said. "We all know what this place is, but I'm not sure whose side we're playing on."

"You know who we work for," Amy said.

"No," Nichole said, then swallowed. "I'm CIA."

If Nichole was expecting a look of surprise, she didn't get it.

"Well," Amy said, "I'm not."

"I know. You're CI-6."

"There is no CI-6."

"You're right," Nichole said. "After today."

"Look, forget this for now. What we have is a homicidal she-bitch out there, trying to kill us all."

"One of yours, no doubt," Nichole said.

"There are only two sides here. Hers and ours. Help me take care of her, we'll sort this out later."

"Either you're against the terrorist, or you're with her."

"That's funny."

Nichole thought it over. "What do you have in mind?"

"There are at least two guns in here, right?"

"Three. David's, Molly's, and my own."

"Ammo?"

"Mine's almost spent. I used two bullets on David's hand. But Molly only used one, as far as I can tell."

"Then we go out there, flank her, then kill her. Jamie here can guard David."

Jamie, who had been listening to this exchange and trying to exact a single shred of sense from it, cleared his throat. "You know, um, this Jamie guy? He's still in the room."

Nichole ignored him, and asked Amy, "Is he one of yours, too?"

"What do you mean?"

"He claims to be a civilian. Is he?"

Amy looked at Jamie. "Yes. As far as I know."

"Wonderful."

On the floor, David started to place another food order. Burger King this time. *Two Whoppers, extra onions, plenty of pickles, along with fries.* He started murmuring about Burger King allegedly cooking the best-tasting fries of all the fast food chains, but that was bull, because none could hold a salt shaker to McDonald's.

"What's wrong with him?" Amy asked.

"You were there when he was shot in the head, weren't you?"

"I didn't know that made you hungry."

Amy and Nichole eyed each other. They looked like two college students stuck in a group project who both clearly hated group projects.

"I'm not sure about you and a gun," Nichole said.

"There's two of us. One of her. It's simple."

"You don't understand. About thirty minutes ago, I fired six shots at her, point-blank, and they went through her like she was a ghost."

"She's flesh and blood. She can be killed."

"Hey," Jamie said. "You don't need to kill anybody."

Nichole ignored him.

"You even field-rated?" she asked Amy.

"I can shoot."

"Hey!" Jamie shouted. "She's our co-worker. She's confused. She needs help. You can't just go and kill her!"

Had everyone gone insane? Why weren't they even responding to him?

Nichole sighed.

"I can do this," Amy said. "I *have* to do this. Even if I die doing it."

"Fine. We do this, we come back here for answers. If you cross me, you *will* die."

Amy knew death.

Hanging upside down, it was easy to spot death.

It was right there. Thirty-six stories below.

Death was a city sidewalk.

Or maybe death was the space between. Even after the fact, it was hard to decide.

Obsessed with heights, Amy had read about the jumpers at the World Trade Center. Oh, so many hours fixed on the image of the infamous "Falling Man"—the anonymous human being who had leapt from one of the burning floors and had been captured by a photographer at a particular moment in time: 9:41:15 A.M. on September 11, 2001. In that moment, all looked strangely ordered, composed. The lines of the building, the lines of his body. One leg, tucked up slightly. The Falling Man looked like he was floating. Frozen in space, as if he were in complete control. *If I just spread my arms and will it, I will stop falling.* This, of course, wasn't the truth.

The more Amy read, the more she understood the true horror. The photograph, which appeared on the front pages of a dozen newspapers on the morning of September 12, 2001, was a piece of freak luck. Photographers were trained to look for symmetry, shapes. At that moment, the Falling Man was in perfect harmony with his surroundings. But the outtakes from the same sequence—snapped almost robotically—reveal the truth. There's nothing symmetrical about falling to your death from a height like the 105th floor of the North Tower. It is a fast and horrific and chaotic death—death at 9.8 meters per second.

That's what death looked like.

That's what Amy Felton stared at for the better part of an hour.

No, that wasn't quite true. She had passed out for much of it.

What brought her back was Ethan.

He was alive in this building. She had no doubt about that. He was smart—so smart. He saw this coming somehow. Showed up to work, just like her, put his bag down, fired up his computer, but noticed something off. A little detail. Which was just like Ethan.

Hanging upside down, she remembered going to the door before being distracted by Molly. Calling out to see if anyone (Ethan?) was there.

It was Ethan behind that door. She knew it now.

And she left him behind.

Yes, death was there. Thirty-six floors below. But it wasn't up here with her. Not yet.

She was closer to Ethan than to death.

Amy sucked in warm air and prepared to sit up, that's it, just think of sitting up, just once, and grabbing hold of the window frame. You only have to grab it once. Pull yourself inside. Kill that murderous cunt. Find Ethan.

Now, standing in the hallway with a gun in her hands, she was ready for the next part.

CLEANUP

Down the hall, Amy saw a blur of motion. No. Not a blur.

Molly.

Amy squeezed the trigger. There was a spray of wood trim and drywall. Molly spun with the blast and bounced off the wall behind her, then dropped out of sight.

"Get down!" Amy cried.

They fell to the floor, guns pointed away from each other.

"Think I got her."

"You sure?"

"We need to look."

"I'll do it," Nichole said.

She crawled on her hands and knees to the edge of the hallway. Glanced around the corner, then ducked her head back in.

"I see legs."

"Molly?"

"I think so. The woman up there is not wearing shoes. When I encountered Molly an hour ago, she didn't have any shoes."

"That's her, then."

"Whoever it is, I'm going to cripple her. A bullet in the ankle will slow her down. We stand up, flank her, it's over."

"We need to kill her."

"No," Nichole warned. "She has to answer for this."

Amy gave her a crooked smile. "You're the CIA agent." She said it in a tone that sounded more like, *You're the idiot.*

"That's right," Nichole said. "I am."

Nichole held up her gun, then flung herself into the hallway. Arm extended, lining up a shot. Looking for that leg. Looking for that piece of ankle.

Instead of firing, she cursed.

"What?" Amy whispered.

Nichole pushed herself off the carpet and back to her original position. Amy didn't need her to say anything, really. She knew what had happened.

The legs were gone.

Ania was lucky in a way. The bullet had passed straight through skin and muscle of her left shoulder. No bone. No joints. No place that couldn't be endured, and later, repaired.

But she was spectacularly unlucky in that the bullet spun her and smashed her against the wall. Muscles that had already been in extremis now refused to function. She lay on the teal blue carpet, partially writhing in agony—this bullet hurt—and unable to execute a simple bodily command, such as: *You must crawl away from this hallway—NOW.*

Someone out there in the hallway had a gun.

Her guess was Amy.

Oh, how she'd underestimated that woman.

Amy Felton was a database warrior, an operations center soldier. There was no evidence she'd actually ever *handled* a gun before.

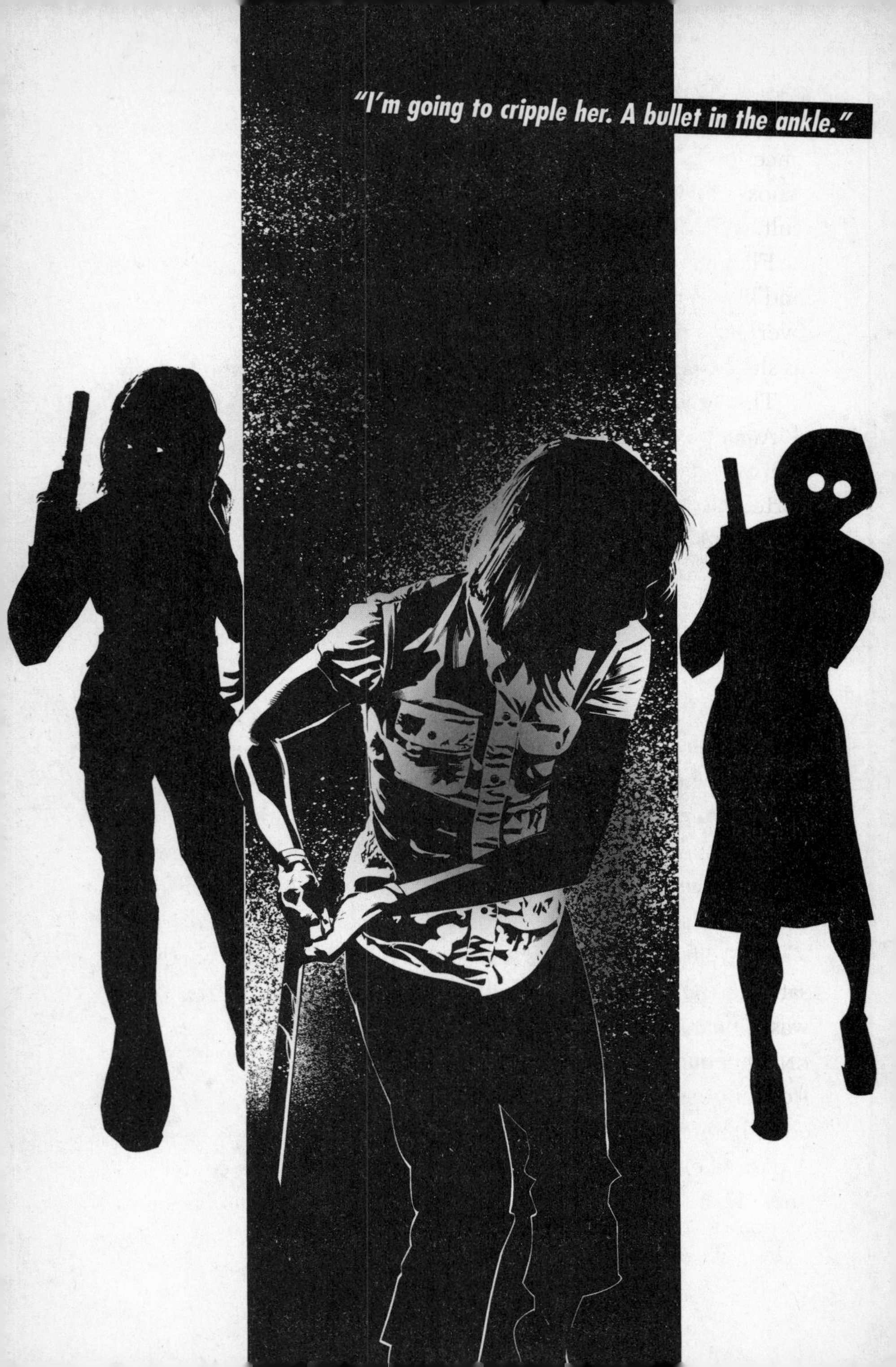
"I'm going to cripple her. A bullet in the ankle."

But it was entirely possible she'd had years of field experience, under a different name, before taking a job with Murphy, Knox. In which case, Ania's job became considerably more difficult.

Flipped over on her belly, Ania was able to use her elbows and knees to clear the hallway in a matter of seconds. She rolled over into the assistants' area, nudged the door closed as quietly as she could.

This bought her a little time.

Ania hated the assistants' area. It was a multipurpose part of the office meant for transcribers, researchers, and other assorted temps. David hired based on a tit-to-hip ratio, as well as eyes. Men rarely set foot in the assistants' area; the domain belonged to women David could conceivably fall into bed with easily and without future entanglement.

Not that David ever did. Far as Ania could discern, he kept his office alliances limited, seeking release elsewhere in the city—usually from personal ads in the back of local alternative newsweeklies. She'd once found a ripped-out square of newspaper tucked in his DayMinder: "Let me swallow your Tastee Throat Yogurt." There was a number printed on the ad. Someone—presumably David—had underlined it twice.

Ania was glad she would be killing David later.

But now it was Amy's turn.

The assistants' area was utterly devoid of weapons. Used PCs sat on top of Formica cubicle desks. Roll-out chairs. Plastic wastebaskets. Ceramic coffee mugs emblazoned with MURPHY, KNOX: PROUD TO CALL THE CITY OF BROTHERLY LOVE HOME . . . 5 YEARS RUNNING! Black plastic in-boxes. A wall of cork, painted pale blue, with pushpins grouped in one corner. A paper trimmer.

A paper trimmer.

Ania quickly examined the handle, the blade, the joint.

Her left arm was useless for the moment.

But her right . . .

She flipped open a compartment on her wrist bracelet and produced a mini Phillips-head screwdriver. She immediately set to work.

She could hear someone approaching.

Nichole motioned to Amy: *the assistants' area.* Amy nodded. There were two ways into the assistants' area: the entrance closest to David's office and another entrance near the central cubicles. Amy took the one near David's office. Nichole covered the other.

A thin trail of blood led to the door closest to Nichole.

Molly was shot.

Molly was bleeding.

Molly was trapped.

Molly was *screwed.*

Ania loosened the fourth screw and flicked it away. The blade was heavy in her hands, the edge sharp. It would take effort to swing the blade with only one arm. But the exertion would be worth it: The weight of the steel would drive the edge even farther into whatever it encountered.

Maybe a human neck.

A face.

They didn't plan it, but Amy and Nichole opened both doors at the same time.

First thing that moved, Amy decided, was getting shot to hell. Even though she had precious few bullets in her gun. But all she needed was one. One shot could flush out her quarry. And once she showed herself, Amy would wrap her hands around the bitch's neck and squeeze and spit in her face until she . . .

Ania heard footsteps to her left.

And to her right.

The ones to the left sounded closer.

She held the heavy blade high.

Stared at the carpet. Waited for a shadow to appear.

Nichole used the classic two-hand stance, gun out in front, ready to blast away at anything hostile. This morning, Molly Lewis certainly qualified.

She'd ducked away once before. She wouldn't this time.

Nichole was thinking about a particular button on Molly's perfect white blouse. It gave her a target. The button that rested a few inches to the left of her heart. Aim for the button, drift right, then blast away. She fixated on that button.

She fixated so much, she didn't fully notice when something cold and wet lashed across her wrists.

Ow.

What had hit her hands?

Oh God.

No.

Nichole staggered backwards.

Where . . .

. . . were her hands?

Ania felt the gunmetal on the nape of her neck. Heard the click.

"Freeze," Amy said.

Still another mistake, Ania realized. Up until a minute ago, she thought she only had one person stalking her. There had been two. Nichole Wise. And Amy Felton.

Nichole had been easy—one swing. Now she was either in shock or busy searching the floor for her hands.

But that had left Ania wide open.

From behind.

And Amy had taken full advantage.

The blade in Ania's hands was too heavy. By the time she swung it even a quarter of the way, Amy could blast her spinal cord to pieces.

"Drop it."

Ania did. The floor of this part of the office, a shared work-space, was covered in linoleum. The heavy blade landed with a dull thud.

"Hands above your head. Lock your fingers together."

Then, she called out, "Nichole? You with me?"

This was all wrong. Somehow Nichole Wise survived her deathblow, and Amy Felton had overcome her fear of heights. Two more disappointments in a long string of them. Had they caught all of that on-screen? Nichole's miraculous resurrection? Amy's courageous climb?

What were they saying now?

It was unacceptable to kill someone only partway. With Amy Felton, it had been calculated. Nichole was different. Nichole was supposed to be dead. Ania should have gone for an insurance shot. But in that moment—when escape to the other office seemed paramount—it hadn't been a priority. Nichole had stopped breathing, thanks to a paralyzing blow to her diaphragm. She should not have been able to draw another breath on her own.

What were they saying about Ania now? Gun to her head, forced to surrender her weapon?

"Let's go," Amy snarled, then grabbed the collar of Ania's shirt, spun her around and pushed her forward, back in the direction where Amy had come from. A few feet down the hall, Amy gave her a violent push, and Ania's head bounced off the drywall. Amy yanked back on Ania's shirt, then pushed her forward again.

"Move it," Amy said. "You've got a date with a window, bitch."

Nichole leaned up against the nearest available wall, intending to ease herself down to the floor, nice and easy. Instead she stumbled. She tried to catch herself with her hands, but no. That couldn't be right. Her arms usually had hands attached to them.

Look. There was one. On the floor.

The other was still attached.

Sort of.

Ania smiled.

. . . smiled.

Ah yes, Amy.

Let's go to your office.

Let's have a date.

On the way to her office, Amy smashed Molly's head against drywall three more times—which was impressive for a journey no more than a dozen feet. The third time, the wall actually shattered, paint chips and dust drizzling down to the carpet.

Amy's office door was slightly ajar. Amy knew she had closed it tight when she had escaped. She hadn't wanted to tip Molly off.

"Why is my door open?"

"Your boyfriend's waiting for you," Molly said, then turned to offer her profile. A crooked creek of blood ran down from her hairline. Her lips were curled into a tight little smile.

Amy pushed Molly's head forward so that it slammed on her door, which had the curious effect of both punishing Molly and causing the door to open all the way.

A second later, Amy wished it hadn't.

Ethan was perched behind her desk, his hands hanging— palms up—off the metal arms of her chair. The delirious smile on his face would have caused Amy's soul to leap, if the smile didn't look so . . . unnatural.

"Ethan?"

Ohgod.

Ethan couldn't be . . .

Ania dropped to the ground, then swept Amy's legs. Amy's face hit wall. The gun tumbled out of her hand.

Those sixteen miserable floors of hauling Ethan Goins up the fire tower were suddenly worth every step.

Look at her suffer.

Ania fixed her blouse the best she could, then walked over to Amy's desk and snatched a pile of Kleenex from a box that was adorned with sunflowers. Stopping the bleeding was key. Lose too much and she'd become light-headed. She needed to finish off Amy, then David, then talk to Jamie. It was almost over.

But Amy was up a lot faster than Ania had predicted.

"I'm going to hurt you," she said, spitting blood from her lips.

Quickly, Ania ran through her mental repertoire. What hadn't she used yet? What could she do to impress the men at the other end of the fiber-optic camera? How could she save this abortion of a morning?

Amy lunged forward.

. . .

Nichole had only one idea in her head: Crawl back to the conference room and do something indescribably nasty to David to force him to reveal the lockdown code. Ideally she needed a torture she could accomplish with little strength, because she didn't know how long she was going to last. And something she could do with no hands. Maybe she could crush his face with her heels.

She couldn't bring herself to look at her severed wrists. She could feel her remaining hand there, hanging by what felt like the thinnest strand of flesh. She knew it wasn't good. Knew she was losing more blood than she should.

Didn't matter. She would crawl with two good knees. Crawl faster than she was losing blood.

No, she couldn't.

She was being stupid. She needed to tie off her wrists. Then continue crawling.

But how?

You can't tie off anything without hands, can you?

She'd try anyway.

Nichole would be damned if she would pass out from blood loss before a final encounter with her nemesis.

Her boss.

She rolled over onto her back, then angrily ripped at her shirt with her teeth. Fine. Let him see me in my bra. As I squeeze my blood into his face. Let that be the last thing he ever sees.

Tastes.

Then the solution came to her:

Kitchen.

Electric range.

A dial that could be turned with her teeth.

Yes.

. . .

Keene needed to stop with the orange juice. He was drinking it compulsively now, and the acid was tearing up his stomach. The old habits were slowly creeping back. Only now with Florida's best, rather than the smoky nectar of the Scottish highlands.

But what he was reading . . . well, it would have driven anyone to drink.

Keene had worked another source.

Keene's second source was high-placed; it was rumored that she was the one who currently acted as a director of CI-6, or whatever you wanted to call their *thing*. She certainly knew enough. Keene never walked away from one of their conversations disappointed.

If this intel could be trusted, then "Murphy, Knox" was not what his good buddy McCoy had claimed it was:

A cover for CI-6 operatives. Fixers. Sleepers. Black baggers. Accident men. Killers. Professionals, mixed in with civilian support, to complete the illusion of a working financial services company.

Nope.

It *was* a financial services company.

Granted, it was a financial services company that was designed to infiltrate and destroy terrorist financial networks. Or for that matter, anyone whose finances needed destroying, international or domestic.

According to Keene's second source, the funding worked both ways. Money poured out of Murphy, Knox, too. Funding training. Weapons. Research. Operations. Anything that you didn't want attached to an official budget line? Simply run it through a guy like Murphy.

So why had McCoy lied to him? He clearly had to know this. He acted like he knew every intimate detail of that office.

And for God's sake—why were more than a half dozen people going to die there this morning?

Jamie stared at the back of the chair he'd been sitting in about . . . oh, what was it? An hour? Two hours? Jamie was bad at noting the passage of time. Whenever he poured himself into his writing, it was as if the digital clock on his computer played tricks on him. He had an arrangement with Andrea during his parental leave: Every morning, he could devote some time to his freelance career, pitching stories to men's magazines.

It was the only way, Jamie had explained, he'd ever be able to quit Murphy, Knox. Leave the Clique behind.

But by the time Jamie felt like real work was being accomplished, time was up. Chase needed his attention. Andrea needed a break. He was glad to give it to them. They were his family. His everything. But every minute away from his desk felt like another minute the dream was delayed.

And now this, stuck in the conference room with his half-dead boss, was like that. Being in that strange place where the clock seemed to be actively working against you.

"Jamie," a voice said. "Are you there?"

God.

It was David.

Amy and Nichole had left clear instructions about what to do if someone—who was not Amy or Nichole—tried to enter the conference room: Aim for the head.

"I'm not going to kill anybody," he'd told them.

"You want to see your kid again?" Nichole had asked.

"You can't make me," he said, feeling like a third-grader the moment the words left his mouth.

Nichole stuffed the third gun in his waistband.

"Do it for your family," she said.

And then they'd left.

They had not told him what to do if David started talking to him. David, the man who started all of this when he tried to force everyone to drink poisoned champagne.

"Jamie . . . please."

"Yeah, I'm here."

"Could I ask a favor?"

"What?"

"May I have a cookie? I'm starving."

As much as he wanted to ignore him, Jamie couldn't. This was a man who'd been shot in the head, asking for a cookie.

Never mind that a man who'd been shot in the head shouldn't be asking for a cookie.

A few weeks before Chase was born, Andrea purchased a children's book from a store near work. "To start his library," she'd said. It was called *If You Give a Mouse a Cookie.* Late one night, Jamie read the book. The point was cute and simple: Give a mouse a cookie, and he'll want something else. And then something else. And something else still, until finally, you've surrendered your soul to a rodent.

Okay, maybe that wasn't exactly the point of the book. But that's what it felt like now. David would ask for a cookie. Then a gallon of milk. Then a gun. And then . . .

"Do you mind?" David asked.

"What kind?" Jamie heard himself saying.

"Anything but a Chessman."

Of course.

Chessmen were for losers.

The conference table was frozen in time. Napkins with cookies stacked on top. Moisture-beaded bottles of champagne. Notebooks. Pens, some uncapped. Molly's white cardboard bakery box—the one that had been holding doughnuts and a gun. Snipped string.

Jamie fished a Milano from the bag and carried it over to David, whose eyes were closed. Jamie knelt down next to him. His head swam with options. He had to proceed carefully.

If you give a boss a cookie . . .

"I have your cookie," he said.

David's eye fluttered open. "Thanks."

"You want it?"

Jamie dangled the cookie above David's open mouth. His boss looked, somewhat absurdly, like a baby bird, waiting to be fed a worm.

"Yes."

"Well, not yet."

David's eyes narrowed. "Really."

"First you're going to tell me how to disable the lockdown so I can get off this floor."

David smirked. "And then I get the cookie?"

"Then you get the cookie."

Jamie felt like he was engaged in a real estate deal with a toddler. Maybe he could throw in a sippy cup, sweeten the offer.

"I like you, Jamie, I really do. You're unlike anybody else in this office. I didn't want you to come in this morning, but my bosses insisted. Said you had to go. I couldn't understand it."

"Then help me."

"I *still* don't understand it."

"If I can get out, I can call an ambulance for you. You don't have to die."

"Especially with you having a newborn baby at home."

"Goddamn it!" Jamie cried. "Tell me how to get off this floor!"

"I wish I could. But the answer is no. You're going to die up here, just like the rest of us."

Jamie felt his blood burn. He was overcome with the urge to smash his fists into David's face, force him to cough up the secret code or pass key or the friggin' *Omega Project*—anything to help him leave this building. *Now.*

Instead, he tightened his fist and pulverized the Milano. The crumbs rained down on David's face. Some of the crumbs landed in the streaks of blood and hung there.

Jamie opened his hand. It was smeared with chocolate from the center of the cookie.

Here he was, trapped on a floor, faced with certain death, and his hands were smeared with blood and chocolate.

Oh, was life absurd.

"That was *mean*," David said, then flicked his tongue out and caught a cookie crumb that had landed near the corner of his mouth. "Mmmm."

Jamie stood up and walked back to the conference table. The champagne bottles were still lined up, beaded with moisture. Maybe he should force-feed David a mimosa. Shut him up permanently.

Uh-uh.

Everything else had gone to hell.

But he was no killer.

Besides, Nichole had kept David alive for a good reason: information. If there was the slightest chance they could beat an escape plan out of him, it would be suicide to throw it away.

But he couldn't stay in here with him any longer. Because he *would* kill him.

"You're not going to leave this floor alive."

"I'll find a way," Jamie said.

"No, you won't," David said. "Even if you could, trust me, you don't want to leave. You think you can just walk away from something like this? You think there aren't people out there who want to make sure you're dead? Along with your family?"

"It would be the last thing you'd ever do."

"Tough talk from a tough guy," David said. "No man wants to ever admit he's powerless to protect his family."

"Oh, suck it."

"Whip it out, faggot."

Jamie took the gun from his waistband and aimed it at David's face.

"Oh, oh, please. *Do* it. Pull the trigger. Show me how tough you are."

Nichole had said there were only two bullets left in this gun. But at this range, it would be a sure shot.

"*Pretty* please."

This is what he wants, Jamie thought. Just like the cookie. The freak wants to die here on this floor. Why are you so eager to please him? He's not your boss anymore. You don't have to listen to him.

"With sugar on top."

Jamie threw the gun on the floor, and headed for the conference room doors.

"*Hey.*"

David was clearly not happy. But Jamie didn't care. He was almost at the doors.

"Hey! Come back here!"

Through the doors.

"I'm going to put the word out!" David screamed. "I'm going to make sure they rape your wife nice and good! They'll skin your son alive! Right in front of her!"

Out the doors.

"*They'll like doing it! They live for this!*"

The wall collapsed far easier than Amy would have imagined. The space around them swirled with atomized plaster dust. It was hard to tell the ceiling from the floor. But Amy trusted her hands. Which were wrapped around Molly's neck and slowly, steadily crushing the air out of her. Her hands were the only thing that mattered now. Her strong hands. They had to be strong for Ethan.

The hallway to the conference room was long. Ridiculously long on elbows and knees and smelling your own cooked flesh. Nichole might as well have been crawling to Harrisburg.

But she just needed to make it to David.

And she would.

If she endured the searing agony of the electric range to stop the bleeding, she could endure the rest of this.

She longed for David in the most physical way possible.

Jamie tried the elevator button, simply because he had to, because wouldn't it be hilarious if all this time David had been lying about the bypass?

He hadn't been lying.

He pressed the button again, mashing his thumb into the plastic key as if he could override the bypass by sheer strength.

Damn it!

The fire tower doors were the only other option. He walked to the one closest to their offices, and was surprised to see a hook and wire hanging from the door handle. Had someone already opened this door and dismantled the nerve gas bomb?

Did he want to take that chance?

Only now, lying on the carpet and being strangled to death, did Ania realize her miscalculation. She'd thought the sight of

Ethan's corpse would incapacitate Amy. But it had the opposite effect. It had energized her. For the first time since childhood, Ania thought she might actually die.

Her left hand, attached to her left arm and damaged shoulder, was completely sapped of strength. Her right hand alone was not powerful enough to overcome the concrete grip of Amy's hands. The awful press of Amy's thumbs into her trachea. The tips of Amy's manicured nails hooked into the back of Ania's neck, as if probing for the place where the brain stem met spinal cord.

Her light-headedness was real now. Reality was being washed away in waves of gray. Not the plaster dust. Ania saw the gray when she closed her eyes.

Ania held her breath and squeezed Amy's wrists with her one good hand. It wasn't much of a defense.

This was not something she had anticipated.

How was Amy doing this?

By thinking of her true love.

It was something out of fairy tales, and Ania loathed fairy tales—at least the few she'd been allowed to read. But perhaps there was true magic in thinking about your true love.

So she thought of Jamie.

Jamie put his hand on the gleaming silver door handle. If he pushed it down, maybe he'd hear the click of the bomb in time. He could jump out of the way, find another way.

But there are no other ways, are there, Jamie?

Andrea, if you can hear me, know that your dumb husband tried the best he could, and this was the only way he could think of to make it back home to you. . . .

· · ·

On the floor, David heard a noise.

He couldn't turn his head to see, but knew the sound well enough. The swishing of the conference room doors. Ah, Jamie was back. He must have seen the futility of his escape. Now was back to kill his boss.

Thank Christ.

"You left your gun here," David said.

"I know," said a voice.

It wasn't Jamie.

But David, from his supine position on the floor, couldn't see anybody. Was he now hearing things? Wouldn't surprise him. He had been shot in the head and was completely *starving*. Nothing to eat all morning but the crumb of a Milano. Cruel tease *that* was.

"Hello, David," said the voice.

A female voice.

Nichole.

He turned his head, and it hurt. But he could see her now. Crawling toward him, with red paint covering her hands. David couldn't even see her hands, there was so much red paint. Why was she nudging the gun with her face? Pushing it toward him. Nosing it so that the barrel was pointed at him? Why didn't she pick the goddamned thing up and get it over with already?

He just wanted to finish his mission and go home.

When Ania was Molly, she thought herself immune to America. And she was. Except for Jamie. He listened. He truly *listened*. He didn't see her as a disposable part of a larger machine. He didn't see her as a life support system for a pussy and a pair of tits—not that she showed them at work. For some reason Jamie put her at ease so much that she had to be careful not to slip into Russian. Jamie felt that much like home.

She wanted to touch him, just hold his hand, ever since the moment she met him.

The only distraction this morning was the thought of Jamie, and the opportunity to hold his hand, even if it meant giving him pain.

The pain would teach him, and serve as a reminder to her, as well.

Everything beautiful can be destroyed.

She was thinking of Jamie, but no surge of adrenaline followed. Only a strange melancholy.

She could be strangled to death here, and Jamie might not even know or care.

Jamie.

With his mangled fingers.

There she found the answer, and knew it was time to simply let go.

Jamie pushed down on the door handle.

For a moment, there was nothing.

No telltale click.

Or hiss.

Or beep.

He pushed the door open a few more inches.

Nichole was straddling him now, and David saw that it wasn't paint on her arms at all. She had bloody stumps where her hands should have been. Okay, there was one hand, kind of just hanging there. Her skin smelled like Chinese food. The sickeningly sweet aroma distracted him from the fact that Nichole wasn't wearing a shirt, and that her pussy was pressed up against his chest. Clothes separated their flesh—and there were those mangled hands—but still, she aroused him. David never thought he'd experience this kind of intimacy with Nichole, who'd been out to destroy him ever since she'd started working for him. Which was a shame. He'd always found her deliciously screwable.

"You have one chance," she said, a tiny bead of blood hanging from one corner of her mouth. "Tell me how to get off this floor."

"I could *so* eat you out right now," David said.

Nichole's eyes widened, and then she leaned forward. For a moment there, David thought she was going to give him a little kiss. Right there on his forehead.

But she was reaching too far up and behind.

Nichole pressed her elbow against the grip of the gun that she had positioned next to David's head. She stuck out her tongue.

I quit, she thought, and thrust her tongue hard against the trigger.

David Murphy died not knowing his mission had been accomplished.

He was still thinking about what Nichole's pussy would look like. He was thinking well-trimmed, but a little loose. Used. He'd heard she'd been messing around with the mail guys for years. Which she had been. He'd watched some of it. Got off on it.

David wore a waterproof watch he never removed, even during sex or masturbation. Lovers would tease him about it. *What, are you going to time me?*

He had worn it ever since he first rented the thirty-sixth floor of 1919 Market Street, and installed detonating devices on the thirtieth floor. And installed the trigger in his wristwatch.

The watch was one of those that monitored your pulse. Constantly, quietly, efficiently.

But it wasn't *exactly* one of those kinds of watches. He'd had it modified so that it had room for the trigger. If his pulse stopped, a signal would travel to the detonating devices six floors below. If David Murphy was to go, everything was to go.

And so it went.

The moment the door opened, there was an explosion.

Jamie screamed and hurled himself backwards, slamming against the opposite wall, then slid to the ground and tried to scuttle away like a crab.

Jesus H. . . .

That wasn't a chemical bomb.

The crazy bastard, he rigged a *real explosive* to the door.

But not here. There was no fire or smoke. The explosion sounded like it was somewhere else in the building.

Was the bomb set somewhere else?

Christ, was David planning on bringing the whole place down?

Twenty floors down, Vincent Marella dreamed he heard an explosion. He woke up to find that his eyes were bleeding and he could barely breathe.

He also heard a man scream.

Amy released her grip momentarily—there was an explosion, somewhere, and it seemed to puzzle her.

That was all that Ania needed.

The lid of one of her wrist compartments flipped up easily.

The blade slid down and landed in her palm. She had taken a chance, releasing her grip on Amy's wrists to dig out her weapon. But what was true love without risks?

Ania used her injured arm to brace Amy's body and her right hand to slide the blade into the hollow of Amy's neck.

Then she sliced down, directly between Amy's breasts and down her stomach to where her belt used to be.

Jamie DeBroux

~~Abony Sutton~~

~~Ethan Goins~~

~~Roxanne Kortwood~~

Molly Lewis

~~Stuart McGraine~~

Nichole Wise

. . .

The bullet that had ripped through David's brains also struck one of the large conference room windows, spiderwebbing it. That was a nice bit of luck, Nichole thought. It wouldn't take much to push the rest of it through. Not to call for help. She was too high up to seriously entertain that. And with the explosion down below, well, attention would be scattered, to say the least, for the time being.

Nah. Nichole Wise, code name Workhorse, was thinking long-term.

If she could sever the stubborn piece of flesh attached to her hand—and a jagged edge of the conference room window might do the trick—she could drop her hand out the window. Thirty-six floors down, wave good-bye. It might take a while, but at some point, some investigator would stumble across it, bag it, and eventually do a fingerprint check. Langley would pop up. Questions would be asked. And maybe the story would finally be told. The story of her miserable years undercover at Murphy, Knox.

Maybe she'd end up a black star, chiseled into the slab of white Vermont marble that was the CIA's Wall of Honor:

IN HONOR OF THOSE MEMBERS
OF THE CENTRAL INTELLIGENCE AGENCY
WHO GAVE THEIR LIVES
IN THE SERVICE OF THEIR COUNTRY

Buddy, you don't know the half of it, Nichole thought.
Then she died.

Jamie DeBroux

~~Avery Fulton~~

~~Ethan Goins~~

~~Roxanne Kentwood~~

Molly Lewis

~~Stuart McGrane~~

~~Nichole Wise~~

. . .

Keene paused by the sea to watch the waves. He wasn't looking forward to the conversation he was about to have.

Farther down on the beach Keene saw another dog—not a three-legged one this time. It was a fully equipped black Lab, and he was running into the crashing waves. A young red-haired mother, no more than thirty, was standing there with two preschoolers, both with reddish-blond hair. They were jumping and laughing at the dog, who rushed into the waves, stopped to relieve his bowels, then raced out of the water again before another wave could wash over him. Speed defecation. Keene had to admire that. The owner needed to be commended. He wondered if the children were trained that way, as well. *Go on. Run into the water, kids. Go potty.*

Keene's mobile rang. It was his second source.

"I didn't think I'd hear back from you," Keene said.

"I didn't think I'd be calling."

"What's going on?"

"There's a lot of activity here on my end."

"Oh?"

"Yeah."

There was a pause.

"Look, just come out with it. Can't be any worse than what I'm already thinking."

"Your man is behind it all."

"What do you mean?"

"David Murphy is a straw man. A burnout case. Your man McCoy plucked him from the wreckage, started to run him. Build him up again. But McCoy was behind everything. Including the financing of a particular tracking device that has been causing us much trouble as of late."

"I see. You just find this out now?"

"That's not fair."

"It's not fair that I've been stationed with a traitor. For *months* now."

"We're a big dumb animal, Will. You know that. Big and strong, but dumb nonetheless. The important thing is you helped us uncover him. If you hadn't asked questions, we wouldn't know. That's the important thing."

"Is it?"

The dog bounded up the shore. The mother and children raced after it. Nothing like a good run after voiding your bowels.

"There's something else."

"You need me to kill him, of course."

"We need you to kill him."

"Uh-huh." Keene swallowed. "I've got a really bad cold, you know."

"I'm sorry, Will."

"Not looking for sympathy. It's just . . . well, it's really a pish day for this."

The mother, children, and black Lab were all headed away from the beach now, the dog's transaction with Mother Nature complete. If Keene were to return to the same spot tomorrow, he would probably see the same event replay. He wondered how much of this dog's shit was in his sea.

"Yeah, I know. But is it ever a good day?"

"You've got a point there."

"What about the other people on that floor in Philadelphia?"

There was a pause.

"That's not something we can embroil ourselves in right now."

"I see."

"I'm sorry."

"No, no. I understand. Hey, it's a lousy day all around then, isn't it?"

"Will . . ."

"Talk to you in a bit. Cheers, now."

CLOSING TIME

Vincent Marella tried to ignore the symptoms, hoist his pal Rickards up, get him out of the fire tower. He grabbed his partner under his arms, but he couldn't resist. He touched the sensitive skin below his eyes, and his fingertips came back bloody. Jesus Christ. He couldn't be checking out now. Not after last year. Not like this. Not like *Center Strike.*

It was so, *so* hard to breathe.

And look.

There was a bloody human tooth on the floor.

Wonderful.

If that explosion up top was real, and he wasn't dreaming it— and well, you know, the high and loud clanging of the fire alarm seemed to indicate that this *wasn't* an event confined to la-la land—then he was seriously screwed. Because in the event of a fire, all elevators shoot down to the lobby level and stay there. The fire towers are the only way out.

Like the fire tower they'd just left, which was apparently full of some kind of nerve agent.

It made him choke.

And it certainly wasn't goddamn Lysol.

Somewhere downstairs in the security office, up on the fake maplewood shelves, there was a thick paperback manual called *Terrorism and Other Public Health Emergencies.* A nice little handout everyone received about a year back.

The manual had first aid tips. Vincent couldn't remember a damn one of them, except wash your skin like crazy. And you could be sure that was the first thing he would do.

If he could get down to that manual, he and Rickards might have a shot here.

After that, he was seriously leaving the goddamned private security business for good, end of story. Did people still sell aluminum siding?

But with the north fire tower out of commission, and the elevators gone, there was only one other way out. The south tower. Unless the terrorists had released the same nerve gas in there, too.

Was that part of their plan? Dose the fire towers and then blow up the building, so everybody inside would die, one way or the other? But why pull this shit on a Saturday, when the building was mostly empty? Didn't make any sense. The broken glass, his run-in with that psycho broad, none of it.

Forget it for now. He'd have plenty of time to scratch his nuts and ponder the myriad possibilities after he quit. Now he needed to drag Rickards to the south tower and pray it was clear.

"You're heavier than you look," Vincent said.

Rickards said nothing.

"Yeah, that's what I thought you'd say."

Get yourself up off the floor, Jamie. C'mon. You're not going to solve anything by sitting here. Try the other fire tower. Try the elevator button again. Try something. Maybe that explosion you heard canceled the bypass. Maybe it made things worse. But you won't know unless you get up and *do something*.

Jamie rounded the corner, back into the elevator bank. Sprinklers were gushing. White lights were flashing. The fire alarm was clanging violently.

And Molly was standing there.

Covered in blood.

From her neck to the tops of her thighs, which were bare. Somehow, she'd lost her skirt. Or she'd taken it off to show off her plain panties, which would have been bone white had they not been soaked with blood. She looked like Carrie White, modeling for Victoria's Secret.

The sprinklers were washing away some of the blood, but not nearly enough.

"We need to talk," Molly said, loud enough to be heard over the alarm.

"What happened to you?" Jamie asked. He meant it literally, but as he spoke the words, he realized he'd meant *mentally,* too. Where was the Molly he'd known? Was she gone for good? Or was she back?

"You have a choice to make in the next minute, and it will be the most important one you'll ever make."

She moved closer to him, one foot in front of the other, making a single, bloody trail up the middle of the carpet.

"Where—?"

"Shhhh. Let me speak. Then you can ask as many questions as you want."

Jamie swallowed.

"Okay," he said.

But he was thinking: I have no weapon. Damn it. He should have taken the gun from the conference room. If only to keep

Molly at bay for a few minutes, until he could figure out an escape plan.

"David was going to kill you. I wanted to *save* you. This is why I'm doing all of this. You may not believe me, but it's all for you."

"You're right," he said, almost shouting. "I don't believe you."

"I cut your hand to convince my superiors that you could withstand pain. And you did. You did as well as could be expected. Now look at you. Seeking a way out. Many men would have curled up and waited to die. That's what Paul would have done."

Paul.

Her husband.

Would have?

She was closer now, which made it easier to hear. Jamie could see that she'd taken a beating, too. Her left shoulder had a wound that looked like it could have been made with a bullet, and her neck was torn and bruised. Her face might have been beaten, too, but it was hard to tell, because her long hair was wet and hanging down in her face. Molly never wore her hair down at the office. It looked strange. Almost as strange as the lack of clothes and the dripping blood.

"I want you to come with me."

"Where?"

"Away."

"What are you talking about?"

"Europe. We can be happy there. You can write. You can spend all of the time you want writing. I know that's what you want to do."

"Europe? Molly, I'm married. And you're . . ."

Insane.

She reached out her hand to touch his cheek and he flinched.

"Shhhh," she said, more quietly now. "Molly Lewis was married, yes. But I am not Molly Lewis. My name is Ania Kuczun."

Anya *who*?

"You can be whoever you want, too. As easy as a snake shedding skin."

Jamie had watched Molly survive a beating at the hands of Nichole. Watched her shoot David in the head. Felt the agony as she paralyzed him with just one simple move, then cut his fingers apart. Who was this woman? And what was she capable of? What did she really want?

Europe?

Wash away the blood, brush her hair, put it back in a conservative ponytail, get her dressed, and Jamie could almost see the old Molly. His office spouse. A quiet, thoughtful, pretty woman who was Andrea's polar opposite.

Sometimes, though, it's the opposites that get you. Draw you in, when you least expect it.

Like a few months ago.

On a walk home from an after-work happy hour.

Hey, I'll walk you to your car. Well, here it is. Nice SUV. Guess I'll be going. Yeah, good hanging with you, too . . . and that's when it gets you, when you find yourself leaning forward to give her a kiss on the cheek but really you're aiming for her lips, and she pulls back, a little startled. And you console yourself by saying, Hey, that would have been stupid. I have a pregnant wife at home.

Still, in that drunken moment, you really wanted that kiss.

The look on her face slides from puzzlement to embarrassment, and then she climbs into her car, and you walk home, and it's really not that far away. The humid night air gives you time to think about what you narrowly avoided.

It's not different in work the next day, or any other day, except maybe she sometimes looks at you oddly or warmly or knowingly. You forget about it. You're about to have a kid.

You have a kid. You come back to work.

On a hot Saturday morning in August.

Those lips you momentarily wanted to kiss are now spotted with blood.

And she's talking about shedding your skin.

"There's something you need to leave behind," Molly said.

"I don't know what you're talking about," Jamie said. "This building is burning. We need to leave. *Now.*"

She moved closer to him. Her lips. Smiling a little. "I have another way out. If you come with me."

"How?"

"It won't hurt much."

Did she really know another way?

It didn't matter. Jamie had trusted her before, and she'd ended up slicing his hand open like a roasted chicken. He wasn't going to fall for the same ploy twice. He might be a public relations flack, but he wasn't brain-dead.

Molly was closer now. Even with the spraying water, he could smell her. The copper penny scent of blood.

So Jamie did the only thing he could think of. He pushed her. Hard. Like they were schoolchildren in a playground.

She stumbled back to the ground.

Jamie bolted.

Keene opened the hall cupboard and lifted the false plywood bottom. Beneath it was his backup gun. A silver Ruger, Speed Six .38 Special. He never thought he'd need one here in Porty. Went through a lot of trouble to get one. Bought it from a fat guy from Haddington named Joe-Bob, as unlikely as that sounded. But he'd planted it months ago, nonetheless. It was hard to shake the Moscow Rules, even though he hadn't been CIA in many, many years.

Build in opportunity but use it sparingly.

He stuffed the gun in his waistband, near the base of his spine. And as he headed up the stairs he recalled another old espionage chestnut:

Everyone is potentially under control of the opposition.

And as he put his hand on the doorknob and thought about killing McCoy . . .

There is no limit to a human being's ability to rationalize the truth.

It wasn't an entirely bad trip down; Vincent fell only once and dropped Rickards twice. If Rickards asked later, Vincent planned on shrugging his shoulders. *I don't know how you got those bruises, man.* His muscles were trembling and it was hard to breathe. But there was no sitting down and taking a breather. The longer they stayed in this tower, the more likely they were going to die.

The guys from the Philadelphia Fire Department had begun to arrive by the time Vincent hit the ground floor. They were scurrying in the lobby and on the sidewalk outside the building. Crap. Two guys in full gear with pickhead axes and Nomex hoods came up to them, tried to take Rickards off his hands.

Vincent pulled back and warned them: "We've been dosed with chemical agents. We need a hazmat team or Homeland Security or whatever you guys are supposed to call out for this stuff."

"Where?"

"I was up on sixteen, the north fire tower. Tell your guys now before they go charging up."

"What about the other one?"

"No idea. And hey—there are people up there. I heard someone yell."

"What floor?"

"I don't know. Up higher than I was. Could be anywhere."

"All right, let's go, move, move!"

There, warning done . . . now he had to get Rickards back to the washup room and find that goddamned *Terrorism* manual. No telling how long it would take for the scientists to show up and analyze this stuff. If he lived through this—if it wasn't blood he felt streaming down his cheeks, though Vincent kind of suspected it was—he was sure he was looking at weeks and weeks of blood tests and cheek swabs and anal pokes. His son would be fascinated. Ask all about it. Question is, does a dad tell his kid about stuff like this? Is it educational?

Vincent Marella was going to do two things after all this was over.

He was seriously going to quit.

And he was going to put *Center Strike* in a garbage can, piss on it, then light it on fire.

Jamie keyed the door code with his good hand, then yanked open the door. He ran down the short hallway and was immediately confused. Why was it dark outside? He couldn't open the nearest office door—it was locked—but he looked through the slats of the window to the outer windows.

That wasn't darkness. It was smoke.

And that was because *the building was on fire*.

He could see the flashes of red in the sky. Fire trucks.

Goddamn David Murphy.

Hang on now. Worry about that later. Jamie needed somewhere else to be, away from Molly. If he could circumvent her, he could make it to the other fire tower. Maybe it was rigged to explode, too. Maybe not. But it was his only option.

That's not true, DeBroux. Molly told you that she has a way out.

Yeah, and she also said it wouldn't "hurt much."

Uh-uh.

But if Molly knew a way out, then there was another way out. Maybe he could hide long enough to find it. Watch Molly take it, then take it himself. Or do both.

Point was, keep moving.

Jamie moved to the right. If he could make it to the abandoned offices and cubicles, he could duck in and out of those, listening for her footsteps (bare feet on carpet, good luck) and eventually make his way around to the other door, then to the elevator bank, then to the other fire tower.

Besides, the other way—toward David's office—was a dead end.

There was nothing else he could do except move to the other side of the floor. That, and try to control his breathing. His lungs were pumping too hard. He had to slow it down. In through the nose, out through the mouth. In through the nose, out through the mouth.

On the other side of the office, Jamie saw the white box with the little cartoon heart on it.

Wait. There *was* something else he could do.

He opened the front panel. Read the instructions quickly. Took the paddles in his hands, even his sore one—he could deal with it for a little while—and used his good thumb to hit the charging button. There was a high-pitched whine.

Sixty seconds to go.

Jamie put his back to the panel, paddles behind his back.

Molly was standing in the hallway.

"You never answered my question," she said.

Keene opened the door and fired the Ruger.

There was no need to play it cute. Keene had a feeling that McCoy would spot a ruse in a microsecond.

But the bullet struck bare wall. Something sliced at his forearm, ripping through skin and muscle. A butcher knife.

"Ah, you cunt."

The gun tumbled from Keene's hand. Keene threw his weight into the door. It slammed into McCoy. Keene pivoted, then booted McCoy in the testicles so hard, it sent him staggering backwards. He smashed his head into the corner of an oak bureau.

Keene, the pain in his forearm overpowering, fell backwards. Landed on his ass. A simple slash across the arm shouldn't hurt so much.

McCoy either had braced himself or didn't actually have testicles, because he recovered quickly. He opened the bottom drawer next to him. Reached below a stack of six T-shirts. Always with his T-shirts. The one on the top said THE BAD PLUS.

He'd hidden a gun under there. It was a Ruger, too.

Build in opportunity but use it sparingly.

They were both students of the old school.

"Have a nice walk?" McCoy said, then shot Keene in the chest.

"Come with me," she said.

"No," Jamie said. Trying to keep his breathing under control.

"You don't have to pretend," she said. "I can give you everything you want."

How many seconds had elasped? Ten? At most?

Keep yourself calm.

Keep her talking.

Molly started walking toward him. "Come with me and we can leave this building. Right now."

"No," Jamie said. "Not until you tell me what this is about. Why everyone on this floor had to die."

"What does it matter? You going to write a book about it?" She smiled.

Jamie could hear the high-pitched whine. Could she?

"I want to know."

Molly was just a few feet away. Jamie pretended to lean back against the wall, frightened. Which was not too difficult to pretend.

Had a half a minute gone by yet?

"This is just a company. We're just employees. I'm going for a promotion. Not just for me. For both of us. And now I want to know if you'll come with me."

"How can I just leave my life behind?"

"Is it really a life you'll miss?"

Behind him, something clicked.

She touched his chest.

Smiled.

Jamie pressed the defibrillator paddles against Molly's chest and squeezed the plastic handles. Prayed it had been enough time.

It had.

There was a loud *pop.*

She yelped. The shock blew her body back across the hall. Down there on the floor, she looked like a puppet with her strings cut.

Jamie droppped the paddles. God bless OSHA, which had started to require these devices in buildings over twenty stories in downtown Philadelphia. Even the abandoned floors of buildings.

The shock wouldn't be enough to kill her. Even from this distance, he could see her chest moving. But it would buy him time until he figured a way off this floor.

Even if he had to lift a desk and hurl it through the glass. Let the firemen below know that there were people up here in need of rescue.

The conference room was his best bet. Maybe he could use that gun to shoot out the glass. Ah, damn it! He kicked himself for not thinking about that before. Shoot the glass and start heaving office furniture out. A chair first, to get their attention. Then the conference room table itself, if he had to.

Jamie started down the hallway but stopped when he felt something on his pant leg.

Fingers.

Yanking the material downward.

"You," Molly said, "never answered my question."

The wound was mortal; Keene knew that. There wasn't much time. The bullet must have nicked quite a few arteries. He could imagine the inside of his chest with miniature leaking hoses, and an imaginary coronary engineer throwing his hands up, exasperated. *What am I supposed to do now? I can't fix this.*

He also had a pain in his arse.

Literally. Something hard, jabbing him in the soft, fleshy part of his cheek.

"You just find out, or have you known for a while? I'm thinking you just found out."

Keene looked at McCoy. His lover had a smirk on his face. Ordinarily, Keene took great pleasure in that smirk. It made him horny.

"I'm not going to sit here and explain it all to you," McCoy said. "I hate that."

"Yeah," Keene said. At least, he thought he said it. It might have been in his mind.

"I will tell you this, though. And this is more of a personal note, though it does cross over slightly into the business end of things."

"Yeah?"

McCoy. Always drawing things out. Forcing you to ask "what?" or "yeah?" or something. Even as he sat here, dying.

"I'm not even gay."

Keene's fingers found the Ruger, under his arse. He had the strength to lift it. So of course he had the strength to squeeze the trigger. Repeatedly. He blasted off the five remaining shots.

Most of the bullets hit McCoy. There was just one miss, making for a grand total of two bullets the next occupant of this flat would have to pry out of the walls.

If they were being observed—which was absurd, but still—people would be tempted to think it was all about the gay comment. But as he felt his lifeforce ebbing away, Keene mentally denied it, saying he was just being a professional to the end.

Doing his job.

Like always.

After all:

There is no limit to a human being's ability to rationalize the truth.

Molly hurled him against the wall.

She tried doing that paralyze-you-with-your-own-fingers thing again, but her hands were slick with blood. Jamie slipped away and tried to crawl across the floor. He felt her hand on his waistband. Jamie kicked backwards, caught her on the leg. She exhaled, then grabbed his ankle, flipped him, and kicked him in the chest with her heel.

It felt like someone had flipped a valve in his chest. Jamie's breath was trapped in his lungs. He couldn't breathe in. He couldn't breathe out. His fingers clawed at the carpet involuntarily, sending fresh waves of agony across his injured hand.

But he wasn't really thinking about that, because more important, *he couldn't breathe.*

Then Molly started dragging him across the floor.

Forty-three hundred miles away from Edinburgh, in a quiet rooming house on the outskirts of Madison, Wisconsin, a woman in a T-shirt and jeans watched the video image of another man shooting his lover to death.

A few minutes later, the shooter—an operative using the name Will Keene—appeared to die, too. It was a sudden and shocking end to months of surveillance. She wasn't sure what this one was all about; her superiors never told her. Just watch them, they said. So she did. As often as she could. They were an interesting pair to watch. Kind of like an old married couple. She never thought it would have ended like this. They genuinely seemed to care about each other. But boom, there it was—the fight, the knife, the guns, and the short conversation before the final, repeated coups de grâce.

That was totally about the gay crack, she thought.

The woman picked up the phone and called her director. People would have to be sent.

As she waited on hold, she idly wondered who'd she be watching next, then thought about pizza.

"If you want to come with me," Molly said, "nod your head once."

Jamie had no choice. Jamie had no air.

She hadn't dragged him far. They were in the conference room. He recognized the ceiling. The floor was hot beneath his back. Smoke was curling and rolling outside the large windows.

"You're going to lose consciousness any second now."

Jamie nodded.

She jammed a palm into his chest. The mystery valve released. Air tried to gush in and out of his lungs at the same time. Jamie turned to the side, curled up, and then vomited.

"There, there," Molly was saying. "Just breathe. The feeling will pass."

The ground was so hot now, Jamie could imagine his own puke sizzling within a matter of moments. Reheating his breakfast. Those Chessmen.

She was rubbing his back now. Jamie opened his eyes and saw two people lying on the floor. It was a woman, topless except for a bra. She was slumped over a guy in a suit. Nichole . . . and David?

Molly rolled him back over, dabbed at his lips with a napkin she must have picked up from the conference room table.

"No offense, but I don't think I'm going to kiss you until after you brush your teeth," she said.

Jamie's mouth and throat burned, and his lungs still felt like they were on the verge of exploding. The rest of his body seemed to be in retreat mode. Sensation dimmed—the normal sensations you feel every second of the day. His skin chilled. His legs went numb. A cold sweat broke out on his forehead. Was he going to die anyway, after all of this?

"One last thing, Jamie," Molly said. "We're going to need to leave something of you behind. Something the investigators will be able to use to harvest some DNA. Blood won't be enough. It burns up too quickly. We need a part of you. Something they'll find, so they won't come looking for you."

Screw you. Let them find me. And David. And Nichole. And Stuart. And Amy. And Ethan. Find everyone who was brought up here this morning to die and figure it out. If he was to die, Jamie wanted Andrea and Chase to know what happened. He didn't want Chase to grow up thinking, *Daddy just didn't come home one day.*

"I'm thinking your hand," she said.

"What?" Jamie croaked.

"It's already injured. And yes, you're a writer. But I'll be there to help. You can dictate. I can transcribe." Molly smiled. "After all, I am an experienced executive assistant."

"No."

"I can numb your arm. I can't say it won't hurt, but it won't be as bad as you think. You can close your eyes. I'll take care of everything."

"*No.*"

"We have to act soon," she said, and stood up. "If you can think of another body part, tell me quick."

Molly turned to face a corner of the conference room. She pushed her wet hair out of her face, best she could. She straightened her bra and panties, as if adjusting a business suit after a ride on the regional rail lines. Then she did the strangest thing of all: She addressed a ghost in the corner of the room: "Boyfriend, I'm ready."

She's insane, Jamie thought.

Truly, truly insane.

"You've watched a demonstration of my abilities," she continued. "You've seen my skills, and how I quickly and decisively respond to evolving circumstances. In the end, despite setbacks, my objectives were achieved. I hope you'll find that I am a creative and determined operative, able to deal with any challenge placed before me."

Who the hell was she talking to? The imaginary voices inside her head that told her to kill, kill, kill?

"In our discussions, you promised escape and refuge at the completion of my demonstration, if you found my performance satisfactory or greater. I ask you now. Do you find me worthy?"

Jamie rolled over, looking for another pair of legs. Maybe someone else was in the conference room. Maybe there was a helicopter floating outside, waiting for them to grab hold of a rope ladder and be taken away to safety.

But there was nobody else in the room. Just the two of them, and their dead coworkers. Stuart hadn't moved an inch since dropping dead a few hours ago. David must have finally died from his head shot. Or something else. Maybe Nichole had finished him off. But then who had killed her?

"Do you?" she asked the corner of the conference room.

Molly, of course. Molly had killed them all. One by one. Why was she sparing him?

Because of an attempted kiss one drunken night a few months ago?

"*Please* answer me," she pleaded.

Jamie made it to his belly and used his good hand to push himself up to his knees. He could see Nichole and David more clearly now. More important, he could see the gun on the floor, under her face. The grip was showing.

"PLEASE ANSWER ME!"

Thirty-five hundred miles away, there was no one who could answer her.

The question was, could Jamie do it?

Could he shoot a woman?

No, not just a woman. Molly Lewis. Crazy as she was—and that was another consideration, her being clearly mentally incapacitated—was it right to shoot a woman you wanted to kiss just a few months ago? Especially if she's not in her right mind?

But Jamie wondered about that. Maybe she was in her right mind. There were bigger things than him at play in this office this morning. Nichole had told him as much. Unless Home Depot was running a sale on chemical weapons, explosives, and poison champagne . . . wasn't it possible that this was something larger and stranger than Jamie would have imagined?

And Molly was at the center of it?

Jamie looked at the gun. Looked at Nichole, who knew what was going on, but refused to tell him.

If you don't already know, then you're not supposed to know.

This was a betrayal beyond reason.

Ania couldn't understand it. Granted, her audition was technically shaky. Nothing had proceeded as planned. But she had improvised her brains out. And in the end, the mission had been accomplished. Her coworkers were dead. Every single one of them—save Jamie. The explosives had been detonated. Again, not according to plan, but the cleansing fire was under way nonetheless. Things had worked out. She'd proved her worth. She deserved a response.

Couldn't they acknowledge her with a simple response?

Was she not worth a mere syllable?

A *yes*?

Or a *no*?

The silence was maddening.

Ania thought of her mother in that dreadful place, hanging on to the promise of a better life. Don't worry, Mama, I'm coming back for you, she'd told her.

Ania had lied.

Lied to *her mother.*

Not a single syllable, and now here she was, in the place of her own nightmares, burning alive, torn apart, covered in blood, trapped with the only man she cared about. The man she'd promised to introduce to Mama.

You'll like him. He's a writer. Just like Josef.

And they were both going to die.

She tried one last time. One last beg for a response. She was owed that much.

She'd put too much into this job for it to end this way.

With nothing.

Could he do it? The gun was right there, on the floor.

Pick it up.

This is a woman who could take a full blast from a defibrillator and pop right back up.

Think about it being the right or wrong thing to do later.

You need to stop her.

Do it.

Do it *now*.

The conference room doors slammed open and two firemen, decked out in helmets and face masks and pickaxes, stormed in.

"*I need an answer!*" Molly screamed at the corner of the room.

"Relax, miss," said the taller one. "We're here to help."

Molly turned around, hands clenched at her sides. She looked strangely lost, even for a woman who was nearly naked and drenched in blood.

"No," Molly said. "You are here for me to punish."

She looked back at the corner of the room, told her invisible friend: "I will show you I am worthy."

Then she cleared three paces and jumped at the taller one, her foot in the air.

Her heel shattered his plastic face mask, sending him staggering backwards.

The other one, his partner, who was shorter, charged forward with the handle of the pickaxe and pinned Molly against the wall.

That didn't last long. She worked a leg up, pressed her foot against the firefighter's chest, then flung him across the room. His back struck the edge of the conference room table. The champagne bottles jolted and tittered. Cookies slid off their plates. The firefighter landed on his face, hands splayed on the floor.

By this time his partner, with a broken face mask, had regained his senses and charged forward.

Molly kicked him in the face again, shattering the rest of his mask. He screamed.

Jamie climbed to his feet and gripped one of the conference room chairs. The chair rolled beneath him, and was heavier than it looked.

He picked it up and swung it at Molly anyway.

Aiming for her back.

She needed to be stopped.

But Molly sensed him. Kicked sideways. Hit the chair. Jamie went tumbling backwards, over the dead bodies of Nichole and David. Jamie kicked out, trying to clear himself of the corpses.

The firefighters, by this point, had enough screwing around.

They remembered their pickaxes had blades.

The shorter one swung at Molly, aiming for her chest. She lifted her forearm to block it, and the blade cut through her metal bracelet. It slipped from her wrist and fell to the floor. The blow had connected with her flesh, though. Molly cried out. Grabbed her wrist. Bent forward.

The taller one took advantage, hurling his pickaxe into Molly's back, high and to the left. She took a few wobbly steps forward, then dropped.

No one spoke for a few moments. Smoke continued to roil

around the building. The air in the conference room itself was beginning to look wavy.

Molly lay with her check pressed against the carpet, staring at Jamie.

He thought about that night a few months ago, that drunken night when he walked her to her car. She had stared at him the same way.

But now something was different.

Now she was pursing her lips.

Blowing him a kiss.

Before her eyes closed.

The shorter firefighter knelt down beside her. Took off his glove. Pressed two stubby fingers to her neck. Shook his head.

"Okay, c'mon," his partner said. Then he turned to Jamie. "Buddy, you okay?"

"Yeah," Jamie said, automatically.

But he wasn't, of course.

"We've gotta get out of here. Now."

"Buddy. You with us?"

Jamie stood up. It all had happened so quickly. Then he remembered what he had been reaching for.

The gun.

Even though the man was dead—his body was right there on the floor, his head covered in a messy halo of blood—his boss's words echoed.

You think you can just walk away from something like this? You think there aren't people out there who want to make sure you're dead? Along with your family?

I'm no killer, Jamie had told David.

But the truth was, he *could* be.

If it was for his family.

Jamie bent over and took the gun out from under Nichole's

face. The metal was hung up on her skin, and she was still warm. Then again, everything in the room was superheating.

He lunged for Molly's body. He needed to be sure.

He needed to put a bullet in her brain.

"Hey *hey*, come on, man," said shorter firefighter, catching Jamie in his extended arm and holding him back. The firefighter didn't see he was holding a gun. "She's gone."

"Smoke's getting real bad in here," his partner said. Jamie could see his eyes and nose beneath the shattered mask. He looked young.

"I have to," Jamie said.

"No you don't."

"She . . ."

"Buddy, she's *gone*. There's another team behind us. They'll get her. Along with everybody else."

Jamie dropped the gun to the carpet.

They all left the building.

OUT OF THE OFFICE

I just want to spend more time with my family.
—POPULAR SAYING

The walk down the south fire tower felt like forever. Jamie had never felt such heat. He was sure he'd passed out at least once. Maybe twice. But he was supported by the arms of the firefighters, whose names he didn't even know. He thought about asking them, but his mouth couldn't form the words. He'd have to find out later. Write them. Thank them. Buy them beers. Introduce them to Andrea, Chase. Cook them meals.

The endless repetition of *staircase, turn, staircase, turn* also felt like it lasted longer than physically possible.

Eventually, though, they reached the ground floor, and Jamie was being placed on a stretcher, and he reached his hand out to thank his rescuers, high-five them, anything, but they were already headed back into the building.

Someone jabbed a needle in his arm and put a mask over his face and rolled him into the back of an ambulance.

He started to drift off, even though it was only the middle of the day. Hard to tell, with the sky outside so black.

He *wanted* to drift off. Maybe he would snap awake and find himself in his usual position in bed: left arm tucked under Andrea's pillow. Her hair, fanned across her pillow. Her scent intoxicating, even in the middle of the night. His hand, resting on her hip. Or if the mood was right, up around the front and higher.

So Jamie drifted a bit, fantasizing that he was home already with Andrea. With Chase in the other room, monitor on, so that the moment he fussed, even a little, they'd hear it, and they could be in there to comfort him in a flash.

He could smell her hair.

Or imagine he could.

Wait.

No.

He couldn't drift off, not yet.

He had to reach Andrea, tell her he was okay. A phone call, *something*. News of the fire was probably all over TV. God, she could probably see the smoke from the front steps of their apartment building. She'd wonder. Check the news. Hear about 1919. Panic. He couldn't do that to her.

Jamie sat up on the stretcher. Pulled the mask from his face. Yanked the needle from his arm.

He reached around to his back pocket to see if he'd put his wallet back there, or left it upstairs. Maybe he could hail a cab, be home in seconds.

Instead he found a card.

And on the front was the cartoon of a duck in little boy pants.

Later, investigators clearing out the floors would discover something odd on the thirty-sixth floor: a badly burned single parachute harness-container containing a Dacron parachute. The brand name was consistent with harnesses and parachutes used for BASE jumping. The pack was found on the floor, but it appeared to have been stuffed over the drop-ceiling tiles on the thirty-sixth floor, just outside the office of Murphy, Knox, CEO David Murphy. As the tiles had burned away, the pack dropped to the ground.

Investigators were at a loss to explain the gear, other than an office thrill-seeker stashing the equipment for a future jump.

But that didn't explain the typewritten note, found inside an envelope deep within the pack:

CONGRATS, it read.

The body of Paul Lewis was discovered that afternoon, when police officers arrived at the Lewis home to inform him that his wife was missing. They were surprised to find him dead, with half-chewed pieces of potato salad in his mouth.

Blood screens came back negative; the death was ruled accidental.

Somebody tipped off a reporter. By the end of the week, over forty-seven newspapers were running the short wire story of one couple's freakishly bad luck.

Names withheld to protect the innocent.

Jamie raced up Twentieth Street, hunting for a pay phone. He seemed to remember one at the corner of Arch Street, near a diner that had recently gone upscale—charging nine dollars for hamburgers and adding seven martinis to the menu.

He glanced back. The top of 1919 was a raging inferno now, with so much smoke pouring from the top, it looked as if all of Center City were on fire. That it all had been sold to the Devil.

Everybody had been so busy, no one noticed that he had just stepped out of the ambulance and started walking.

Toward home.

There was a phone on Arch Street, just as he'd remembered it. The steel line connecting the handset to the box looked badly damaged, but there was still a dial tone. Jamie punched in his calling card number, then his home phone. Three rings, then the machine picked up.

Hi, you've reached us. If you're calling, you know who we are. Leave a message, and one of us will get back to you. If we feel like it.

Jamie, being funny.

Beep.

"Honey, it's me, if you're there pick up. I don't know if you saw the news, but I'm fine, I'm out of the building, so you don't have to worry. Are you there?"

Nothing.

"Sweetie, if you're there, please pick up."

No Andrea.

"Okay . . . I'm walking home right now. I'll be there in five minutes. I love you."

Jamie paused another few seconds, just in case. Their apartment was oddly shaped: hallway, kitchen, living room, and office on one floor, then a semi-subterranean floor with two bedrooms and a small space connecting the two. Andrea could easily be downstairs, changing Chase's diaper. It happened enough.

But usually she picks up by now. . . .

Forget that. Hang up, walk home, hug your wife and kid. Start to tell her the story you'll probably be telling her the rest of your lives.

Then tell her—in as serious a voice as you can muster—that you think it's time you quit your job.

Andrea would crack up at that.

Wouldn't she?

You think you can just walk away from something like this? You think there aren't people out there who want to make sure you're dead? Along with your family?

Stop it.

Jamie quickened his pace, blasting by the Franklin Institute, then the main branch of the Free Library, then Starbucks, then the old Granary Building and Spring Garden and the long-closed bodega and then finally the dry cleaners, which told him he had reached Green Street. The path from Market to Green was a gradual uphill. Most days that Jamie walked home from work, he ended up a sweaty mess.

Today, none of that mattered. Not the humidity. The sun. The fire. None of it.

Jamie reached the front door and remembered: his keys.

Damn it! His keys. In his bag, back on the thirty-sixth floor.

Jamie hammered the button next to his name. Please, Andrea, hear the buzzer and answer. Let me hear that click. Your voice on this cheap-ass plastic brown box. Jamie pressed the button again.

Nothing.

He couldn't stand this.

He pressed other buttons. His neighbors, whom he hardly knew. It wasn't exactly a social building. Having a kid didn't make them very popular, either.

C'mon, somebody answer. Give me a click.

C'mon.

Forget it. Jamie walked back down the front stairs, found a large stone in a square of dirt next to a tree, then walked back up and hurled it through the glass. He reached in, unlocked the door, and proceeded back to his apartment. He'd pay the damage. He'd pay it gladly. Smile as he wrote the check.

Their apartment was down the hall, toward the back. He was about to apply the same technique—kick in it, pay for the damages later—but saw it was already ajar.

Andrea never, ever left it open.

She was afraid of Philadelphia.

I'm going to make sure they rape your wife nice and good! They'll skin your son alive! Right in front of her!

He rushed down the hall past the kitchen into the living room where the TV was on, and it was local news, covering the fire with helicopters and reporters on the street, asking inane questions about what had happened, but Jamie didn't care about that. He wanted to see Andrea and Chase *now.* He hurled himself down the creaky wooden stairs that led to their bedrooms.

It was dark down there, which wasn't unusual. Andrea kept the lights low while Chase napped.

"Andrea!" Jamie shouted.

He heard something coming from the baby's room.

A small cry.

A tiny little *wah.*

Oh, thank Christ.

Jamie rounded the bend and looked into Chase's room. Andrea was there in the wooden rocking chair, holding Chase in her arms, humming to him. Only Andrea looked different. She was only wearing underwear.

"Andrea?"

The room was dark. He needed to see them. Touch them. Smell them.

His hand found the light switch. But before he could flip it, she spoke.

"You didn't tell me he looks just like you."

Jamie turned on the lights.

And he screamed.

Acknowledgments

The creator of *Severance Package* would like to single out the following staff members for exemplary service:

Executive Officers: Meredith, Parker, and Sarah Swierczynski, Allan Guthrie, Marc Resnick, David Hale Smith, Angela Cheng Caplan, Danny Baror, and Shauyi Tai.

Corporate Benefactors: Matthew Baldacci, Bob Berkel, Julie Gutin, Sarah Lumnah, Lauren Manzella, Andrew Martin, Matthew Sharp, Eliani Torres, Tomm Coker, Dennis Calero, and the entire team at St. Martin's Minotaur.

Silent Partners: Axel Alonso, Ray Banks, Lou Boxer, Ed Brubaker, Ken Bruen, Aldo Calcagno, Jon Cavalier, Nick Childs, Michael Connelly, Bill Crider, Paul Curci, Albin Dixon, Father Luke Elijah, Loren Feldman, Ron Geraci, Greg Gillespie, Maggie Griffin, Paul Guyot, Ethan Iverson, Jon and Ruth Jordan, Jennifer Jordan, McKenna Jordan, Deen Kogan, Terrill Lee Lankford, Joe R. Lansdale, Paul Leyden, Laura Lippman, Michelle Monaghan, H. Keith Melton, Karin Montin, Edward Pettit, Tom Piccirilli, Will Rokos, Greg Rucka, Warren Simons, Kevin Burton Smith, Mark Stanton, David Thompson, Andra Tracy, Peter Weller, Dave White, and all my friends and family.

About the Author

DUANE SWIERCZYNSKI is the author of *The Blonde* (St. Martin's Minotaur) and the writer for the Monthly Marvel Comics series *Cable*. Until recently he was the editor-in-chief of the *Philadelphia City Paper*, and almost never wanted to kill his employees.

Visit him at www.duaneswierczynski.com.

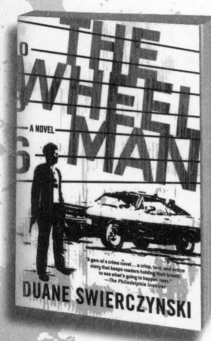
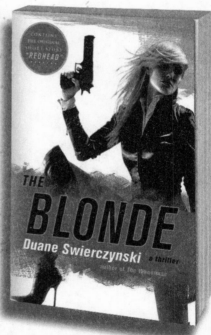